JF   Colfer, Eoin.
COL   Artemis Fowl

ARTEMIS FOWL

THE LOST COLONY

OTHER BOOKS BY EOIN COLFER

ARTEMIS
FOWL
THE LOST COLONY

EOIN COLFER

MIRAMAX BOOKS
HYPERION BOOKS FOR CHILDREN
NEW YORK

First American Edition
1 3 5 7 9 10 8 6 4 2

Printed in the United States of America
This book is set in 13.5-point Perpetua.
Reinforced binding

ISBN 0-7868-4956-8

Library of Congress Cataloging-in-Publication Data on file.

Visit www.artemisfowl.com

For Badger. The man. The legend.

ARTEMIS FOWL

THE LOST COLONY

CHAPTER 1: BLAST TO THE PAST

Barcelona, Spain

Happy was not a word often used to describe Artemis Fowl's bodyguard. *Jolly* and *contented* were also words that were rarely applied to him or to people in his immediate vicinity. Butler did not get to be one of the most dangerous men in the world by chatting with anyone who happened to stroll past, unless the chat concerned exit routes and concealed weapons.

On this particular afternoon, Butler and Artemis were in Spain, and the bodyguard's Eurasian features were even more taciturn than normal. His young charge, as usual, making Butler's job more complicated than it needed to be. Artemis had insisted that they stand on the sidewalk of Barcelona's Passeig de Gràcia for over an hour in the afternoon sun, with only a few slender trees to provide them with cover from the heat or possible enemies.

This was the fourth unexplained trip to foreign locations in as many months. First Edinburgh, then Death Valley in the American West, followed by an extremely arduous trek to doubly landlocked Uzbekistan. And now Barcelona. All to wait for a mysterious *visitor*, who had not as yet made an appearance.

They made an odd couple on the busy pathway. A huge, muscular man: forties, Hugo Boss suit, shaven head. And a slight teenager: pale, raven-haired, with large piercing blue eyes.

"Why must you circle so, Butler?" asked Artemis, irritated. He knew the answer to his own question, but according to his calculations, the expected visitor to Barcelona was a minute late, and he allowed his annoyance to transfer to the bodyguard.

"You know perfectly well why, Artemis," replied Butler. "In case there is a sniper or an audiotech on one of the rooftops. I am circling to provide maximum cover."

Artemis was in the mood to demonstrate his genius. This was a mood in which he frequently found himself. And, as satisfying as these demonstrations were for the fourteen-year-old Irish boy, they could be intensely irritating for anyone on the receiving end.

"Firstly, it is hardly likely that there is a sniper gunning for me," he said. "I have liquidated eighty percent of my illegal ventures and spread the capital across an extremely lucrative portfolio. Secondly, any audiotech trying to eavesdrop on us may as well pack up and go home, as the third button on your jacket is emitting a solinium pulse that whites out any surveillance tape, human or fairy."

Butler glanced at a passing couple who were bewitched by Spain and young love. The man had a camcorder slung around his neck. Butler fingered his third button guiltily.

"We may have ruined a few honeymoon videos," he noted.

Artemis shrugged. "A small price to pay for my privacy."

"Was there a third point?" asked Butler innocently.

"Yes," said Artemis, a touch testily. Still no sign of the individual he was expecting. "I was about to say that if there is a gunman on one of these buildings, it's that one directly to the rear. So you should stay behind me."

Butler was the best bodyguard in the business, and even he couldn't be a hundred percent sure which rooftop a potential gunman would be on.

"Go on. Tell me how you know. I know you're dying to."

"Very well, since you ask. No sniper would position himself on the rooftop of Casa Milà, directly across the street, because it is open to the public and so his access and escape would probably be recorded."

"His or her," corrected Butler. "Most metal men are women these days."

4

"His or her," amended Artemis. "The two buildings on the right are somewhat screened by foliage, so why handicap yourself?"

"Very good. Go on."

"The cluster behind us is financial buildings with private security stickers on the windows. A professional will avoid any confrontation he is not being paid for."

Butler nodded. It was true.

"And so, I logically conclude that your imaginary sniper would pick the four-story construction to our rear. It is residential, so access is easy. The roof affords him *or her* a direct line of fire, and the security is possibly dismal or, more than likely, nonexistent."

Butler snorted. Artemis was probably right. But in the protection game, *probably* wasn't nearly as comforting as a Kevlar vest.

"You're *probably* right," admitted the bodyguard. "But only if the sniper is as smart as you are."

"Good point," said Artemis.

"And I imagine you could put together a convincing argument for any one of these buildings. You just picked that one to keep me out of your line of vision, which leads me to believe that whoever you're expecting will turn up outside Casa Milà."

Artemis smiled. "Well done, old friend."

Casa Milà was an early twentieth-century dwelling designed by the Spanish art nouveau architect Antoni

Gaudí. The façade consisted of curved walls and balconies topped by twisted ironworks. The walkway outside the building was thronged with tourists lining up for an afternoon tour of the spectacular house.

"Will we recognize our visitor among all these people? Are you sure that he is not already here? Watching us?"

Artemis smiled, his eyes glittering. "Believe me, he is not here. If he were, there would be a lot of screaming."

Butler scowled. Once, just once, he would like to get all the facts before they boarded the jet. But that wasn't the way Artemis worked. To the young Irish genius, the *reveal* was the most important part of his schemes.

"At least tell me if our contact will be armed."

"I doubt it," said Artemis. "And even if he is, he won't be with us for more than a second."

"A second? Just beaming down through outer space, is he?"

"Not space, old friend," said Artemis, checking his wristwatch. "Time." The boy sighed. "Anyway, the moment has passed. It seems as though I have brought us here for nothing. Our visitor has not materialized. The chances were slim. Obviously there was nobody at the other end of the rift."

Butler didn't know what rift Artemis was referring to; he was simply relieved to be leaving this insecure location. The sooner they could get back to Barcelona Airport the better.

The bodyguard pulled a mobile phone from his pocket and hit a number on the speed dial. The person on the other end picked up on the first ring.

"Maria," said Butler. "Collection, *pronto*."

"*Sí*," replied Maria tersely. Maria worked for an exclusive Spanish limousine company. She was extremely pretty and could break a breeze block with her forehead.

"Was that Maria?" said Artemis, mimicking casual conversation perfectly.

Butler was not fooled. Artemis Fowl rarely asked casual questions.

"Yes, that was Maria. You could tell because I used her name when I spoke to her. You don't usually ask so many questions about the limo driver. That's four in the past fifteen minutes. Will *Maria* be picking us up? Where do you think *Maria* is right now? How old do you think *Maria* is?"

Artemis rubbed his temples. "It's this blasted puberty, Butler. Every time I see a pretty girl, I waste valuable mind space thinking about her. The girl at that restaurant, for instance. I've glanced in her direction a dozen times in the past few minutes."

Butler gave the pretty girl in question an automatic bodyguard's once-over.

She was twelve or thirteen, did not appear to be armed, and had a mane of extremely tight blond curls. The girl was studiously working her way through a selection of *tapas* while a male guardian, perhaps her father, read the paper. There was another man at the table who was struggling to stow a set of crutches under his chair. Butler judged that the girl was not a direct threat to their safety, though indirectly she could cause trouble if Artemis were unable to concentrate on his plan.

Butler patted his young charge on the shoulder. "It's normal to be distracted by girls. Natural. If you hadn't been so busy saving the world these past few years, it would have happened sooner."

"Nevertheless, I have to control it, Butler. I have things to do."

"Control puberty?" snorted the bodyguard. "If you manage that, you'll be the first."

"I generally am," said Artemis.

And it was true. No other teenager had kidnapped a fairy, rescued their father from the Russian *Mafiya*, and helped put down a goblin revolution by the tender age of fourteen.

A horn honked twice. From across the intersection, a young lady gestured through an open limousine window.

"It's *Maria*," said Artemis, then caught himself. "I mean, let us go. Maybe we'll have better luck at the next site."

Butler took the lead, stopping traffic with a wave of one massive palm. "Maybe we should take Maria with us. A full-time driver would make my job a lot easier."

It took Artemis a moment to realize that he was

being ribbed. "Very funny, Butler. You were joking, weren't you?"

"Yes, I was."

"I thought so, but I don't have a lot of experience with humor. Apart from Mulch Diggums."

Mulch was a kleptomaniac dwarf who had stolen from, and for, Artemis on previous occasions. Diggums liked to think of himself as a funny fairy, and his main sources of humor were his own bodily functions.

"If you can call that humor," said Butler, smiling in spite of himself at his own memories of the pungent dwarf.

Suddenly Artemis froze—in the middle of a heaving intersection.

Butler glowered at the three lanes of city traffic, a hundred impatient drivers leaning on their horns.

"I feel something," breathed Artemis. "Electricity."

"Could you please feel it on the other side of the road?" asked Butler.

Artemis stretched out his arms and felt a tingle on his palms.

"He's coming, after all, but several yards off target. Somewhere there is a constant that is not constant."

A shape formed in the air. From nothing came a cluster of sparks and the smell of sulfur. Inside the cluster, a gray-green thing appeared, with golden eyes, chunky scales, and great horned ears. It stepped out of nowhere and onto the road. It stood erect, five feet high, humanoid, but there was no mistaking this creature for human. It sniffed the air through slitted nostrils, opened a snake's mouth, and spoke.

"Felicitations to Lady Heatherington Smythe," it said in a voice of crushed glass and grating steel. The creature grasped Artemis's outstretched palm with a four-fingered hand.

"Curious," said the Irish boy.

Butler wasn't interested in *curious*. He was interested in getting Artemis away from this creature as quickly as possible.

"Let's go," he said brusquely, laying a hand on Artemis's shoulder.

But Artemis was already gone. The creature had disappeared as quickly as it had come, taking the teenager with him. The incident would make the news later that day, but strangely enough, in spite of the hundreds of tourists armed with cameras, there would be no pictures.

The creature was insubstantial, as though it did not have a proper hold on this world. Its grip on Artemis's hand was soft with a hard core, like bone wrapped in foam rubber. Artemis did not try to pull away; he was fascinated.

"Lady Heatherington Smythe?" repeated the creature, and Artemis could hear that it was scared. "Dost this be her estate?"

Hardly modern syntax, thought Artemis. But definitely English. Now, how does a demon exiled in Limbo learn to speak English?

The air buzzed with power, and white electrical bolts crackled around the creature, slicing holes in space.

A temporal rent. A hole in time.

Artemis was not overly awed by this; after all, he had seen the Lower Elements Police actually *stop* time during the Fowl Manor siege. What did concern him was that he was likely to be whisked away with the creature, in which case the chances of him being returned to his own dimension were small. The chances of him being returned to his own time were minuscule.

He tried to call out to Butler, but it was too late. If the word *late* can be used in a place where time does not exist. The rent had expanded to envelop both him and the demon. The architecture and population of Barcelona faded slowly like spirits, to be replaced first by a purple fog, then a galaxy of stars. Artemis experienced feverish heat, then bitter cold. He felt sure that if he materialized fully he would be scorched to cinders, then his ashes would freeze and scatter across space.

Their surroundings changed in a flash, or maybe a year; it was impossible to tell. The stars were replaced by an ocean, and they were underneath it. Strange deep-sea creatures loomed from the depths, luminous tentacles scything the water all around them. Then there was a field of ice, then a red landscape, the air filled with fine dust. Finally they were looking at Barcelona again. But different. The city was younger.

The demon howled and gnashed its pointed teeth, abandoning all attempts to speak English. Luckily, Artemis was one of two humans in any dimension who spoke Gnommish, the fairy language.

"Calm yourself, friend," he said. "Our fate is sealed. Enjoy these beautiful sights."

The demon's howl ceased abruptly, and he dropped Artemis's hand.

"Speak you fairy tongue?"

"Gnommish," corrected Artemis. "And better than you, I might add."

The demon fell silent, regarding Artemis as though he were some kind of wondrous creature. Which, of course, he was. Artemis, for his part, spent what could possibly be the last few moments of his life observing the scene before him. They were materializing at a building site. It was the Casa Milà, but not yet completed. Workmen swarmed across scaffold erected at the front of the building, and a swarthy bearded man stood scowling at a sheet of architectural drawings.

Artemis smiled. It was Gaudí himself. How amazing.

The scene solidified, colors painting themselves brighter. Artemis could smell the dry Spanish air now, and the heavy tangs of sweat and paint.

"Excuse me?" said Artemis in Spanish.

Gaudí looked up from the drawings, and his scowl was replaced with a look of utter disbelief. There was a boy stepping from thin air. Beside him a cowering demon. The brilliant architect absorbed every detail of the tableau, committing it to his memory forever.

"*Sí?*" he said hesitantly.

Artemis pointed to the top of the building. "You've got some mosaics planned for the roof. You might want to rethink those. Very derivative."

Then boy and demon disappeared.

Butler had not panicked when a creature had stepped out a the hole in time. Then again, he *was* trained not to panic, no matter how extreme the situation. Unfortunately, nobody else at the Passeig de Gràcia intersection had attended Madam Ko's Personal Protection Academy, and so they proceeded to panic just as loudly and quickly as they could. All except the curly-haired girl and the two men with her.

When the demon appeared, the public froze. When the creature disappeared, they unfroze explosively. The air was rent with the sounds of shouting and screaming. Drivers abandoned their cars, or simply drove them into store windows to escape. A wave of humans withdrew from the point of materialization as though repelled by an invisible force. Again, the girl and her companions bucked the trend, actually running toward the spot where the demon had shown up. The man with the crutches displayed remarkable agility for one who was supposedly injured.

Butler ignored the pandemonium, concentrating on his right hand. Or rather, where his right hand had been a second earlier. Just before Artemis fizzled into another dimension, Butler had managed to get a grip on his shoulder. Now the disappearing virus had claimed his own hand. He was going wherever Artemis had gone. He could still feel his young charge's bony shoulder in his grip.

Butler fully expected his arm to disappear, but it didn't. Just the hand. He could still feel it in an underwater pins-and-needles kind of way. And he could still feel Artemis.

"No, you don't," he grunted, tightening his invisible grip. "I've put up with too much hardship over the years for you to vanish on me now."

And so Butler reached down through the decades and yanked his young charge back from the past.

Artemis didn't come easy. It was like dragging a boulder through a sea of mud, but Butler was not the kind of person who gave up easily, either. He planted his feet and put his back into it. Artemis popped out of the twentieth century and landed sprawling in the twenty-first.

"I'm back," said the Irish boy, as if he had simply returned from an everyday errand. "How unexpected."

Butler picked his principal up and gave him a per-functory examination.

"Everything is in the right place. Nothing broken. Now, Artemis, tell me, what is twenty-seven multiplied by eighteen point five?"

Artemis straightened his suit jacket. "Oh, I see, you're checking my mental faculties. Very good. I suppose it's conceivable that time travel could affect the mind."

"Just answer the question!" insisted Butler.

"Four hundred and ninety-nine point five, if you must know."

"I'll take your word for it."

The giant bodyguard cocked his head to one side. "Sirens. We need to get out of this area, Artemis, before I'm forced to cause an international incident."

He hustled Artemis to the other side of the road, to the only car still idling there. Maria looked a little pale, but at least she had not abandoned her clients.

"Well done," said Butler, flinging open the rear door. "Airport. Stay off the highway as much as possible."

Maria barely waited until Butler and Artemis were belted before burning rubber down the street, ignoring the traffic lights. The blond girl and her companions were left on the roadside.

Maria glanced at Artemis in the mirror. "What happened out there?"

"No questions," said Butler curtly. "Eyes on the road. Drive."

He knew better than to ask questions himself. Artemis

would explain all about the strange creature and the shining rift when he was ready.

Artemis remained silent as the limousine swung down toward Las Ramblas and from there into the labyrinthine back streets of downtown Barcelona.

"How did I get here?" he said eventually, musing aloud. "Or rather, why aren't we there? Or why aren't we *then*? What anchored us to this time?" He looked at Butler. "Are you wearing any silver?"

Butler grimaced sheepishly. "You know I never usually wear jewelry, but there is this." He shot one cuff. There was a leather bracelet on his wrist with a silver nugget in the center. "Juliet sent it to me. From Mexico. It's to ward off evil spirits, apparently. She made me promise to wear it."

Artemis smiled broadly. "It was Juliet. She anchored us." He tapped the silver nugget on Butler's wrist. "You should give your sister a call. She saved our lives."

As Artemis tapped his bodyguard's wristband, he noticed something about his own fingers. They *were* his fingers, no doubt about it. But different, somehow. It took him a moment to realize what had happened.

He had, of course, done some theorizing on the hypothetical results of interdimensional travel, and concluded that there could possibly be some deterioration of the original, as with a computer program that has been copied once too often. Streams of information could be lost in the ether.

As far as Artemis could tell, nothing had been lost, but now the index finger on his left hand was longer than the second finger. Or more accurately, the index finger had swapped places with the second finger.

He flexed the fingers experimentally.

"Hmm," noted Artemis Fowl. "I am unique."

Butler grunted.

"Tell me about it," he said.

CHAPTER 2: **D⊙⊙DAH DAY**

Haven City, The Lower Elements

Holly Short's career as an elfin private investigator was not working out as well as she'd hoped. This was mainly because the Lower Elements' most popular current events show had run not one, but two specials on her over the past few months. It was difficult to go undercover when her face was forever popping up on cable reruns.

"Surgery?" suggested a voice in her head.

This voice was not the first sign of madness. It was her partner, Mulch Diggums, communicating from his mike to her earpiece.

"What?" she said, her voice carrying to her own microphone, a tiny flesh-colored chip glued to her throat.

"I'm looking at a poster of your famous face, and I'm thinking that you should have some cosmetic surgery if we want to stay in business. And I mean real business, not this bounty hunting game. Bounty hunters are the lowest of the low."

Holly sighed. Her dwarf partner was right. Even criminals were considered more trustworthy than bounty hunters.

"A few implants and a reshaped nose, and even your best friend wouldn't recognize you," continued Mulch Diggums. "It's not as if you're a beauty queen."

"Forget it," said Holly. She was fond of the face she had. It reminded her of her mother's.

"What about a skin spray? You could go green, disguise yourself as a sprite."

"Mulch? Are you in position?" snapped Holly.

"Yep," came the dwarf's reply. "Any sign of the pixie?"

"No, he's not up and about yet, but he will be soon. So stop the chatter and just get ready."

"Hey, we're partners now. No more criminal and police officer. I don't have to take orders from you."

"Get ready, *please*."

"No problem. Mulch Diggums, low-life bounty hunter, signing off."

Holly sighed. Sometimes she missed the discipline of the Lower Elements Police Reconnaissance Squad. When an order was given, it was followed. Although, if she were honest, Holly had to admit she had gotten herself into trouble more than once for disobeying a direct command.

She had only survived in LEPrecon for as long as she had because of a few high-profile arrests. *And* because of her mentor, Commander Julius Root.

Holly felt her heart lurch as she remembered, for the thousandth time, that Julius was dead. She could go for hours without thinking about it, then it would hit her—every time like the first time.

She had quit the LEP because Julius's replacement had actually accused her of murdering the commander. Holly figured with a boss like that, she could do the Fairy People more good outside the system. It was starting to look like she had been dead wrong. In her time as LEPrecon Captain she had been involved in putting down a goblin revolution, thwarting a plan to expose the subterranean fairy culture to the humans, and reclaiming stolen fairy technology from a Mud Man in Chicago. Now she was tracking a fish smuggler who had skipped out on his bail. Not exactly national security stuff.

"What about shin extensions?" said Mulch, interrupting her thoughts. "You could be taller in hours."

Holly smiled. As irritating as her partner was, he could always cheer her up. Also, as a dwarf, Mulch had special talents that came in very handy in their new line of business. Until recently, he had used these skills to break *into* houses and *out* of prisons, but now he was on the side of the angels, or so he swore. Unfortunately, all fairies knew that a dwarf's vow to a non-dwarf wasn't worth the spit-sodden handshake that sealed the deal.

"Maybe you could get a brain extension," Holly retorted.

Mulch chortled. "Oh, brilliant. I must write that one down in my witty retorts book."

Holly was trying to come up with an actual witty retort, when their target appeared at the motel room door. He was a harmless-looking pixie, barely two feet high, but you didn't have to be tall to drive a truck of fish. The smuggling bosses hired pixies as drivers and couriers because they looked so innocent and childlike. Holly had read this pixie's profile, and she knew that he was anything but innocent.

Doodah Day had been smuggling livestock to illegal restaurants for more than a century. In smuggling circles he was something of a legend. As an ex-criminal, Mulch was privy to criminal folklore and was able to supply Holly with all kinds of useful information that wouldn't find its way into an LEP report. For instance, Doodah had once made the heavily patrolled Atlantis–Haven run in under six hours without losing a fish from the tank.

Doodah had been arrested in the Atlantis Trench by a squad of LEP water sprites. He had skipped out en route from a holding cell to the courthouse, and now Holly had tracked him here. The bounty on Doodah Day was enough to pay six months' rent on their office. The plaque on their door read: *Short and Diggums. Private Investigators.*

Doodah Day stepped out of his room, scowling at the world in general. He zipped his jacket then headed south toward the shopping district. Holly stayed twenty steps back, hiding her face underneath a hood. This street had traditionally been a rough spot, but the Council was putting millions of ingots into a major revamp. In five years, there would be no more goblin ghetto. Huge, yellow multi-mixers were chewing up old sidewalks and laying down brand new paths behind them. Overhead, public service sprites unhooked burned-out sun strips from the tunnel ceiling and replaced them with new molecule models.

The pixie followed the same route that he had for the past three days. He strolled down the road to the nearest plaza, picked up a carton of vole curry at a kiosk, then bought a ticket to the twenty-four hour movie theater. If he stayed true to form, Doodah would be in there for at least eight hours.

Not if I can help it, thought Holly. She was determined to get this case wrapped by close of business. It wouldn't be easy. Doodah was small, but he was fast. Without weapons or restraints, it would be almost impossible to contain him. *Almost* impossible, but there was a way.

Holly bought a ticket from the gnome attendant, then settled into a seat two rows behind the target. The theater was pretty quiet at this time of day. There were maybe fifty patrons besides Holly and Doodah. Most of them weren't even wearing theater goggles. This was just somewhere to put in a few hours between meals.

The theater was running The Hill of Taillte trilogy nonstop. The trilogy told a cinematic version of the events surrounding the Hill of Taillte battle, where the humans had finally forced the fairies underground. The final part of the trilogy had cleaned up at the AMP Awards a couple of years ago. The effects were splendid, and there was even a special edition interactive version, where the player could become one of the minor characters.

Looking at the movie now, Holly felt the same pang of loss as she always did. The People should be living aboveground; instead they were stuck in this technologically advanced cave.

Holly watched the sweeping aerial views and slow motion battles for forty minutes, then she moved into the aisle and threw off her hood. In her LEP days, she would simply have come up behind the pixie and stuck her Neutrino 3000 in his back, but civilians were not allowed to carry weapons of any kind, and so a more subtle strategy would have to be employed.

She called the pixie from the aisle. "Hey, you. Aren't you Doodah Day?"

The pixie jumped from his seat. He fixed his fiercest scowl on his features and threw it Holly's way. "Who wants to know?"

"The LEP," replied Holly. Technically, she had not

identified herself as a member of the LEP, which would be impersonating a police officer.

Doodah squinted at her. "I know you. You're that female elf. The one who tackled the goblins. I've seen you on digital. You're not LEP anymore."

Holly felt her heartbeat speed up. It was good to be back in action. Any kind of action.

"Maybe not, Doodah, but I'm still here to bring you in. Are you going to come quietly?"

"And spend a few centuries in the Atlantis pen? What do you think?" said Doodah Day, dropping to his knees.

The little pixie was gone like a stone from a sling, crawling under the seats, jinking left and right.

Holly pulled up her hood and ran toward the fire exit. That's where Doodah would be going. He went this way every day. Every good criminal checks the exit routes in whatever building he visits.

Doodah was at the exit before her, crashing through the door like a dog through a hatch. All Holly could see was the blue blur of his jumpsuit.

"Target on the move," she said, knowing her throat mike would pick up whatever she said. "Coming your way."

I hope, thought Holly, but she didn't say it.

In theory, Doodah would make for his bolt hole, a small storage unit over on Crystal Street, which was set up with a small cot and air-conditioning unit. When the pixie got there, Mulch would be waiting. It was a classic

human-hunting technique. Beat the grass and be ready when the bird flies. Of course, if you were human, you shot the bird, then ate it. Mulch's method of capture was less terminal, but equally revolting.

Holly stuck close, but not too close. She could hear the pitter-patter of the pixie's tiny feet scurrying along the theater's carpet, but she couldn't see the little fellow. She didn't want to see him. It was vital that Doodah believe he had gotten away; otherwise he wouldn't make for his bolt hole. In her LEP days, there would be no need for this kind of close-up pursuit. She would have had complete access to five thousand surveillance cameras dotted throughout Haven, not to mention a hundred other gadgets and gimmicks from the LEP surveillance arsenal. Now there was just her and Mulch. Four eyes and some special dwarf talents.

The main door was still flapping when Holly reached it. Just inside, an outraged gnome was flat on his behind, covered with nettle smoothie.

"A little kid," he complained to an usher. "Or a pixie. It had a big head, I know that much. Hit me right in the gut."

Holly skirted the pair, shouldering her way onto the plaza outside. Outside—relatively speaking. Everything was inside when you lived in a tunnel. Overhead, the sun strips were set to midmorning. She could trace Doodah's progress by the trail of chaos in his wake. The vole kiosk was overturned. Lumpy gray-green curry congealed on the flagstones. And lumpy gray-green footsteps led to the plaza's northern corner. So far, Doodah was behaving very predictably.

Holly pushed her way through the ragged line of curry customers, keeping her eyes on the pixie's footsteps.

"Two minutes," she said for Mulch's benefit.

There was no reply, but there shouldn't be, not if the dwarf was in position.

Doodah should take the next service alley and cut across to Crystal. Next time, she resolved, they would go after a gnome. Pixies were too fast. The fairy Council did not really like bounty hunters, and tried to make life as difficult for them as possible. There was no such thing as a licensed firearm outside the LEP. Anyone with a weapon, without a badge, was going to prison.

Holly rounded the corner expecting to see the tail end of a pixie blur. Instead she saw a ten-ton yellow multi-mixer bearing down on her. Obviously Doodah Day had finished being predictable.

"D'Arvit!" swore Holly, diving to one side. The multi-mixer's front rotor chewed through the plaza's pavement, spitting it out at the rear in inch-perfect slabs.

She rolled into a crouch and reached for the Neutrino blaster, which had been on her hip, until recently. All she found was air.

The multi-mixer was swinging around for a second run, bucking and hissing like a mechanical Jurassic carnivore. Giant pistons thumped, and rotor blades carved scythe-like through whatever surface fell beneath their blades. Debris was shoveled into the machine's belly to be processed and shaped by heated plates.

It reminds me a bit of Mulch, thought Holly. Funny what crosses your mind when your life is in danger.

She backpedaled away from the mixer. Yes it was big, but it was slow and unwieldy. Holly glanced upward to the cab, and there was Doodah expertly manipulating the gears. His hands flashed across the knobs and levers, dragging the metal behemoth toward Holly.

All around was pandemonium: shoppers howling, emergency sirens sounding. But Holly couldn't worry about that now. Priority one. Stay alive. Terrifying as this situation might be to the general public, Holly had years of LEP training and experience. She'd escaped the grasp of far quicker enemies than this multi-mixer.

As it turned out, Holly was mistaken. The multi-mixer was slow as a whole, but some of its parts were lightning fast. For example, the containment paddles—two ten-foot-high walls of steel that slotted out on either side of the front rotor to contain any debris that might be thrown up by the rotor blades.

Doodah Day, an instinctive driver of any vehicle, saw his opportunity and took it. He overrode the safety and deployed the paddles. Four pneumatic pumps instantly pressurized and literally blew the paddles into the wall on both sides of Holly. They bit deep, sinking six inches into the stone.

Holly's confidence drained down into her boots. She was trapped with a hundred curved strip blades tearing up the ground before her.

"Wings," said Holly, but only her LEP suit had wings, and she had given up the right to wear that.

The paddles contained the vortex created by the blades and turned it back on itself. The vibration was terrific. Holly felt her teeth shake in her gums. She could see ten of everything. Her whole world was bad reception. Beneath her feet the blades greedily chewed the pavement. Holly jumped at the left-hand paddle, but it was well lubricated and slipped out of her grasp. Her luck was equally bad with the other paddle. The only other possible avenue was straight ahead, and that wasn't really an option, not with the deadly rotor waiting.

Holly shouted at Doodah. Maybe her mouth formed actual words, but she couldn't be certain, not with the shaking and the noise. Blades snicked through the air, grabbing for her. With each pass they tore strips from the ground beneath her feet. There wasn't much ground left. Soon she would be feeding the multi-mixer. She would be shredded, passed through the machine's innards, and finally laid as a pavement slab. Holly Short would literally be part of the city.

There was nothing to do. Nothing. Mulch was too far

away to be of any assistance, and it wasn't likely that any civilian would attempt to mount a rogue mixer, even if they had known she was trapped between the paddles.

As the blades closed in, Holly gazed toward the computer-generated sky. It would have been nice to die on the surface. Feel the heat of the real sun warm her brow. It would have been nice.

Then the rotor stopped. Holly was sprayed with a shower of half-digested debris from the mixer's stomach. A few stone slivers scratched her skin, but that was the extent of her injury.

Holly wiped the grime from her face and looked up. Her ears rang with the engine's aftershock, and her eyes watered from the dust that settled on her like dirty snow.

Doodah peered down at her from the cab. His face was pale but fierce.

"Leave me alone!" he shouted down. His voice seemed weak and tinny to Holly's damaged eardrums.

"Just leave me alone!"

And he was gone, scurrying down the access ladder, maybe heading for his bolt hole.

Holly leaned against one of the paddles, allowing herself a moment to recover. Tiny sparks of magic blossomed on her many cuts, sealing them. Her ears popped, whined, and flexed as the magic automatically targeted her eardrums. In seconds, Holly's hearing was back to normal.

$$\mathbb{D} \ \lozenge \ \text{\textcircled{\tiny{co}}} \ \text{\textcircled{\tiny{\texttheta}}} \ \text{\textcircled{\tiny{co}}} \ \mathscr{R} \ \text{\textcircled{\tiny{\textbeta}}} \ \bullet \ \boxtimes \ \text{\textcircled{\tiny{\texttheta}}} \ | \ \text{\textreferencemark} \ \blacklozenge \ \text{\textcircled{\tiny{\textbullet}}} \ \text{\textcircled{\tiny{\texttheta}}} \ \lozenge \ \text{\textreferencemark} \ \boxtimes$$

She had to get out of there. And there was only one way. Over the rotor. Past the blades. Holly tipped one gingerly with a finger. A droplet of blood oozed from a tiny cut, only to be sucked back in by a blue spark of magic. Those blades would cut her to ribbons if she slipped, and there wouldn't be enough magic under the world to stitch her back together again. But the rotor was her only way out, otherwise she would have to wait until LEPtraffic arrived. It would have been bad enough causing this kind of damage with the weight of LEP public liability insurance behind her, but as a freelancer she'd probably be thrown in jail for a couple of months while the courts decided what to charge her with.

Holly threaded her fingers between the blades and gripped the first bar on the rotor. It would be just like climbing a ladder. A very sharp, potentially fatal, ladder. She stepped on a lower bar and boosted herself up. The rotor groaned and dropped six inches. Holly held on, because it was safer than letting go. Blades quivered an inch from her limbs. Slow and steady. No false moves.

One bar at a time, Holly climbed the rotor. Twice, a blade nicked her flesh, but the wounds were not serious and were quickly sealed by blue sparks. After a brief eternity of utter concentration, Holly pulled herself onto the hood. The hood was filthy and hot, but at least it wasn't sharper than a centaur's tongue.

"He went that way," said a voice from ground level.

Holly looked down to see a large frowning gnome in a city services uniform pointing toward Crystal Street.

"He went that way," repeated the gnome. "The pixie who threw me out of my mixer."

Holly stared at the burly public services guy. "That tiny pixie threw *you* out?"

The gnome almost blushed. "I was getting out anyway, he just tipped me over." He suddenly forgot all about his embarrassment. "Hey, aren't you Polly something? Polly Little? That's it. The LEP hero."

Holly climbed down the cab ladder. "Polly Little. That's me."

Holly landed running, her boots crunching on pebbles of crushed pavement.

"Mulch," she said. "Doodah is coming your way. Be careful. He's a lot more dangerous than we thought."

Dangerous? Maybe, maybe not. He hadn't killed her when he'd had the chance. It would seem that the pixie had no stomach for murder.

Doodah's stunt with the multi-mixer had caused chaos in the plaza. Traffic police, nicknamed Wheelies, were pouring in, and civilians were pouring out. Holly counted at least six LEPtraffic magna-bikes and two cruisers. She was keeping her head down, when one of the traffic officers hopped off his bike and grabbed her shoulder.

"Did you see what happened, missy?"

Missy? Holly was tempted to twist the hand on her

shoulder and flip the officer into a nearby recycler. But this was not the time for outrage; she needed to redirect his attention.

"Why, thank goodness you're here, officer," she twittered in a voice at least an octave higher than her normal tones. "Over there, by the multi-mixer. There's blood everywhere."

"Blood!" exclaimed the Wheelie, delighted to hear it. "Everywhere?"

"Absolutely everywhere."

The traffic cop dropped Holly's shoulder. "Thank you, missy. I'll handle it from here."

He strode purposefully toward the multi-mixer, then turned back.

"Excuse me, missy," he said, recognition glimmering in his eye, just out of reach. "Don't I know you?"

But the hooded elf had disappeared.

Ah, well, thought the Wheelie. I should probably go look at the blood everywhere.

Holly ran toward Crystal Street, though she felt sure there was no need for haste. Doodah had either decided that there was too much heat on him to reveal his bolt hole, or Mulch had him. Either way it was out of her control. Once again she lamented the loss of LEP backup. In her Recon days, all it would have taken was a quick order into her helmet microphone, and every street in the area would be cordoned off.

She skirted a street-cleaning robot and turned onto Crystal. The narrow street was a service lane for the main shopping plaza, and consisted mostly of delivery bays. The rest of the units were rented out for storage. Holly was surprised to find Doodah directly in front of her, rummaging in his pocket, presumably for the access chip to his unit. Something must have held him up for a minute. Maybe he had ducked behind a crate to avoid the Wheelies. Whatever. She had another shot at him.

Doodah looked up, and all Holly could do was wave.

"Morning," she said.

Doodah shook a tiny fist at her. "Don't you have better things to do, elf? All I do is smuggle a few fish."

The question cut Holly deeply. Was this really the best way to help the People? Surely, Commander Root had wanted more from her. In the past few months she had gone from top priority surface operations to chasing down fish smugglers in a back alley. That was quite a drop.

She showed Doodah her hands. "I don't want you to get hurt, so stand perfectly still."

Doodah chuckled. "Hurt? By you? Not likely."

"No," said Holly. "Not by me. By him." She pointed at the patch of mud under Doodah's feet.

"Him?" Doodah looked down, suspecting a trap. His suspicions were absolutely correct. The ground beneath his feet fizzled slightly as the surface earth shivered and bounced.

⊖β℞⊃◊⊗ • ⅋β⚘ • ৪⊖◊◊ • ◊ ℞⊃◊

"What?" said Doodah, lifting one foot. He would doubtless have stepped off the patch if he'd had time. But what happened next, happened very quickly.

The ground did more than just collapse, it was sucked from below Doodah with a sickening slurping sound. A hoop of teeth cut through the earth, followed by a huge mouth. There was a dwarf on the other end of the mouth, and he breached the ground like a dolphin jumping, driven apparently by gas from his rear end. The ring of teeth closed around Doodah, swallowing him to the neck.

Mulch Diggums, for of course it was he, settled back into his tunnel, taking the unfortunate pixie with him. Doodah, it has to be said, did not look quite so cocky as he had a second ago.

"A d . . . dwarf," he stammered. "I thought your people didn't like the law."

Holly peered into the hole. "Generally they don't. But Mulch is an exception. You don't mind if he doesn't answer you himself. He might accidentally bite your head off."

Doodah squirmed suddenly. "What's he doing?"

"I imagine he's licking you. Dwarf spittle hardens on contact with air. As soon as he opens his mouth, you'll be locked up tight as a chick in an egg."

Mulch winked at Holly. It was about as much gloating as he could pull off at the moment, but Holly knew that he would spend the next several days boasting about his skills.

Dwarfs can tunnel through miles of earth. Dwarfs have

jet-powered rear ends. Dwarfs can produce two gallons of rock spittle every hour. What have you got? Besides a famous face that keeps blowing our cover?

Holly peered into the hole, the toe of one boot hooked over the edge. "Okay, partner. Good job. Now, can you please spit out the fugitive."

Mulch was happy to oblige. He hawked Doodah onto the lane's surface, then clambered up himself, rehinging his jaw.

"This is disgusting," moaned Doodah, as the viscous spittle solidified on his limbs. "It stinks, too."

"Hey," said Mulch, injured. "The smell is not my fault. If you'd rented storage on a cleaner street . . ."

"Oh yeah, stinky? Well, this is what I think of you." Doodah attempted a pixie hex gesture, but fortunately the rock spittle froze his arm before he could complete it.

"Okay, you two. Cut it out," said Holly. "We have thirty minutes to get this little guy to the LEP before the spittle loosens up."

Mulch peered over her shoulder toward the mouth of the lane. He turned suddenly pale underneath his coating of wet earth, and his beard hair bristled nervously.

"You know something, partner," he said. "I don't think we're going to need thirty minutes."

Holly turned away from her prisoner. There were half a dozen elves blocking the entrance to the lane. They were LEP, or something very like it. They wore plain clothes

⊗ • ∪ ⚛ ⟩ ⑧ ⚡ • ⨍ ⚛ • ⚛ ℈ • ⊙ ⚛ ◊ • ⨍

with no markings or insignias of any kind. They were official, though. The heavy artillery cradled in their elbows attested to that. Holly noticed with some relief that none of the guns were pointed at her or Mulch.

One of the elves stepped forward, popping the visor on her helmet.

"Hello, Holly," she said. "We've been looking for you all morning. How've you been?"

Holly swallowed a relieved sigh. It was Wing Commander Vinyáya, a longtime supporter of Holly and Julius Root. Vinyáya had blazed the trail for all females in the forces. In a five-hundred-year career, she had done everything from leading a Retrieval team to the dark side of the moon, to heading up the liberal vote on the fairy Council. In addition to this, she had been Holly's flight instructor in the academy.

"Fine, Commander," said Holly.

Vinyáya nodded at the solidifying mass of rock spittle.

"Keeping busy, I see."

"Yes. That's Doodah Day. The fish smuggler. Quite a catch."

The Commander frowned. "You're going to have to cut him loose, Holly. We have bigger snails to pop."

Holly placed her boot on Doodah's midriff. She was reluctant to jump through LEP hoops, even for an undercover wing commander.

"What kind of snails?"

Vinyáya's frown deepened, cutting a slash between her brows.

"Can we talk in the car, Captain? The regulars are on the way."

Captain? Vinyáya had referred to her by her old rank? What was going on here? If the regulars were LEP, who were these fairies?

"I don't trust the force as much as I used to, Commander. You need to give me something before we go anywhere."

Vinyáya sighed. "Firstly, Captain, we're not the force. Not the one you think, anyway. Secondly, you want me to give you something? I'll give you two words. Care to hazard a guess what they are?"

Holly knew at once. She felt it.

"Artemis Fowl," she whispered.

"That's right," confirmed Vinyáya. "Artemis Fowl. Now, are you and your partner prepared to come with us?"

"Where are you parked?" asked Holly.

Vinyáya and her mysterious unit obviously had a serious budget. Not only were their weapons state of the art, but their transportation was way out of the usual LEP league. Within seconds of scraping Doodah Day and slipping a tracker into his boot, Holly and Mulch were strapped into lounger seats in the back of a stretch armored vehicle. They weren't prisoners, exactly, but Holly couldn't help feeling that she wasn't in control of her destiny any-more.

Vinyáya took off her helmet, shaking out long silver hair. Holly was surprised.

The commander smiled. "You like the color? I got fed up dying it."

"Yes. It suits you."

Mulch raised a finger. "Sorry to interrupt the salon chat, but who are you people? You're not LEP, I'll bet my bum-flap on it."

Vinyáya swiveled to face the dwarf. "How much do you know about demons?"

Mulch checked the vehicle's cooler and was delighted to find sim-chicken and nettle beer. He liberated both. "Demons. Not a lot. Never seen one myself."

"What about you, Holly? Remember anything from school?"

Holly was intrigued. Where could this conversation be going? Was this a test of some kind? She thought back to her history classes in Police Academy.

"Demons. The Eighth Family of the Fairy People. Ten thousand years ago, after the battle of Taillte, they had refused to move underground, opting instead to lift their island out of time and live there in isolation."

Vinyáya nodded. "Very good. So they assembled their circle of warlocks and cast a time spell over the island of Hybras."

Mulch burped. "They disappeared off the face of the earth, and no one's seen a demon since."

"Not quite true. A few have popped up over the centuries. One quite recently, in fact. And guess who was there to meet him?"

"Artemis," said Holly and Mulch simultaneously.

"Exactly. Somehow he was able to predict what we couldn't. We knew when, but our where was off by several feet."

Holly sat forward. Interested. Back in the game.

"Did we get Artemis on film?"

"Not exactly," replied Vinyáya cryptically. "If you don't mind, I'll leave the explaining to someone more qualified than me. He's back at base." And she would say no more on the subject. Most infuriating.

Mulch wasn't one for patience.

"What? You're just going to take a nap? Come on, Vinyáya, tell us what little Arty is up to."

Vinyáya would not be drawn. "Relax, Mr. Diggums. Have another nettle beer, or some spring water." The commander took two bottles from the cooler and offered one to Mulch.

Mulch studied the label. "Derrier? No thanks. You know how they put the bubbles in this stuff?"

Vinyáya's mouth twitched with the ghost of a smile. "I thought it was naturally carbonated."

"Yeah, that's what I thought until I got a prison job at

the Derrier plant. They employ every dwarf in the Deeps. They made us sign confidentiality contracts."

Vinyáya was hooked. "So go on, tell me. How *do* they get the bubbles in?"

Mulch tapped his nose. "Can't say. Breach of contract. All I *can* say is it involves a huge vat of water and several dwarfs using our . . . eh"—Mulch pointed to his rear end—". . . natural talents."

Vinyáya gingerly replaced her bottle.

As Holly sat back in her comfortable gel chair, enjoying yet another of Mulch's tall tales, a niggling thought nudged through. She realized that Commander Vinyáya had avoided answering the dwarf's initial question. *Who were these people?*

Ten minutes later, that question was answered.

"Welcome to Section Eight Headquarters," said Vinyáya. "Forgive my theatrics, it's not often we get to *wow* people."

Holly didn't feel very *wowed*. They had pulled into a multi-story car park several blocks down from Police Plaza. The stretch armored vehicle followed the curved arrows up to the seventh floor, which was stuffed below the craggy ceiling. The driver parked in the least accessible, darkest space, then switched off the engine.

They sat for several seconds in the damp darkness, listening to rock-water drip from stalactites onto the roof.

"Wow," said Mulch. "This is something. I guess you people spent all your money on the car."

Vinyáya smiled. "Just wait."

The driver ran a quick proximity scan on the dashboard scanner, and came up clean. He then took an infrared remote from the dash and clicked it through the transparent plastic roof at the rock face overhead.

"Remote-controlled rocks," said Mulch dryly, delighted at the opportunity to exercise his sarcasm muscle.

Vinyáya did not respond; she didn't have to. What happened next shut Mulch up all on its own. The parking space rose hydraulically, sending the car catapulting toward the rock face above. The rocks did not move out of the way. There was no doubt in Holly's mind that when rock went up against metal, the rock would win. It made no sense, of course, that Vinyáya would bring them here only to crush the entire party. But there was no time to consider this in the half second that it took the stretch vehicle to reach the hard unforgiving rock.

In truth, the rock wasn't hard or unforgiving. It was digital. They passed right through to a smaller car port built into the rock.

"Hologram," breathed Holly.

Vinyáya winked at Mulch. "Remote-controlled rocks," she said. She flipped open the rear door and stepped out into an air-conditioned corridor.

"The entire headquarters has been hewn from the rock.

Actually, most of the cave was already here. We just lasered off a corner here and there. Forgive all the cloak-and-dagger stuff, but it's vital that what we do here at Section Eight remains secret."

Holly followed the commander through a set of automatic doors and down a slick corridor. There were sensors and cameras every few paces, and Holly knew that her identity had been verified at least a dozen times before they reached the steel door at the end of the corridor.

Vinyáya plunged her hand into a plate of liquid metal at the door's center.

"Flux metal," she explained, pulling her hand out. "The metal is saturated with nano-sensors. There's no way to fake your way through this door. The nano-sensors read everything from my handprint to my DNA. Even if someone cut off my hand and stuck it in here, the sensors would read a lack of pulse."

Holly folded her arms. "All this paranoia in one place. I think I can guess who your technical consultant is."

The door whooshed back, and standing on the other side was exactly the person Holly had expected to see.

"Foaly," she said fondly, stepping through to embrace the centaur.

Foaly hugged her warmly, stamping his rear hooves with delight.

"Holly," he said, holding her at arm's length. "How have you been?"

"Busy," replied Holly.

Foaly frowned. "You look a little skinny."

"Amazingly, so do you!" Holly laughed.

Foaly had lost a little weight since she had last seen him. And his coat was glossy and groomed.

Holly patted his flank. "Hmm," she mused. "You're using conditioner, and you're not wearing the brain probe–proof tinfoil hat. Don't tell me you have a little lady centaur tucked away somewhere."

Foaly actually blushed. "It's early days yet, but I'm hopeful."

The room was packed from floor to ceiling with state-of-the-art electronics. In fact, some of it was in the floors and ceiling, including wall-size gas view screens and an incredibly realistic sim-sky overhead.

Foaly was obviously proud of what he had put together. "Section Eight has the budget. I get the very best of everything."

"What about your old job?"

The centaur scowled. "I tried working for Sool, but it didn't work out. He's destroying everything Commander Root built. Section Eight headhunted me discreetly at a speed-dating weekend. They made me an offer and I accepted. I get plenty of fawning adoration here, not to mention a huge salary hike."

Mulch had a quick nosey-around and was irritated to find that there wasn't a single crumb of food in the room.

"None of that salary went on vole curry, I suppose?"

Foaly raised an eyebrow at the dwarf, who was still coated with tunnel dirt.

"No. But we do have a shower room. You do know what a shower is, don't you, Diggums?"

Mulch's beard hair bristled. "Yes, I do. And I know a donkey when I see one, too."

Holly stepped between them. "Okay, you two. No need to take up where you left off. Let's hold off on the traditional insults until we find out where we are, and why we're here."

Mulch lowered himself gleefully onto a cream-color couch, fully aware that some of his mucky coating would rub off on the furniture. Holly sat beside him, but not too close.

Foaly activated a wall screen, then touched it gently to navigate to the program he wanted.

"I love these new gas screens," he snickered. "Electric pulses heat the particles to different temperatures, causing the gas to turn different colors, forming pictures. Of course, it's a lot more complicated than that, but I'm dumbing it down for the convict."

"I was completely exonerated," objected Mulch. "As you well know."

"The charges were dropped," Foaly pointed out. "You were not exonerated. It's a different thing. Slightly."

"Yes, like a centaur and a donkey are different things. Slightly."

Holly sighed. It was almost like old times. Foaly was the LEP technical consultant who had steered her through many operations, and Mulch was their reluctant helper. It would be difficult for a stranger to believe that the dwarf and the centaur were actually good friends. She supposed this irritating bickering was how the males of every species showed affection.

A life-size picture of a demon flashed up on the screen. Its eyes were slitted, and its ears were crowned with spikes.

Mulch jumped. "D'Arvit!"

"Relax," said Foaly. "It's computer generated. Amazing picture quality, though. I grant you." Foaly enlarged the face until it filled the screen.

"Full-grown buck demon. Post warp."

"Post warp?"

"Yes, Holly. Demons do not grow like other fairies. They are quite cuddly until they hit puberty, then their bodies undergo a violent and painful spasm, or warp. After eight to ten hours they emerge from a cocoon of nutrient slime as demons. Before that, they are simply imps. Not the warlocks, though, they never warp. Their magic blossoms. I don't envy them. Instead of acne and mood swings, a pubescent warlock demon gets lightning bolts shooting out of his fingers. If he's lucky."

"Where do they shoot out of if he's unlucky? And why do we care about any of this?" asked Mulch, cutting to the chase.

"We care because a demon popped up recently in Europe and we didn't get to him first."

"So we heard. Demons are coming back from Hybras now?"

"Maybe, Holly." Foaly tapped the screen, splitting it into smaller sections. Demon pictures appeared in each one. "These demons have materialized momentarily through-out the past five centuries. Luckily, none of them have stayed around long enough to be captured by the Mud Men." Foaly highlighted the fourth picture. "My pre-decessor managed to hold on to this one for twelve hours. He got a silver medallion onto him, and there was a full moon."

"That must've been a special moment," said Mulch.

Foaly sighed. "Didn't you learn anything in school? Demons are unique among all the creatures of the earth. Their island, Hybras, is actually an enormous moon rock that came down during the Triassic period when the moon was hit by a meteorite. From what we can glean from fairy cave paintings and virtual models, this moon rock punched into a magma stream and more or less got itself welded to the surface. Demons are descended from lunar microorganisms that lived inside the rock. They are subject to a strong physical and mental lunar attraction; they even levitate during the full moon. And it is this attraction that pulls them back into our dimension. They have to wear silver to repel the lunar pull. Silver is the most effective dimensional anchor. Gold works, too, but sometimes you leave bits of yourself behind."

"So let's say we believe all this interdimensional lunar attraction baloney," said Mulch, doing his utmost to wind Foaly up. "What has that go to do with us?"

"It has everything to do with us," snapped Foaly. "If the humans capture a demon, who do you think will be next under their microscope?"

Vinyáya took up the backstory. "That is why, five hundred years ago, Council Chairman Nan Burdeh set up Section Eight to monitor demon activity. Luckily, Burdeh was a billionaire, and when she died, she left her entire fortune to Section Eight. Hence the rather impressive setup. We are a very small, covert division of the LEP, but everything we have is the best. Over the years our brief has expanded to include secret missions that are too sensitive to entrust to regular LEP. But demonology is still our priority. For five centuries our finest minds have been studying the ancient demon texts, trying to predict where the next demon will pop up. Generally our calculations are correct and we can contain the situation. But twelve hours ago something happened in Barcelona."

"What happened?" asked Mulch, a reasonable question for once.

Foaly opened another box on the screen. Most of the picture was white. "This happened."

Mulch peered at the box. "A very small snowstorm?"

Foaly wagged a finger at him. "I swear, if I weren't such a fan of mockery myself, I would have you tossed out of here on your combustible behind."

Mulch accepted the compliment with a gracious nod.

"No, this is not a small snowstorm. This is whiteout. Someone was blocking our scopes."

Holly nodded. Scopes was the shop name for the shrouded trackers attached to human communications satellites.

"You can see that whatever happened in our little snowstorm must have been pretty unusual, because the Mud Men are very eager to get away from it."

On screen, humans outside the whiteout zone were wildly running away or driving their cars into walls.

"Human news programs reported several sightings of a lizardlike creature appearing out of thin air for several seconds. Of course there are no photographs. I had calculated that there would be an appearance, but more than three feet to the left, and we had set up an Elldee, sorry, light-distortion projector accordingly. Unfortunately, although we got the time right, the exact location was wrong. Somehow, whoever was inside that ball of interference got the location exactly right."

"So Artemis saved us," noted Holly.

Vinyáya was puzzled. "Saved us? How?"

"Well, if it hadn't been for that interference, our demon friend would have been all over the Internet by now. And

48

you think that Artemis was inside the ball of interference."

Foaly grinned, obviously delighted with his own cunning. "Little Arty thought he could outwit me. He knows the LEP keeps him under constant surveillance."

"Even though they promised not to," interjected Holly.

Foaly ignored this technicality, plowing on. "So Artemis sent out decoys to Brazil and Finland, but we put a satellite on all three. Took a big chunk out of my budget, I can tell you."

Mulch groaned. "I am either going to barf, or fall asleep, or both."

Vinyáya slammed a fist into her palm. "Right. I've had enough of the dwarf. Let's just toss him into a holding cell for a few days."

"You can't do that," objected Mulch.

Vinyáya grinned nastily at him. "Oh, yes I can. You wouldn't believe the powers Section Eight has. So shut up, or listen to your own voice bouncing back at you from steel walls."

Mulch locked his mouth and threw away the key.

"So we know Artemis was in Barcelona," continued Foaly. "And we know a demon appeared. Artemis was at several other possible materialization sights, too, but no demons showed up. He's involved somehow."

"How do we know that for sure?" asked Holly.

"Here's how," said Foaly. He tapped the screen, enlarging a section of the Casa Milà's roof.

• ♗ ◉ • ♘ ⊖ ℱℬ • ⑧ ⅋ ℬ ℱ ⊃ ⅋ ℱ • ⊖ ℬ •

Holly stared at the picture for several seconds, looking for whatever it was she was supposed to see.

Foaly gave her a hint. "This is a Gaudí building. You like Gaudí? He designed some lovely mosaics."

Holly looked harder. "Oh my God," she said suddenly. "It can't be."

"Oh, but it is." Foaly laughed and enlarged a particular rooftop mosaic until it filled the entire wall screen. There were two figures in the picture stepping from a hole in the sky. One was obviously a demon, and the other was clearly Artemis Fowl.

"But that's impossible. That building must be a hundred years old."

"Time is the key to this whole thing," said Foaly. "Hybras has been lifted out of time. A demon who gets sucked off the island drifts through the centuries like a temporal nomad. This demon obviously got hold of Artemis and took him along for the ride. They must have appeared to one of Gaudí's artists, or maybe even the man himself."

Holly paled. "You mean Artemis is . . ."

"No, no. Artemis is home in bed. We've pulled a satellite out of orbit to keep twenty-four/seven watch on him."

"How is this possible?"

Foaly said nothing, so Vinyáya answered the question. "I'll take this one, because Foaly doesn't like saying the words.

We don't know, Holly. This affair leaves a lot of important questions unanswered. That's where you come in."

"How? I don't know anything about demons."

Vinyáya nodded craftily. "Yes, but you know a lot about Artemis Fowl. I believe you keep in touch."

Holly shrugged. "Well, I wouldn't say we really . . ."

Foaly cleared his throat, then called up an audio file on the system.

"Hey, Artemis," said a recording of Holly's voice. "I've got a little problem you might be able to help me with."

"Happy to help, Holly," said Artemis's voice. "Something difficult, I hope."

"Well, there's this pixie I'm after, but he's a fast one."

Foaly switched off the file. "I think we can say you're in contact."

Holly smiled sheepishly, hoping nobody would ask who gave Artemis a fairy communicator.

"Okay, I call from time to time. Just to keep an eye on him. For the greater good."

"Whatever your reasons," said Vinyáya, "we need you to contact him again. Go to the surface and find out how he can predict demon appearances so accurately. According to Foaly's calculations, there isn't a demon appearance due for six weeks, but we would like to know where exactly it's going to be."

Holly took her time to think about this.

"In what capacity would I be contacting Artemis?"

"Full captain, your old rank. Of course, now you'd be working for Section Eight. Everything you do for us would be hush-hush."

"A spy?"

"A spy, but with excellent overtime and medical insurance."

Holly jerked a thumb at Mulch. "What about my partner?"

The dwarf jumped to his feet. "I don't want to be a spy. Far too dangerous." He winked slyly at Foaly. "But I could be a consultant, for a fee."

Vinyáya scowled. "We're not prepared to grant Diggums a surface visa."

Mulch shrugged. "Good. I don't like the surface. It's too close to the sun and I have sensitive skin."

"But we *are* prepared to compensate him for loss of earnings."

"I don't know if I'm ready to put on the uniform again," said Holly. "I like working with Mulch."

"Let's call this mission a probationary term. Do this one for us. See if you like the way we operate."

Holly mulled it over. "What color is the uniform?"

Vinyáya smiled. "Matte black."

"Okay," said Holly. "I'm in."

Foaly hugged her again. "I knew you'd do it. I knew it. Holly Short cannot resist adventure. I told them."

Vinyáya saluted stiffly. "Welcome on board, Captain

Short. Foaly will complete your briefing and get you set up. I expect you to make contact with the subject as soon as possible."

Holly returned the salute. "Yes, Commander. Thank you, Commander."

"Now, if you'll excuse me, I have a debriefing with a pixie we've managed to place inside the goblin triads. He has been wearing a scale suit for six months, and he's having a bit of an identity crisis."

Vinyáya left, her silver mane rippling behind her. The automatic doors closed with barely a whisper.

Foaly dragged Holly from her seat.

"I have so much to show you," he babbled excitedly. "The fairies here are nice, but a bit on the square side. Sure they ooh and aah, but no one appreciates me like you do. We have our own shuttle port, you know. And field equipment! You are not going to believe the spec. Wait until you see the new Shimmer Suits. And the helmet! Holly, this thing comes home on its own. I built in a series of mini-thrusters into the skin. It can't fly, but it can bounce and roll. The thing is beyond genius."

Mulch covered his ears. "Same old Foaly. Modest to a fault."

Foaly aimed a kick at Mulch, pulling it at the last second.

"Keep it up, Diggums. I could snap at any moment. I am half beast, remember."

⊕ • ⼽ ⚛ ⊕ • ⊕ ⚛ • ⚛ ⼌ ⼁ • ⊕ ▢ • ⽥ ⼌

Mulch moved the hoof away from his face with a finger. "I can't help it," he whined. "All this melodrama. Someone has to poke fun."

Foaly turned once more to his precious wall screen. He selected and enlarged an artist's impression of the island of Hybras.

"I know this all sounds very cloak-and-dagger, and I know you think I'm making an anaconda out of a stink worm. But believe me, somewhere on that island there is an unsuspecting demon who is about to take a reluctant visit to Earth and make life very difficult for us."

Holly stepped close to the screen. Where was that reluctant demon? she wondered. And did he have any idea that he was about to be snatched from his own dimension and propelled into another?

As it happened, Holly's questions were inaccurate on two counts. Firstly, the demon in question was not actually a demon, he was just an imp. And secondly, the *imp* in question was anything but reluctant. In fact, visiting Earth was his dearest wish.

CHAPTER 3: **FİRST İɱPRESSİON**

The Island of Hybras, Limbo

One night, Imp N°1 dreamed he was a demon. He dreamed his horns were curved and pointed. His hide was coarse and armored, and his talons were sharp enough to rip the hide from a wild boar's back. He dreamed the other demons cowered before him, then scurried away lest he injure them while in the throes of his battle spasms.

That night he dreamed this magnificent dream, then awoke to find he was still merely an imp. Of course, technically he did not have this dream at night. The sky over Hybras is forever tinged with the red glow of dawn. But N°1 thought of his rest period as night, even though he'd never seen one.

Imp N°1 dressed quickly and rushed into the hallway to

check his reflection in the lodge mirror, just in case he *had* warped in his sleep. But there was no change. Still the same unimpressive figure as usual. One hundred percent imp.

"*Grrr,*" he said to his image, but even the Nº1 in the mirror was unconvinced. And if he couldn't scare himself, then he was not a scary creature and might as well get a job changing baby imps' diapers.

There was *some* potential in the mirror. Imp Nº1 had the general skeletal structure of a proper demon. He was about the same height as a sheep sitting on its rear. His skin was gray as moon dust and pebbled with armored plating. Spiraling red runes wound their way around his chest, up along his neck, and across his forehead. His eyes had striking orange irises, and his jaw had a noble jut about it, or so he liked to think, though others had called it protruding. He had two arms, slightly longer than an average human ten-year-old, and two legs, slightly shorter. Fingers and toes, eight of each. So nothing weird there. One tail, more of a stump, actually, but excellent for burrowing holes if you're hunting for grubs. All in all, your typical imp. But at fourteen years old, Nº1 was the oldest imp in Hybras. Roughly fourteen years old, that is. It was hard to be exact when it was always dawn. "The hour of power," as the warlocks used to call it before they got sucked into the depths of cold space. *The hour of power.* Very catchy.

Hadley Shrivelington Basset, a demon who was actually six months N°1's junior, but already fully fledged, strolled down the tiled corridor on his way to the washroom. His horns corkscrewed impressively and his ears had at least four points. Hadley enjoyed parading his new demon self in front of the imps. Generally, demons shouldn't even bunk in the imp lodge, but Basset seemed in no hurry to move out.

"Hey, imp," he said, snapping his towel at N°1's behind. It connected with a sharp crack. "Are you going to warp any time soon? Maybe if I get you angry enough."

The towel stung, but N°1 didn't get angry. Just nervous. Everything made him nervous. That was his problem.

Time for a quick subject change. "Morning, Basset. Nice ears."

"I know," said Hadley, tipping the points one after another. "Four points already, and I think there's a fifth coming up. Abbot himself only has six points."

Leon Abbot, the hero of Hybras. The demons' self-proclaimed savior.

Hadley snapped N°1 again with the towel.

"Don't you get a pain in your face looking in the mirror, imp? Because you're giving me a pain in mine."

He put his hands on his hips, threw back his head, and laughed. It was all very dramatic. You'd think there was an artist in the wings doing sketches.

"Eh, Basset. You're not wearing any silver."

The laughing stopped, to be replaced by a froglike gurgle. Shrivelington Basset bolted down the lodge corridor without pause for more bullying. Nº1 knew scaring people half to death shouldn't give him any satisfaction, and generally it wouldn't. But for Basset, he'd make an exception. Not wearing silver on your person is much more than a fashion disaster for a demon or imp. For them it could be fatal, or worse. Painful for all eternity. This rule usually only applied when an imp or demon was near the volcano crater, but luckily Basset was too scared to remember that.

Nº1 ducked back into the senior imp dorm, hoping his roommates were still snoring. No such luck. They were knuckling the sleep from their eyes and already searching for the target of their daily ribbing, which was, of course, him. He was by far the oldest in the senior dorm, no one else had made it to fourteen without warping. It was getting to the point where he was a permanent fixture. Each night his legs protruded from the foot of the bed, and his blanket barely covered the swirling moon markings on his chest.

"Hey, Runt," called one. "Are you going to warp today, do you think? Or will pink flowers grow out of my armpits?"

"I'll check your armpits tomorrow," sniggered another.

More abuse. This time from a couple of twelve-year-old imps who were so pumped up that they were likely to warp before class. But they were right. He would have gone for the pink flowers option, too.

Runt was his imp nickname. They didn't have real names, not until after they warped. Then they would be given a name from the sacred text. Until that moment, he was stuck with N°1, or Runt.

He smiled good-naturedly. It didn't pay to antagonize his dorm-mates. Even though they were smaller than him today, they could be a lot bigger tomorrow.

"I'm feeling pumped," he said, flexing his biceps. "Today is going to be my day."

Everyone in the dorm was excited. Tomorrow they could be out of this room for good. Once they warped, they were transferred to decent accommodations, and nothing in Hybras was off-limits.

"Who do we hate?" shouted one.

"Humans!" came the reply.

The next minute or so was spent howling at the ceiling. Imp N°1 joined in, but he wasn't really feeling it.

It shouldn't be "who do we hate," he thought. It really should be "whom."

But this probably wasn't a good time to bring that up.

Imp School

Sometimes N°1 wished he had known his mother. This was not a very demonlike desire, so he kept it to himself.

〇 🗲 ◗ 🗲 • ◎ ◗ 🦀 • ✢ 🗲 🗲 • ❢ 🗲 ▷ ▷ ◗

Demons were born equal, and whatever they made of themselves, they did with their claws and teeth. As soon as the female laid an egg, it was tossed in a bucket of mineral-enriched mud and left to hatch. Imps never knew who their family was, and therefore everyone was their family.

But still, some days, when his self-esteem had taken a bit of a pounding, Nº1 couldn't help gazing wistfully across at the female compound on his way to school, and wondering which one was his mother.

There was one demoness with red markings like his own, and a kind face. Often she smiled across the wall at him. She was looking for her son, Nº1 had realized. And from that day he smiled back. They could both pretend to have found each other.

Nº1 had never experienced a feeling of belonging. He ached for the time when he could wake up and look forward to what lay ahead. That day hadn't come yet, and it wasn't likely to, not as long as they lived in Limbo. Nothing would change. Nothing *could* change. Well, that wasn't strictly true. Things could get worse.

Imp School was a low stone building with little ventilation and hardly any light. Perfect for most imps. The stench and the smoky fire made them feel hard done-by and warlike.

Nº1 longed for light and fresh air. He was uniquely different, a brand new point on the compass. Or maybe an old one. Nº1 often thought that perhaps he could be a warlock. True, there hadn't been a warlock in the demon pride since they'd lifted out of time, but maybe he was the first, and that was why he felt so differently about almost everything. N°1 had raised his theory with Master Rawley, but the teacher had cuffed his ear hole and sent him digging grubs for the other imps.

There was another thing. Why couldn't they, just once, have a cooked meal? What would be so horrible about a soft stew and maybe even a few spices? Why did imps delight in chomping their food down before it stopped wriggling?

As usual, N°1 was the last to school. The other dozen or so imps were already in the hall, reveling in the thoughts of another day spent hunting, skinning, butchering, and possibly even warping.

N°1 wasn't feeling particularly hopeful. Maybe today would be his day, but he doubted it. The warp spasm was brought on by bloodlust, and N°1 had never felt the slightest urge to hurt any other creature. He even felt bad for the rabbits he ate, and sometimes dreamed that their little spirits were haunting him.

Master Rawley sat at his bench, sharpening a curved sword. Every now and then he would hack a chunk from the bench and grunt with satisfaction. The desk surface was littered with various weapons for hacking, sawing, and cutting. And of course one book. A copy of *Lady Heatherington Smythe's Hedgerow*. The book Leon Abbot had brought back from the old world. The book that would save them all, according to Abbot himself.

When Rawley had sharpened the blade to a silver crescent, he banged the hilt of the weapon on his bench.

"Sit down," he roared at the imps. "And make it fast, you shower of stinking rabbit droppings. I've got a fresh blade here that I'm just itching to test."

The imps hurried to their places. Rawley would not cut them, but he was certainly not above strapping their backs with the flat of his sword. And then again, maybe he would cut them.

N°1 squashed in on the end of the fourth row. Look tough, he told himself. Sneer a bit. You're an imp!

Rawley sank his blade into the wood, leaving it there quivering. The other imps grunted. Impressed. All N°1 could think was: *Show off*. And: *He's ruined that bench*.

"So, pig slime," said Rawley. "You want to be demons, do you?"

"Yes, Master Rawley!" roared the imps.

"You think you have what it takes?"

"Yes, Master Rawley!"

Rawley spread his muscled arms wide. He threw back a green head and roared. "Well then, let me hear it!"

The imps screamed and stomped, bashed their desks with weapons, and clattered each other on the shoulders. N°1 avoided as much of the ruckus as possible while doing his best to seem involved. Not an easy trick.

Finally Rawley settled them down. "Well, we'll see. This morning is a big morning for some of you, but for others it will be just be one more day of dishonor, grub hunting with the females." He stared pointedly at N°1. "But before we get to oozing, we have to do some snoozing."

Much groaning from the imps.

"That's right, girls. History time. Nothing to kill and nothing to eat, just knowledge for the sake of it." Rawley shrugged his giant knotted shoulders. "It's a waste of time, if you ask me. But I'm under orders here."

"That's right, Master Rawley," said a voice from the doorway. "You're under orders."

The voice belonged to Leon Abbot himself, paying one of his surprise visits to the school. Abbot was immediately surrounded by adoring imps clamoring to receive a friendly cuff on the ear, or to touch his sword.

Abbot endured this adoration for a moment, then brushed the imps aside. He elbowed Rawley out of the prime spot at the head of the class, then waited for silence. He didn't have to wait long. Abbot was an impressive specimen, even if you didn't know a thing about his past. He was almost five feet tall, with curved ram horns that jutted from his forehead. His armored scales were deep red and covered his entire torso and forehead. Very impressive, and of course difficult to penetrate. You could bash away with an ax all day at Abbot's chest and get nowhere. Indeed, one of his party tricks was to challenge anyone in the room to hurt him.

Abbot threw back his rawhide cloak and slapped his chest. "Right, who wants to have a go?"

Several imps nearly warped right then and there.

"Make a line, ladies," said Rawley, as if he were still in control.

The imps piled to the head of the class and hammered Abbot with fist, foot, and forehead. They bounced off, every one. Much to Abbot's amusement.

Idiots, thought N°1. As if they could possibly succeed.

Actually, N°1 had a theory about armored scales. A few years ago he had been toying with a discarded baby armored scale, and he'd noticed that they were made of dozens of layers, which made them almost impossible to breach head-on, whereas if you went at them at an angle with something hot . . .

"What about you, Runt?"

The raucous laughter of his classmates stomped all over N°1's thoughts.

N°1 physically twitched with shock as he realized that not only had Leon Abbot spoken to him, he had actually used his dormitory nickname.

"Yessir, pardon me? What?"

Abbot thumped his own chest. "You think you can get through the thickest plates on Hybras?"

"I doubt they're the thickest," said N°1's mouth before his brain had a chance to catch up.

"*Raahhr!* Are you insulting me, impling?"

Being called *impling* was even worse than being called Runt. The term impling was generally reserved for the recently hatched.

"No, no, of course not, Master Abbot. I just thought that, naturally, some of the older demons would have more layers on their scales. But yours are probably tougher—no dead layers on the inside."

Abbot's slitted eyes squinted at N°1. "You seem to know a lot about scales. Why don't you try to get through these."

N°1 tried to laugh it off. "Oh, I really don't think—"

But Abbot wasn't smiling. "I really *do* think, Runt. Get your stumpy tail up here before I give Master Rawley license to do what he has wanted to do for a long time."

Rawley pulled his blade from the bench and winked at N°1. This was not a friendly you-and-I-share-a-secret wink; it was a let's-see-what-color-your-insides-are wink.

N°1 sloped reluctantly to the head of the class, passing the smoldering embers of last night's fire. Wooden meat skewers jutted from the coals. N°1 paused for a beat, gazing at the sharp skewers and thinking that if he had the guts, one of those would probably do the trick.

Abbot followed his gaze. "What? You think a meat skewer is going to help you?" The demon snorted. "I was buried in molten lava once, Runt, and I'm still here. Bring one up. Do your worst."

"Do your worst," echoed several of N°1's classmates, their loyalties obvious.

N°1 reluctantly selected a wooden needle from the fire. The handle was solid enough, but the tip was black and flaky. N°1 tapped the skewer against his leg to dislodge loose ash.

Abbot grabbed the meat skewer from N°1's hand and held it aloft.

"This is your chosen weapon," he said mockingly. "The Runt thinks he's hunting rabbits."

The jeers and hoots broke over N°1's furrowed brow like a wave. He could feel one of his headaches coming on. He could always count on one to show up just when it was least wanted.

"This is probably a bad idea," he admitted. "I should just pound on your armored plates like those other morons . . . I mean my classmates."

"No, no," said Abbot, handing back the skewer. "You go ahead, little bee, prick me with your sting."

Prick me with your sting, warbled N°1 in a highly insulting imitation of the pride leader. Of course he didn't warble this aloud. N°1 was rarely confrontational outside his head.

Aloud he said, "I'll do my best, Master Abbot."

"I'll do my best, Master Abbot," warbled Abbot in a

highly insulting imitation of imp N°1, as loudly as he could.

N°1 felt beads of sweat spiral down his stumpy tail. There really was no good way out of this situation. If he failed, then he was in for another bout of jeering and mild personal injury. But if he won, then he *really* lost.

Abbot knocked on the crown of his head. "Hello, Runt. Let's get moving. There are imps here waiting to warp."

N°1 stared at the tip of the skewer and allowed the problem to take over. He placed the flat of his right hand on Abbot's chest. Then, wrapping his fingers tightly around the thick end, he twisted the skewer upward into one of Abbot's armored scales.

He twisted slowly, concentrating on the point of contact. The scale grayed slightly with ash, but no penetration. Acrid smoke twirled around the skewer.

Abbot chuckled, delighted. "Trying to start a fire there, Runt? Should I summon the water brigade?"

One of the imps threw his lunch at N°1. It slid down the back of his head. A lump of fat, bone, and gristle.

N°1 persisted, rolling the skewer between thumb and forefinger. He rolled faster now, feeling the skewer take hold, burning a slight indent.

N°1 felt an excitement build in him. He tried to contain it, to think about consequences, but he couldn't. He was on the point of success, here. He was just about to accomplish with brains something all these other idiots couldn't do with brawn. Of course they would pummel him, and Abbot would invent some excuse to undermine his achievement, but Nº1 would know. And so would Abbot.

The skewer penetrated just a fraction. Nº1 felt the plate give way, perhaps a single layer. The little imp felt something he had never felt before. Triumph. The feeling built inside him, irresistible, unquenchable. It became more than a feeling. It transformed into a force, rebuilding some forgotten neural pathways, releasing an ancient energy inside Nº1.

What's happening? wondered Nº1. Should I stop? Can I stop?

Yes and *no* were the answers to those questions. Yes, he should stop, but no, he couldn't. The force flowed through his limbs, raising his temperature. He heard voices chanting inside his mind. Nº1 realized that he was chanting with them. Chanting what? He had no idea, but somehow his memory knew.

The strange force throbbed in Nº1's fingers in time with his heartbeat, then pulsed out of his body into the skewer. The pin turned to stone. Wood morphed to granite before his eyes. The rock virus spread along the shaft, rippling like water. In the flash of a spark, the skewer was completely made of stone. It expanded slightly into the breach in Abbot's armored plate.

The expansion cracked the plate open half an inch.

Abbot heard the noise, so did everybody else. The demon pride leader flicked his eyes downward and realized instantly what was going on.

"Magic," he hissed. The word was out before he could stop it. With a vicious swipe, he swatted the skewer away from his torso into the fire.

Nº1 stared at his throbbing hand. Power still shimmered around his fingertips, a tiny heat haze.

"Magic?" he repeated. "That means I must be a—"

"Shut your stupid mouth," snapped Abbot, covering the cracked scale with his cloak. "Obviously I don't mean actual magic. I mean trickery. You twist the handle on that skewer to make it crack, then you *ooh* and *aah* as though you have actually achieved something."

Nº1 pulled at Abbot's cloak. "But your scale?"

Abbot drew the cloak tighter. "What about my scale? There's not a mark on it. Not so much as a smear. You believe me, don't you?"

Nº1 sighed. This was Leon Abbot; the truth meant nothing. "Yes, Master Abbot. I believe you."

"I can tell by your insolent tone that you do not. Very well, proof, then." Abbot whipped back his cloak, revealing an unblemished scale. For a moment, Nº1 thought he saw a blue spark playing about where the mark had definitely been, but then the spark winked itself out. Blue sparks. Could it be magic?

Abbot jabbed the imp's chest with a rigid finger. "We've

talked about this, N°1. I know you think you're a war-lock. But there are no warlocks; there haven't been since we lifted out of time. You are not a warlock. Forget that idiotic notion and concentrate on warping. You're a disgrace to your race."

N°1 was about to risk a protest when he was grabbed roughly by the arm.

"You slippery little snail," shouted Rawley, spittle spattering N°1's face. "Trying to trick the pride leader. Get back to your place. I'll deal with you later."

N°1 could do nothing but return to the bench and bear the insults of his classmates. And there were plenty of those, usually accompanied by a missile or blow. But somehow N°1 ignored these latest humiliations, staring instead at his own hand. The one that had turned wood to stone. Could it be true? Could he actually be a war-lock? And if he was, would that make him feel better or worse?

A toothpick bounced off his forehead onto the bench. There was a sliver of gray meat stuck to the end. N°1 glanced up to find Rawley grinning at him.

"Been trying to get that out for weeks. Wild boar, I think. Now, pay attention, Runt, Master Abbot is trying to educate you."

Oh yes, the history lesson. It was amazing how much Leon Abbot managed to insert himself into demon history. To hear him tell it, you would think that he had single-handedly saved the 8th Family, in spite of the meddling warlocks.

Abbot studied the hooked talons on his fingertips. Each one could gut a large pig. If Abbot's own stories were true, he had warped at age eight while wrestling one of the island's wild dogs. His fingernails had actually changed into talons during the fight, lacerating the dog's side.

N°1 found this story highly unlikely. It took hours to warp fully, sometimes days, but Abbot expected them to believe that *his* warp was instantaneous. Hogwash. And yet all the other imps lapped up these self-glorifying legends.

"Of all the demons who fought in the last battle at Taillte," droned Abbot in what he probably thought was a good voice for history lessons, but in what N°1 thought was a boring enough voice to turn soft cheese hard, "I, Leon Abbot, am the last."

Convenient, thought N°1. Nobody left around to argue. He also thought: You look your age, Leon. Too many barrels of pork fat.

N°1 was an uncharitable imp when in a bad mood.

It is the nature of out-of-time spells that the aging process is drastically slowed. Abbot had been a young buck when the warlocks had lifted Hybras out of time, and so the spell, combined with good genes, had kept him and his huge ego alive ever since. Possibly a thousand years. Of course, that was a thousand years in normal time. In Hybras time a millennium meant very little. A couple of centuries could skip by in the blink of an eye on the island. An imp could wake up one morning to find that he'd evolved. A while back, every demon and imp in Hybras got up one morning with a stubby tail where his magnificent long one used to be. For a considerable time after that, the most common noises on the island were the sounds of demons falling down, or swearing as they got up again.

"After that great battle in which the demon battalions were the bravest and fiercest in the People's army," continued Abbot to hoots of approval from the imps, "we were defeated by treachery and cowardice. The elves would not fight, and the dwarfs would not dig traps. We had no choice but to cast our spell and regroup until the time was right to return."

More hooting, plus stamping of feet.

Every time, thought N°1. Do we have to go through this every time? These imps act like they'd never heard this story before. When is someone going to stand up and say: "Excuse me. Old news. Move on."

"And so we breed. We breed and grow strong. Now our army has more than five thousand warriors, surely enough to defeat the humans. I know this because I, Leon Abbot, have been to the world and returned to Hybras alive."

This was Abbot's golden nugget. This was where anyone who stood against him withered and blew away. Abbot had not come directly to Limbo with the rest of Hybras. For

some reason he had been diverted to the human future, then sucked across to Hybras. He had seen the human camps and actually brought his knowledge home. How all this happened was a bit hazy. According to Abbot, there had been a great battle, he'd defeated fifty or so men, then a mysterious warlock had lifted him out of time again. But not before he'd grabbed a couple of things to bring back.

Since the warlocks had been explosively removed from the 8th Family, nobody had much of a clue about magic anymore. Normal demons had no magic of their own. It had been thought that all the warlocks had been sucked into space during the transferal of Hybras from Earth to Limbo, but according to Abbot, one had survived. This warlock was in league with the humans and had only helped the demon leader under threat of grievous injury.

N°1 was highly skeptical of this version of events. First of all, because it came from Abbot, and secondly, because warlocks were being cast, once more, in a bad light. Demons seemed to forget that if it hadn't been for the warlocks, Hybras would have been overrun by humans.

On this particular day, N°1 was feeling a special attachment to the warlocks, and he did not appreciate their memory being sullied by this loudmouth braggart. Hardly a day went by where N°1 did not spend a moment praying for the return of the mysterious warlock who had helped Abbot. And now that he was certain of magic in his own blood, N°1 would pray all the harder.

"The moon separated me from the rest of the island during the great journey," continued Abbot, his eyes half closed as if the memory had him in a swoon. "I was powerless to resist her charms. And so I traveled through space and time until I came to rest in the new world. Which is now the world of men. The humans clamped silver on my ankles, tried to make me submit, but I would not." Abbot hunched his massive shoulders and roared at the roof. "For I am demonkind! And we will never submit!"

Needless to say, the imps went into overdrive. The entire room heaved with their exertions. In Nº1's opinion, Abbot's entire performance was wooden to say the least. The *we will never submit* speech was the oldest page in Abbot's book. Nº1 rubbed his temples, trying to ease the headache. There was worse to come, he knew. First the book, then the crossbow, if Abbot didn't deviate from the script. And why would he? He hadn't in all the years since his return from the new world.

"And so I fought!" shouted Abbot. "I kicked off their shackles and Hybras called me home, but before I took my leave of the hated humans, I fought my way to their altar and stole away with two of their blessed objects."

"The book and the bow," muttered Nº1, rolling his orange eyes.

"Tell us what you stole!" begged the others on cue, as if they didn't know.

"The book and the bow!" proclaimed Leon Abbot, pulling the objects from beneath his robe as if by magic.

As if by magic, thought Nº1. But not actual magic, because then Abbot would be a warlock, and he couldn't possibly be a warlock, as he had already warped, and warlocks did not warp.

"Now we know how the humans think," said Abbot, waving the book. "And how they fight," he proclaimed, brandishing the crossbow.

I don't believe any of this for a minute, thought Nº1. Or I wouldn't, if we had "minutes" in Limbo. Oh, how I wish I were on Earth with the last warlock. Then there would be two of us, and I would find out what really happened when Leon Abbot came calling.

"And armed with this knowledge, we can return when the time spell fades, and retake the Old Country."

"When?" cried the imps. "When?"

"Soon," replied Abbot. "Soon. And there will be humans enough for us all. They will be crushed like the grass beneath our boots. We will tear their heads off like dandelion flowers."

Oh, please, thought Nº1. Enough plant similes.

It was quite possible that Nº1 was the only creature on Hybras who had ever even thought the human word *simile*. Saying it aloud would have certainly earned him a thrashing. If the other imps knew that his human vocabulary also included words like *grooming* and *decoration*, they would string him up for sure. Ironically he had learned these words from *Lady Heatherington Smythe's Hedgerow*, which was supposed to be a school text.

"Tear their heads off," shouted one imp, and it quickly became a chant, taken up by everyone in the room.

"Yes, tear their heads off," said Nº1, trying it out, but there was no feeling in his voice.

What's my motivation? he wondered. I've never even met a human.

The imps climbed onto their benches, bobbing in primal rhythm.

"Tear their heads off! Tear their heads off!"

Abbot and Rawley urged them on, flexing their claws and howling. A sickly sweet smell clogged the air. Warp muck. Someone was entering the warp spasm phase. The excitement was bringing on the change.

Nº1 felt nothing. Not so much as a twinge. He tried his best, squeezing his eyelids together, letting the pressure build in his head, thinking bloody thoughts. But his true feelings shattered the false visions of bloodlust and carnage.

It's no use, he thought. I am not that kind of demon.

Nº1 stopped chanting and sat, head in hands. No point in pretending; another change cycle was passing him by.

Not so the other imps. Abbot's theatrics had opened a natural well of testosterone, bloodlust, and bodily fluid.

One by one, they succumbed to the warp spasm. Green gunge flowed from their pores, slowly at first, then in bubbling gushes. They all went under, every one of them. It must be some kind of record, so many imps warping simultaneously. Of course Abbot would take the credit.

The sight of the fluid brought on fresh rounds of howling. And the more the imps howled, the faster the gunge spurted. N°1 had heard it said that humans took several years to make the transition from childhood to adulthood. Imps did it in a few hours. And a change like that is going to hurt.

The howls of exultation changed to grunts of pain as bones stretched and horns curled, the gunge-coated limbs already lengthening. The smell was sweet enough to make N°1 gag.

Imps toppled to the floor all around. They thrashed for a few seconds, then their own fluids mummified them. They were cocooned like enormous green bugs, strapped tight by the hardening gunge. The schoolroom was suddenly silent, except for the crack of drying nutrient fluid and a rustle of flames from the stone fireplace.

Abbot beamed, a toothy smile that seemed to split his head in half.

"A good morning's work, wouldn't you say, Rawley? I got them all warping."

Rawley grunted his agreement, then noticed N°1. "Except the Runt."

"Well, of course not," began Abbot, then caught himself. "Yes. Absolutely, except the Runt."

Nº1's forehead burned under Rawley and Abbot's scrutiny.

"I want to warp," he said, looking at his fingers. "I really do. But it's the hating thing. I just can't manage it. And all that slime. Even the thought of that stuff all over me makes me feel a bit nauseous."

"A bit what?" said Rawley suspiciously.

Nº1 realized that he needed to dumb it down for his teacher.

"Sick. A bit sick."

"Oh." Rawley shook his head in disgust. "Slime makes you sick? What kind of imp are you? The others live for slime."

Nº1 took a deep breath and said something aloud that he had known for a long time.

"I'm not like the others." Nº1's voice trembled. He was on the verge of tears.

"Are you going to cry?" asked Rawley, his eyes bugging. "This is too much, Leon. He's going to cry now, just like a female. I give up."

Abbot scratched his chin. "Let me try something."

He rummaged in a cape pocket, surreptitiously fixing something over his hand.

Oh, no, thought Nº1. Please no. Not Stony.

Abbot raised a forearm, his cloak draped over it. A

• ⏐◯♗✧♟♀℞ • ⊍♗⊅⊖⚷ • ⚸◯⊖℞

ministage. A puppet human poked his head over the leather cape. The puppet's head was a grotesque ball of painted clay, with a heavy forehead and clumsy features. N°1 doubted that humans were this ugly in real life, but demons were not known for their artistic skills. Abbot often produced Stony as a visual incentive for those imps who were having difficulty warping. Needless to say, N°1 had been introduced to the puppet before.

"*Grrr,*" said the puppet, or rather Abbot said, as he waggled the puppet. "*Grrr*, my name is Stony the Mud Man."

"Hello, Stony," said N°1 weakly. "How've you been?"

The puppet held a tiny wooden sword in its hand. "Never mind how I've been. I don't care how you've been, because I hate all fairies," said Abbot in a squeaky voice. "I drove them from their homes. And if they ever try to come back, I will kill them all."

Abbot lowered the puppet. "Now, how does that make you feel?"

It makes me feel that the wrong demon is in charge of the pride, thought N°1, but aloud he said, "Eh, angry?"

Abbot blinked. "Angry? Really?"

"No," confessed N°1, wringing his hands. "I don't feel anything. It's a puppet. I can see your fingers through the material."

Abbot stuffed Stony back in his pocket.

"That's it. I've had it with you, N°1. You will never earn a name from the book."

Once demons warped, they were given a human name from *Lady Heatherington Smythe's Hedgerow*. The logic being that learning the human language and possessing a human name would help the demon army think like humans, and therefore defeat them. Abbot may have hated the Mud Men, but that wasn't to say he didn't admire them. Also, politically, it was a good idea to have every demon on Hybras calling each other by names that Leon Abbot had procured for them.

Rawley grabbed N⁰1's ear and dragged him from his seat to the rear of the classroom. A metal grille on the floor covered a shallow, pungent dung pit.

"Get to work, Runt," he said gruffly. "You know what to do."

N⁰1 sighed. He knew only too well. This wasn't the first or second time he'd had to endure this odious task. He hefted a long-handled gaff from a peg on the wall and pulled the heavy grille from its groove. The smell was rank but not unbearable, as a crust had formed on the dung's surface. Beetles crawled across the craggy skin, their legs clicking like claws on wood.

N⁰1 uncovered the pit completely, then selected his nearest classmate. There was no way of telling which classmate it actually was because of the slime cocoon. The only movements were small air bubbles around the mouth and nose. At least, he hoped it was the mouth and nose.

N⁰1 bent low and rolled the cocoon along the floor and

into the dung pit. The warping imp crashed through the crust, taking a dozen beetles with him into the muck below. A gush of dung stink washed over N^o1, and he knew his skin would smell for days. The others would wear their pit stink proudly, but for N^o1 it was just another badge of shame.

It was arduous work. Not all the warping imps were still. Several struggled inside their cocoons, and twice demon claws punctured the green chrysalis inches from N^o1's skin.

He persisted, groaning loudly in the hope that Rawley or Leon Abbot would lend a hand. It was a vain hope. The two demons were huddled at the head of the classroom, poring over *Lady Heatherington Smythe's Hedgerow*.

Eventually, N^o1 rolled his last classmate into the dung pit. They were piled in there like meat in a thick stew. The nutrient-rich dung would accelerate their warp, ensuring they reached full potential. N^o1 sat on the stone floor, catching his breath.

Lucky you, thought N^o1. Dunked in dung.

N^o1 tried to feel envious, but even being near the pit made him gag; the thoughts of being immersed in it, surrounded by cocooned imps, made his stomach churn.

A shadow fell across the flagstones before him, flickering in the firelight.

"Ah, N^o1," said Abbot. "Always an imp, never a demon, eh? What am I going to do with you?"

N°1 stared at his own feet, clicking his baby talons on the floor.

"Master Abbot, sir. Don't you think? Isn't there the tiniest chance?" He took a deep breath and raised his eyes to meet Abbot's. "Couldn't I be a warlock? You saw what happened with the skewer. I don't want to embarrass you, but you saw it."

Abbot's expression changed instantly. One second he was playing the genial master, the next his true colors shone through.

"I saw nothing," he hissed, heaving N°1 to his feet. "Nothing happened, you odious little freak of nature. The skewer was coated with ash, nothing more. There was no transformation. No magic."

Abbot drew N°1 close enough to see the slivers of trapped meat between his yellowed teeth. The next time he spoke, his voice seemed different somehow. Layered. As though an entire choir were singing in harmony. It was a voice that could not be ignored. Magical?

"If you are a warlock. Then you should really be on the other side, with your relative. Wouldn't that be for the best? One quick leap, that's all it would take. Do you understand what I am saying to you, Runt?"

N°1 nodded, dazed. What a lovely voice. Where had that come from? The other side—of course that's where he should go. One small step for an imp.

"I understand, sir."

"Good. The subject is closed. As Lady Heatherington Smythe would say, 'Best foot forward, young sir, the world awaits.'"

N°1 nodded just as he knew Abbot wanted him to, but inside, his brain churned along with his stomach. Was this to be the whole extent of his life? Forever mocked, forever different. Never a moment of light or hope. Unless he crossed over.

Abbot's suggestion was his only hope. *Cross over.* N°1 had never seen the appeal of jumping into a crater before, but now the notion seemed nigh on irresistible. He was a warlock, there couldn't be any doubt. And somewhere out there, in the human world, there was another like him. An ancient brother who could teach him the ways of his kind.

N°1 watched Abbot stride away. Off to exercise his power on some other part of the island, possibly by belittling the females in the compound, another of his favorite pastimes. Then again, how bad could Abbot be? After all, he had given N°1 this wonderful idea.

I cannot stay here, thought N°1. I must go to the volcano.

The notion took firm hold of his brain. And in minutes it had drowned out all the other notions in his head.

Go to the volcano.

It pounded inside his skull, like waves breaking on the shore.

Obey Abbot. Go to the volcano.

Nº1 brushed the dust from his knees.

"You know what," he muttered to himself, in case Rawley could hear. "I think I'm going to the volcano."

•) ꙮ • ⊕ ▢ ⚔ ⊕ • ⊕ ▢ • ꙮ ß ⊗ • ∪

CHAPTER 4: MISSION IMPOSSIBLE

The Bellini Theatre, Catania, Southern Sicily

Artemis Fowl and his bodyguard, Butler, relaxed in a private box at the stage-left side of Sicily's world-famous Bellini Theatre. Perhaps it is not altogether accurate to say Butler *relaxed*. Rather, he *appeared* to relax, as a tiger appears to relax in the moment before it strikes.

Butler was even less happy here than he had been in Barcelona. At least for the Spain trip he'd had a few days to prepare, but for this jaunt he barely had time to catch up on his martial arts routines.

As soon as the Fowl Bentley had pulled up at Fowl Manor, Artemis had disappeared into his study, firing up his computers. Butler took the opportunity to work out, freshen up, and prepare dinner: onion marmalade tartlets, rack of lamb with garlic gratin, and a red berries crepe to finish.

Artemis broke the news over coffee.

"We need to go to Sicily," he said, toying with the biscotti on his saucer. "I made a breakthrough on the time spell figures."

"How soon?" asked the bodyguard, mentally listing his contacts on the Mediterranean island.

Artemis looked at his Rado watch and Butler moaned.

"Don't check your watch, Artemis. Check the calendar."

"Sorry, old friend. But you know time is limited. I can't risk missing a materialization."

"But on the jet you said that there wasn't another materialization due for six weeks."

"I was wrong, or rather, Foaly was wrong. He missed a few new factors in the temporal equation."

Artemis had filled Butler in on the 8th Family details as the jet soared over the English Channel.

"Allow me to demonstrate," said Artemis. He put a silver salt shaker on his plate "Let us say that this salt shaker is Hybras. My plate is where it is: our dimension. And your plate is where it wants to go: Limbo. With me so far?"

Butler nodded reluctantly. He knew that the more he understood, the more Artemis would tell him, and there wasn't much space in a bodyguard's head for quantum physics.

"So, the demon warlocks wanted to move the island from plate A to plate B, but not through space, through time."

"How do you know all this?"

"It's all in the fairy Book," replied the Irish teenager. "Quite a detailed description, if a bit flowery."

The Book was the fairy bible, containing their history and commandments. Artemis had managed to obtain a copy from a drunken sprite in Ho Chi Minh City years earlier. It was proving to be an invaluable source of information.

"I doubt the Book has too many charts and graphs," noted Butler.

Artemis smiled. "No, I got the specifics from Foaly, not that he knows he's sharing information."

Butler rubbed his temples. "Artemis, I warned you not to mess with Foaly. The decoy thing is bad enough."

Artemis was fully aware that Foaly was tracking him and any decoys he sent out. In fact, he only sent out the decoys to make Foaly dip into his funds. It was his idea of a joke.

"I didn't initiate the surveillance," objected Artemis. "Foaly did. I found more than a dozen devices on my computers alone. All I did was reverse the spike to get into some of his shared files. Nothing classified. Well, maybe a few. Foaly's been busy since he left the LEP."

"So what did Foaly's files tell you?" said Butler resignedly.

"They told me about magic. Basically, magic is energy, and the ability to manipulate energy. To move Hybras from A to B, the demon warlocks harnessed the power of their volcano to create a time rent, or tunnel." Artemis rolled his napkin into a tube, popped the salt shaker into it, and deposited the shaker on Butler's plate.

"Simple as that?" said Butler doubtfully.

"Not really," said Artemis. "In fact, the warlocks did an exceptional job, considering the instruments available to them at the time. They had to calculate the power of the volcano, the size of the island, the energy of each individual demon on the island, not to mention the reverse pull of lunar attraction. It's amazing that the spell worked as well as it did."

"There was a glitch?"

"Yes. According to the Book, the warlocks induced the volcano, but the force was too strong. They couldn't control it, and the magic circle was broken. Hybras and the demons were transported, but the warlocks were blasted into space."

Butler whistled. "That's quite a glitch."

"It's more than a glitch. The demon warlocks were all killed, so now the rest of the pride are stuck in Limbo, held by a magical spell that was never meant to be permanent, without a warlock to bring them back."

"Couldn't Foaly go and get them?"

"No. It would be an impossible mission to re-create the

same circumstances. Imagine trying to steer a feather in a sandstorm, then land the feather on a particular grain of sand, except you don't know where the grain is. And even if you did know where the grain was, demon magic can only be controlled by a demon. They are by far the most powerful of warlocks. "

"Tricky," admitted Butler. "So tell me why these demons are popping up here now?"

Artemis corrected him with a wagging finger. "Not just here, and not just now. The demons have always felt an attraction to their home world, a combination of lunar and terrestrial radiations. But a demon could only be pulled back if he was at his end of the time tunnel mouth, the crater, and not wearing a dimensional anchor."

Butler fingered his wristband. "Silver."

"That's right. Now, because of massively increased radiation levels worldwide, the pull on demons is much stronger and reaches critical level with greater frequency."

Butler was struggling to keep up. Sometimes it was not easy being a genius's bodyguard.

"Artemis, I thought we weren't going into specifics."

Artemis continued regardless. He was hardly going to stop now, in midlecture.

"Bear with me, old friend. Nearly there. So now, energy spikes occur more often than Foaly thinks."

Butler raised a finger. "Ah, yes, but the demons are okay as long as they stay away from the crater."

Artemis raised a triumphant finger. "Yes!" he crowed. "That's what you would think. That's what Foaly thinks. But when our last demon was off course, I ran the equation from back to front. My conclusion is that the time spell is decaying. The tunnel is unraveling."

Artemis allowed the napkin tube to widen in his hand. "Now the catchment area is bigger, as is the deposit area. Pretty soon, demons won't be safe anywhere on Hybras."

Butler asked the obvious question. "What happens when the tunnel decays altogether?"

"Just before that happens, demons all over Hybras will be plucked off the island, silver or no silver. When the tunnel collapses, some will be deposited on Earth, more on the moon, and the rest scattered through space and time. One thing is for sure, not many of them will survive, and those that do will be locked up in laboratories and zoos."

Butler frowned. "We need to tell Holly about this."

"Yes," agreed Artemis. "But not just yet. I need one more day to confirm my figures. I'm not going to Foaly with nothing but theory."

"Don't tell me," said Butler. "Sicily, right?"

So now they were in the Massimo Bellini Theatre, and Butler had barely half an idea why they were there. If a demon materialized on that stage, then Artemis was right, and the fairy People were in major trouble. And if the fairies were in trouble, then it was up to Artemis to help them. Butler was actually quite proud that his young charge was doing something for somebody else for a change. Even so, they had only a week to complete their task and return to Fowl Manor, because in seven days Artemis's parents returned from Rhode Island, where Artemis Fowl Senior had finally taken possession of an artificial bio hybrid leg, to replace the one he had lost when the Russian Mafiya blew up his ship.

Butler peered out of the box at the hundreds of golden arches and the thirteen hundred–odd people enjoying the evening's performance of Bellini's *Norma*.

"First a Gaudí building, now this theater," commented the bodyguard, his words audible only to Artemis, thanks to their box's isolation and the booming volume of the opera. "Don't these demons ever materialize somewhere quiet?"

Artemis replied in a whisper. "Just let the sublime music flow over you, enjoy the show. Don't you know how difficult it is to get a box for a Vincenzo Bellini opera? Especially *Norma*. *Norma* combines the requirements of both a coloratura and a dramatic soprano. And the soprano is excellent, comparable to Callas herself."

Butler grunted. Perhaps it was difficult for *ordinary* people to get a box in the theater, but Artemis had simply called his billionaire environmentalist friend, Giovanni Zito. The Sicilian had gladly surrendered his own box in exchange for two cases of the finest Bordeaux. Hardly surprising, since Artemis had recently invested more than ten million dollars in Zito's water purification research.

"A Sicilian drinking Bordeaux?" Artemis had chuckled on the phone. "You should be ashamed of yourself."

"Keep your watch pointed at the stage," directed Artemis, interrupting Butler's thoughts. "The chances are minuscule that a demon will be caught without silver, even away from the crater, but if one does show up, I want it on film to prove to Foaly that my theory is correct. If we don't have incontrovertible proof, the fairy Council will never take action."

Butler checked that his watch crystal, which doubled as a camera lense, was angled toward the stage. "The camera is fine, but if you don't mind, I won't be letting the sublime music flow over me. I have enough to do keeping you safe."

The Bellini Theatre was a bodyguard's nightmare. Multiple entrances and exits, more than a thousand patrons that refused to be frisked, hundreds of golden arches that could conceal a gunman, and countless nooks, crannies, and corridors that probably didn't appear on the theater plan. Nevertheless, Butler was reasonably confident that he had done all he could to protect Artemis.

Of course, there were certain things that bodyguards could not guard against, as Butler was about to find out. Invisible things.

Artemis's phone vibrated gently. Usually Artemis

deplored the kind of person who kept their phone on during a performance, but this phone was special and he never turned it off. It was the fairy communicator given to him by Holly Short, plus a few modifications and add-ons made by Artemis himself.

The phone was the size and shape of a quarter with a pulsing red crystal at its center. This was a fairy omnisensor, which could interface with any communications system, including the human body. The phone was disguised as a rather ostentatious ring on Artemis's middle finger. Artemis twisted the ring so that the phone sat on his palm, then closed his middle fingers, extending his thumb and little finger. The sensor would decode vibrations in his little finger and send them as voice patterns. It would also use the bones in his hand to transmit the caller's voice to the tip of his thumb.

Artemis looked for all the world like a young boy talking on an imaginary phone.

"Holly?" he said.

Butler watched as Artemis listened for a few moments, hung up and twisted the phone back into ring position.

He looked steadily at Butler. "Don't draw your weapon," he said.

Which of course had Butler reaching for the butt of his Sig Sauer.

"It's fine," said Artemis reassuringly. "Someone is here. A friend."

Butler's hand dropped to his side. He knew who it was.

Holly Short materialized in the velvet-covered seat beside Artemis. Her knees were drawn to her chin, and her pointed ears were covered by a black helmet. As she fizzled into the visible spectrum, a full-face visor collapsed into sections and stored itself in her helmet. Her arrival among the humans was covered by the theater's darkness.

"Afternoon, Mud Boys," she said, smiling. Her hazel eyes sparkled impishly, or more accurately, *elfishly*.

"Thanks for calling ahead," said Butler sarcastically. "Wouldn't want to spook anyone. No shimmer?"

Usually when fairies used their magic to shield, the only thing visible was a slight shimmer, like a heat haze. Holly's entrance had been completely undetectable.

Holly patted her own shoulder. "New suit. Made entirely from smart wafers. It vibrates with me."

Artemis studied one of the wafers, noting the microfilaments in the material. "Foaly's work? Section Eight issue."

Holly could not hide her surprise. She punched Artemis playfully on the shoulder. "How do you know about Section Eight? Aren't we allowed any secrets?"

"Foaly shouldn't spy on me," said Artemis. "Where there's a way in, there's a way back. I suppose I should congratulate you on the new job. And Foaly, too." He nodded at the tiny lense over Holly's right eye. "Is he watching us now?"

94

"No. He's trying to figure out how you know what he doesn't. We're taping, though."

"I presume you're talking about demons."

"I might be."

Butler stepped between them, interrupting the verbal sparring that was bound to follow.

"Before you two get into negotiations, how about a real hello?"

Holly smiled fondly at the huge bodyguard. She activated the electronic wings built into her suit and hovered to his eye level. Holly kissed his cheek, then wrapped her arms all the way around his head. They barely made it.

Butler rapped her helmet. "Nice equipment. Not run-of-the-mill Lower Elements Police."

"No," agreed Holly, removing the helmet. "This Section Eight stuff is years ahead of standard LEP. You get what you pay for, I suppose."

Butler plucked the helmet from her hands. "Anything an old soldier would be interested in?"

Holly pressed a button on her wrist computer. "Check out the night vision. It's as clear as . . . well . . . day. And the clever thing is that the filter reacts to light as it passes through, so no more being blinded by camera flashes."

Butler nodded appreciatively. Night vision's major drawback had historically been that it left the soldier vulnerable to sudden flashes of light. Even a candle flame could blind the wearer momentarily.

Artemis cleared his throat. "Excuse me, Captain. Are you two going to weep salty tears of admiration over a helmet all night, or do we have matters to discuss?"

Holly winked at Butler. "Your master calls. I'd better see what he wants."

Holly deactivated her wings and settled into the chair. She folded her arms, looking Artemis straight in the eyes.

"Okay, Mud Boy, I'm all yours."

"Demons. We need to talk about demons."

Holly's eyes lost their playful twinkle. "And why *are* you so interested in demons, Artemis?"

Artemis opened two shirt buttons and pulled out a gold coin on a leather necklace. The coin had a circular hole in the center. Put there by a blast from Holly's laser.

"You gave this to me after you saved my father's life. I owe you. I owe the People. So now I'm doing something for them."

Holly wasn't entirely convinced. "Usually before you do anything for the People, you negotiate a fee."

Artemis accepted the accusation with a slight nod. "It's true. It *was* true, but I have changed."

Holly folded her arms. "And?"

"And it's nice to find something Foaly missed, even if I did stumble onto it by accident."

"And?"

Artemis sighed. "Very well. There is another factor."

"I thought so. What do you want? Gold? Technology?"

"No. Nothing like that."

Artemis sat forward in his seat. "Have you any idea how difficult it is to have had all those thrilling adventures with the LEP, and suddenly not be a part of that world anymore?"

"Yes," replied Holly. "Actually, I do."

"I went from *saving the world* to *geometry* in a week. I'm bored, Holly. My intellect is not being challenged. So when I came across the demon gospel in the Book, I realized that here was a way to be involved without affecting things. I could simply observe, and perhaps refine Foaly's calculations."

"Which are not actually in the Book," Holly pointed out. "Simply observe, my foot."

Artemis waved Holly's point away. "Some harmless hacking. The centaur started it. So I began traveling to materialization sights, but nothing happened until Barcelona. A demon showed up, all right, except he showed up in the wrong place, and late. I simply stumbled across him. I would be floating in prehistoric space right now if Butler hadn't anchored me to this dimension with silver."

Holly stifled a laugh. "So it was luck. The great Artemis Fowl trumps the mighty Foaly thanks to dumb luck."

Artemis was miffed. "Informed luck I think is a better description. Anyway, that is unimportant. I have recalculated with the new figures, and my conclusions, if borne out, could be calamitous for the People."

"Go on, tell me. In short words, though; you wouldn't believe the amount of science I had to listen to today."

"This is serious, Holly," snapped Artemis. His outburst was followed by a chorus of shushes from the audience.

"This is serious," he repeated in hushed tones.

"Why?" asked Holly. "Surely it's just a matter of sharing your new figures and letting Foaly take care of the rest with light-distortion projectors?"

"Not quite," said Artemis, settling back in his chair. "If a demon appears on that stage in the next four minutes, then soon there won't be enough projectors to go around. If I'm right, and the time spell is unraveling, then Hybras and everyone on it will soon be dragged back into this dimension. Most of the demons won't make it alive, but those who do could pop up anywhere and at any time."

Holly switched her gaze to the stage. A raven-haired woman was holding ridiculously high notes for a ridiculously long time. Holly wondered would the woman even notice a demon popping out of the air for a second or two. There wasn't supposed to be a materialization today. If there was, then that would mean Artemis was right, as usual, and a lot more demons were on the way. If that happened, then Artemis Fowl and Holly Short would be up to their necks in the whole saving-the-fairy-race thing yet again.

Holly glanced sideways at Artemis, who was studying the stage through a pair of opera glasses. She would never

tell him, but if a human had to be involved with saving the Fairy People, then Artemis was probably the best man, or boy, for the job.

The Island of Hybras, Limbo

N°1 struggled up toward the first rocky ridge on the side of the volcano. Several demons passed him on the trail, but not one tried to talk him out of it. In fact, he'd bumped into Hadley Shrivelington Basset, who had offered to scratch a map on a piece of bark for him. N°1 suspected that if he did take the big dimensional jump, no one would miss him any more than they would miss their favorite crossbow target. Except perhaps the demoness with red markings who smiled at him. The one from the compound. Maybe she would miss him a little. N°1 stopped in his tracks when he realized that the only demon who would care when he was gone was one he had never spoken to.

He moaned aloud. How depressing was that!

N°1 trudged onward past the final warning, which, with typical demon subtlety, was in the form of a blood-reddened wolf skull mounted on a stick.

"What's that even supposed to mean?" muttered N°1 as he passed the sign. "A wolf's head on a stick. Big wolf barbecue tonight. Bring your own wolf."

Barbecue. Another word from Lady Heatherington Smythe.

N°1 sat on the ridge, wiggling his rump to dig a little trench for his tail. Might as well be comfortable before jumping the few hundred feet into the mouth of a steaming volcano. Of course, even if he didn't get whisked away to the New Country, he still wouldn't be vaporized by the lava. No, he would probably be dashed against the rocks on the way down. What a cheery thought.

From his seat on the ridge, N°1 could see the jagged mouth of the crater and the rhythmic wisps of smoke that drifted skyward like the breath of a sleeping giant. It was the nature of the time spell that things progressed as though Hybras were still attached to the rest of the world, albeit at a different pace. So the volcano still bubbled and occasionally burped up a skinny column of flame even though there was no earth beneath it.

If N°1 were honest with himself, his resolve was wavering. It was easy to imagine hopping into an inter-dimensional crater when you were rolling your cocooned classmates into a becrusted dung pit. It had seemed then, as the flakes of ash had fluttered down on him, that things could not get any worse. And there had been something in Abbot's voice that made the idea seem irresistible. But now, sitting on the ridge, with a gentle wind cooling his chest plates, things didn't seem quite as bleak. At least he was alive, and there was no guarantee that the crater led anywhere except into the belly of the volcano. None of the other demons had made it back alive. They came back, all right. Some encased in blocks of ice, some burned to a crisp, but none hale and hearty like the pride leader. Although, for some reason, when N°1 thought about Abbot, the many moments of cruelty he had suffered at the pride leader's whim seemed hazy, hard to focus on. All he could remember was that beautiful insistent voice telling him to cross over.

Moon madness. That was the heart of the matter. Demonkind were attracted to the moon. It sang to them, agitating particles in their blood. They dreamed of it at night and ground their teeth at its absence. At any hour of the so-called day here on Hybras, demons could be seen stopping in their tracks to gaze at the space where the moon used to be. It was part of them, a live organic part; and on an atomic level, they belonged together.

There were threads of the time spell still in the crater. Wisps of magic that curled about the mountaintop snagging any demon stupid enough to be caught without silver. And coded inside the magic was the song of the moon, calling the demons back, enticing them with visions of white light and weightlessness. Once those pale tendrils had a grip on a demon's mind, he would do anything to be closer to the source. The magic and moon madness would pour energy into the atoms of his being, vibrating his very electrons to a new orbit, changing his molecular structure, pulling him through time and space.

But there was only Abbot's word that this journey

would end on Earth. It could end on the moon, and as much as demons loved the moon, they knew that nothing survived on its barren surface. The elders said that sprites could not fly close without freezing to death, spiraling to earth with frozen wings and blue faces.

For some reason, N°1 wanted to take the journey today. He wanted the moon to call him into the crater, then deposit him somewhere where another warlock existed. Someone who would teach him to control his strange powers. But, he miserably admitted, he didn't have the courage. He could not just hurl himself into a rocky crater. The volcano's base was littered with the charred corpses of those who had imagined the moon calling to them. How could he know if the moon's power was truly beckoning, or if it was simply wishful thinking.

N°1 rested his face in his hands. Nothing for it but to return to the school. The imps in the pit would need turning, or their hides could suffer dung lividity marks.

He sighed. This was not the first time he had made this desperate journey. But now N°1 really thought he would do it. Abbot was in his head, urging him on. This time he could almost bear the idea of the rocks rushing toward him. Almost.

N°1 toyed with the silver bangle on his wrist. It would have been so easy to slip off this trinket and just disappear.

Slip it off, then, little one, said a voice in his head. *Slip it off and come to me.*

N°1 was not surprised by the voice. Actually, it was more a feeling than a voice. N°1 had supplied the words himself. He often conversed with voices in his head. There was no one else to talk to. There was Flambard the shoemaker, and Lady Bonnie the spinster, and his favorite, Bookie the lisping gossip.

This voice was new. More forceful.

A moment without silver, and a new world could be yours.

N°1's bottom lip jutted as he considered. He could remove the bangle, he supposed, just for a moment. What harm could it do? He was nowhere near the crater, and the magic rarely strayed beyond the volcano.

No harm. No harm at all. One little tug.

The ridiculous notion had N°1 now. Taking off the bangle could be like a practice run for the day when he finally worked up the courage to feel the moon madness. His fingers traced the runes on the bangle. They were precisely the same as the markings on his chest. A double charm. Repelling the moon magic. Removing one meant that the force of his own markings was reversed, pulling him straight toward the moon.

Take it off. Reverse the power.

N°1 watched his fingers grip the bangle's rim. He was in a daze, a buzzing fugue. The new voice had coated his mind with fog and was in control.

We will be together, you and I. You will bask in my light.

Bask in my light? thought the last conscious sliver of

Nº1. This new voice is quite the drama queen. Bookie is not going to like you.

Take it off, little one.

Nº1 watched his hand tug the bangle over his knuckles. He was powerless to stop himself, not that he wanted to.

Moon madness, he realized with a jolt. All the way over here. How can that be?

Something in him knew. The warlock part of him, perhaps.

The time spell is breaking down. No one is safe.

Nº1 saw the bangle, his dimensional anchor, slip from his fingers and spin to the ground. It seemed to happen in slow motion—the silver flowed and rippled like sunlight through water.

Nº1 felt the tingle that comes when every atom in your body is overloaded with energy and boosted into a gaseous form. It really should be terribly painful, but the body doesn't really know how to respond to this kind of cell damage, and so throws up a pathetic tingling.

There was no time to scream. All Nº1 could do was disappear into a million flashing pinpoints of light, which quickly wound themselves into a tight band following a path to another dimension. In seconds there was nothing left to show that Nº1 had ever been there but a spinning silver bangle.

It would be a long time, relatively speaking, before

anyone missed him. And no one would care enough to come looking.

The Bellini Theatre, Sicily

To look at Artemis Fowl, you would have thought that he was here simply for the opera. One hand trained a pair of opera glasses on the stage, the other hand conducted expertly, following the score note for note.

"Maria Callas is the acknowledged seminal Norma," he said to Holly, who nodded politely, then rolled her eyes at Butler. "But I have a confession: I actually prefer Montserrat Caballé. She took the role on in the seventies. Of course, I have only heard recordings, but to me, Caballé's performance is more robust."

"Really," said Holly. "I'm trying to care, Artemis. But I thought it was all supposed to be over when the fat lady sings. Well, she's singing, but it doesn't appear to be over."

Artemis smiled, exposing his incisors. "That's Wagner you're thinking of."

Butler did not participate in the opera-related chitchat. To him it was just another layer of distraction to be zoned out. Instead he decided to test the night-vision filter on Holly's new helmet. If it could indeed overcome the whiteout problem, as Holly claimed, then he would have to ask Artemis to procure one for him.

Needless to say, Holly's helmet would not fit on

Butler's head. In fact, it would barely slot over his fist, so the bodyguard folded the filter's left wing out until he could squint through it by holding the helmet to his cheek.

The effect was impressive. The filter successfully equalized the light throughout the building. It boosted or dimmed so that every person in the building was seen in the same light. Those on the stage appeared caked in make-up, and those in the boxes had no shadows to hide in.

Butler panned across the boxes, satisfying himself that there was no threat present. He saw plenty of nose-picking and hand-holding, sometimes by the same people. But nothing obviously dangerous. But in a second-tier box adjacent to the stage, there was a girl with a head of blond curls, all dressed up for a night of theater.

Butler immediately recalled seeing the same girl at the materialization site in Barcelona. And now she was here, too? Coincidence? There was no such thing. In the bodyguard's experience, if you saw a stranger more than once, either they were following you, or you were both after the same thing.

He scanned the rest of the box. There were two men behind the girl. One, in his fifties—paunchy, expensive tuxedo—was filming the stage with his cell phone camera. This was the first man from Barcelona. The second man was there, too—possibly Chinese, wiry, spiked hair. He had apparently not yet recovered from his leg injury and was adjusting one of his crutches. He flipped it around, removed a rubber grip from the foot, then nestled it against his shoulder like a rifle.

Butler automatically stepped between Artemis and the man's line of fire. Not that the crutch was aimed at his charge; it was pointed stage right, three feet from the soprano. Just where Artemis was expecting his demon to show up.

"Holly," he said in a low, calm voice, "I think you should shield."

Artemis lowered his opera glasses. "Problems?"

"Maybe," replied Butler. "Though not for us. I think somebody else knows about the new materialization figures, and I think they're planning to do more than just observe."

Artemis tapped his chin with two fingers, thinking fast. "Where?"

"Tier two. Beside the stage. I see one possible weapon trained on the stage. Not a standard gun. Maybe a modified dart rifle."

Artemis leaned forward, gripping the brass rail. "They plan to take the demon alive, if one turns up. In that case, they will need a distraction."

Holly was on her feet. "What can we do?"

"It's too late to stop them," said Artemis, a frown slashing his brow. "If we interfere, we may upset the distraction, in which case the demon will be exposed. If these people are clever enough to be here, you may be sure their plan is a good one."

Holly claimed her helmet, slotting it over her ears. Air pads automatically inflated to cradle her head. "I can't just let them kidnap a fairy."

"You have no choice," snapped Artemis, risking the audience's displeasure. "Best-case—and most likely—scenario, nothing happens. No materialization."

Holly scowled. "You know as well as I do that fortune never sends the best-case scenario our way. You have too much bad karma."

Artemis had to chuckle. "You're right, of course. Worst-case scenario, a demon appears, they anchor it with the dart rifle, we interfere, and in the confusion the demon is swept up by the local *polizia* and we all end up in custody."

"Not good. So we just sit back and watch."

"Butler and I sit back and watch. You get over there and record as much data as possible. And when these people go, you go after them."

Holly activated her wings. They slid from her backpack, crackling blue as the flight computer sent a charge through them.

"How much time do I have?" she asked as she faded from sight.

Artemis checked the stopwatch on his watch.

"If you hurry," he said, "none."

* * *

Holly launched herself out over the audience, controlling her trajectory by using the joystick built into the thumb of her glove. Invisible, she soared above the gathered humans. With the aid of her helmet's filters, she could clearly see the occupants of the stage-side box.

Artemis was wrong. There was time to stop this. All she had to do was throw the shooter's aim off a little. The demon would never get anchored, and Section Eight could track these Mud Men at their leisure. It was simply a matter of touching the marksman's elbow with her buzz baton to make him lose control of all his motor functions for a few seconds. Plenty of time for a demon to appear, then disappear.

Then Holly smelled burning ozone and felt heat on her arm. Artemis was not wrong. There was no time. Someone was coming.

N°1 appeared on the stage, more or less intact. The trip had cost him the last knuckle on his right index finger, and about two gigabytes' worth of memories. But they were mostly bad memories, and he had never been very good with his hands.

Dematerialization isn't a particularly painful process, but materialization happens to be a thoroughly enjoyable one. The brain is so happy to register all the body's essential bits and bobs coming together again that it releases a surge of happy endorphins.

N°1 looked at the nub where his previously whole index finger used to be.

"Look," he said, tittering. "No finger."

Then he noticed the humans. Scores of them, arranged in rings, rising up to the heavens. N°1 knew instantly what this must be.

"A theater. I'm in a theater. With only seven and a half fingers. *I* have only seven and a half fingers, not the theater." This observation brought on another fit of giggles, and that would have been about it for N°1. He would have been whisked off to the next stop on his interdimensional jaunt, had not a human near the stage aimed a tube at him.

"Tube," said N°1, proud of his human vocabulary, pointing with the finger that wasn't altogether there.

After that, things happened very quickly. A flurry of events blurred like mixed stripes of vivid paint. The tube flashed; something exploded over his head. A bee stung N°1 on the leg, a female screamed piercingly. A herd of animals, elephants perhaps, passed directly below him. Then most disconcertingly, the ground disappeared from beneath his feet and everything went black. The blackness was rough against his fingers and face.

The last thing N°1 heard before his own personal blackness claimed him was a voice. It was not a demon's voice, the tones were lighter. Halfway between bird and boar.

"Welcome, demon," said the voice, then sniggered.

They know, thought N°1, and he would have panicked had the chloral hydrate seeping into his system through a leg wound allowed such exertions. They know all about us.

Then the knockout serum caressed his brain, tipping him off a cliff into a deep dark hole.

Artemis watched events unfold from his box. A smile of admiration twitched at the corners of his mouth as the plan unrolled smoothly, like the most expensive Tunisian carpet. Whoever was behind this was good. More than good. Perhaps they were related.

"Keep your camera pointed at the stage," Artemis said to Butler. "Holly will get the box."

Butler was squirming to cover Holly's back, but his place was at Artemis's side. And after all, Captain Short could look after herself. He made sure his watch crystal was trained on the stage. Artemis would never let him forget it if he missed even a nanosecond of the action.

Onstage, the opera was almost over. Norma was leading Pollione to the pyre, where they were both to be burned. All eyes were upon her. Except those involved in a drama of the fairy kind.

The music was lush and layered, providing an unwitting sound track to the real-life drama unfolding in the theater.

It began with an electric crackle downstage right. Barely noticeable, unless you were expecting it. And even if some patrons did notice the glow, they were not alarmed. It could easily be a reflected blotch of light, or one of the special effects these modern theater directors were so fond of.

So, thought Artemis, feeling the excitement buzz in his fingertips. Something is coming. Another game begins.

The *something* began to materialize inside the crackling blue envelope. It took on a vague, humanoid shape. Smaller than the last one, but definitely a demon, and definitely *not* a reflected blotch of light. Initially the shape was insubstantial, wraithlike, but after a second it became less transparent and more of this world.

Now, thought Artemis. Anchor it, and tranquilize it, too.

A slender silver tube poked from the shadows on the opposite side of the theater. There was a small pop, and a dart sped from the tube's mouth. Artemis did not need to follow the dart's path. He knew that it was headed straight into the creature's leg. The leg would be best. A good target, but unlikely to be fatal. A silver tip with some kind of knockout cocktail.

The creature was trying to communicate now, and making wild gestures. Artemis heard a few gasps from the audience as patrons noticed the shape inside the light.

Very well. You have anchored it. Now you need a distraction. Something flashy and loud, but not particularly dangerous. If somebody gets hurt, there will be an investigation.

Artemis switched his gaze to the demon. Solid now in

the shadows. Around him the opera steamrolled toward act four's crescendo. The soprano lamented hysterically, and every eye in the theater was riveted on her. *Almost* every eye. But there are always a few bored audience members at an opera, especially by the time act four comes along. Those particular eyes would be wandering around the hall, searching for something, anything, interesting to watch. Those eyes would land on the little demon downstage right, unless they were distracted.

Right on cue, a large stage lamp broke free of its clamp in the rigging and swung on its cable into the back canvas. The impact was both flashy and loud. The bulb exploded, showering the stage and orchestra pit with glass fragments. The bulb's filament glowed with a magnesium glare, temporarily blinding everyone staring at it. Which was almost the entire audience.

Glass rained down on the orchestra, and the musicians panicked, fleeing en masse toward the greenroom, dragging their instruments behind them. A cacophony of squealing strings and overturned percussion instruments shattered any echoes of Bellini's masterpiece.

Nice, thought Artemis appreciatively. *The clamp and the filament were rigged. The stampeding orchestra is a lucky bonus.*

Artemis noted all of this out of the corner of his eye. His main focus was the diminutive demon, lost in the shadows behind a canvas flat.

Now, if it were me, thought the Irish teenager, I would have Butler drop a black sack over that little creature and whisk him out the stage door into a four-wheel drive. We could be on the ferry to Ravenna before the theater crew got the bulb changed.

What actually happened was slightly different. A stage trapdoor opened beneath the demon, and the creature disappeared on a hydraulic platform.

Artemis shook his head in admiration. Fabulous. His mysterious adversaries must have hijacked the theater computer system. And when the demon appeared, they simply sent a command to open the appropriate trapdoor panel. Doubtless there was someone waiting below to transfer the sleeping demon to an idling vehicle outside.

Artemis leaned over the railing, gazing into the audience below. As the houselights were brought up, the theater patrons rubbed their dazzled eyes and spoke in the sheepish tones that follow shock. There was no talk of demons. No pointing and screaming. Artemis had just witnessed the perfect execution of a perfect plan.

He gazed across to the box on the far side of the stage. The three occupants stood calmly. They were simply leaving. The show was over and it was time to go. Artemis recognized the pretty girl from Barcelona and her two guardians. The thin man seemed to have recovered from his leg injury, as his crutches were now tucked underneath one arm.

The girl wore a self-satisfied smile, the kind that usually decorated Artemis's own face after a successful mission.

It's the girl, Artemis realized with some surprise. *She is the brains here.*

This girl's smile, a reflection of his own, rankled Artemis. He was not accustomed to being two steps behind. No doubt she believed that victory was hers. She may have won this battle, but the campaign was far from over.

It's time, he thought, that this girl know she has an opponent.

He brought his hands together in a slow hand clap.

"Brava," he called. *"Brava, ragazza!"*

His voice carried easily above the heads of the audience. The girl's smile froze on her lips and her eyes searched for the source of this compliment. In seconds she located the Irish teenager, and their eyes locked.

If Artemis had been expecting the girl to quail and tremble at the sight of him and his bodyguard, then he was disappointed. True, a shadow of surprise flitted across her brow, but then she accepted the applause with a nod and royal wave. The girl said two words before she left. The distance was too great for Artemis to actually hear them, but even if he hadn't long since trained himself to lipread, it would have been easy to guess what they were.

"Artemis Fowl," she said. Nothing more. There was a game beginning here. No doubt about it. How intriguing.

Then a funny thing happened. Artemis's clapping hands were joined by a scattering of others from various spots in the theater. The applause grew from hesitant beginnings to a crescendo. Soon the patrons were on their feet and the bewildered singers were forced to take several curtain calls.

On his way through the lobby minutes later, Artemis was highly amused to overhear several audience members gushing over the unorthodox direction of the opera's final scene. The exploding lamp, mused one buff, was doubtless a metaphor for Norma's own falling star. But no, argued a second. The lamp was obviously a modernistic interpretation of the burning stake that Norma was about to face.

Or perhaps, thought Artemis as he pushed through the crowd to find a light Sicilian mist falling on his forehead, the exploding lamp was simply an exploding lamp.

CHAPTER 5: ĪⅢPRĪSOⅡED

Captain Holly Short of Section 8 followed the abductors to a Land Rover Discovery, and from there to the Ravenna ferry. Their captive had been transferred from a canvas sack into a stout golf bag, which was then topped off with the heads of several clubs. It was a very slick operation. Three adult male humans and one teenage female. Holly was only mildly surprised to see that a young girl was involved. After all, Artemis Fowl was little more than a child, and he managed to involve himself in far more complex plots than this.

The Land Rover was returned to a Hertz rental agency in Italy, and from there the group took a first-class sleeper carriage on an overnight bullet train along the western coast. It made sense to travel by train. There was no need to pass the golf bag through an X-ray machine.

Holly didn't need to worry about X-ray machines, or

indeed any form of human security device. Wearing her Section 8 Shimmer Suit, she was invisible to any kind of ray the border police could throw at her. The only way to find a shielded fairy was to accidentally hit one with a stone, and even then you would probably only get an invisible smack on the ear for your trouble.

Holly slipped into the sleeper carriage and deposited herself on an unused luggage rack over the girl's head. Below her, the three humans propped the golf bag against the table and stared at it as if . . . as if there were a demon inside.

Three men and one girl. It would be easy to take them. She could knock them out with her Neutrino, then get Foaly to send in some techs to do mindwipes. Holly was itching to free the poor demon. It would take mere seconds. The only thing stopping her were the voices in her head.

One of those voices belonged to Foaly, the other to Artemis.

"Hold your position, Captain Short," advised Foaly. "We need to see how far this goes."

Section 8 had become very interested in Holly's mission since the demon abduction. Foaly was keeping a dedicated line to her helmet open.

Holly's helmet was soundproof, yet she was still nervous talking in such close proximity to the targets. The trick in this situation is to train oneself to speak without any of the usual accompanying gestures. This is harder than it sounds.

"That poor demon will be terrified," said Holly, lying perfectly still. "I have to get it out of there."

"No," said Artemis sharply. "You have to see the bigger picture, Holly. We have no idea how big this organization is, or how much they know about the Fairy People."

"Not as much as you. Demons don't carry the fairy Book. They're not much for rules."

"At least you have something in common," said Butler.

"I could use the *mesmer* on them," Holly offered. The *mesmer* was one of the tricks in every fairy's magical bag. It was a siren's song that could have any human happily spilling his guts. "That would *make* them tell me what they know."

"And only what *they* know," Artemis pointed out. "If I were running this organization, everyone would be told only what they needed to know. Nobody would know everything, except me, of course."

Holly resisted the urge to thump something in frustration. Artemis was right, of course. She had to hang back and see how this situation played out. They needed to spread their net as wide as possible in order to catch all the members of this group.

"I'll need backup," Holly whispered. "How many agents can Section Eight spare?"

Foaly cleared his throat but didn't answer.

"What is it, Foaly? What's going on down there?"

"Ark Sool caught wind of the abduction."

The mere mention of that gnome's name drove Holly's blood pressure up a few points. Commander Ark Sool was the reason she had quit the LEP in the first place.

"Sool! How did he find out about it so quickly?"

"He's got a source somewhere in Section Eight. He called in Vinyáya. She had no option but to hand over all the facts."

Holly groaned. Sool was the king of red tape. As the dwarfs said, *He couldn't make a decision if he was holding a jug of water and his bum-flap was on fire*.

"What's the word?"

"Sool is going for damage limitation. The blast walls are up, and aboveground missions have been canceled. No further action pending a meeting of the Council. If the manure hits the air circulator, Sool isn't going to be the one taking the blame. Not on his own."

"Politics," spat Holly. "Sool only cares about his precious career. So you can't send me anyone?"

Foaly chose his words carefully. "Not officially. And no one official. I mean, it would be impossible for anyone, a consultant, say, to get past the blast walls carrying something you might need, if you see what I mean."

Holly understood exactly what Foaly was trying to tell her.

"Ten four, Foaly. I'm on my own. Officially."

"Exactly. As far as Commander Sool knows, you are

simply shadowing the suspects. You are only to take action if they decide to go public. In that case your orders are, and I'm quoting Sool here, to 'take the least complicated and most permanent course of action.'"

"He means vaporize the demon?"

"Sool didn't say that, but that's what he wants."

Holly despised Sool more with every heartbeat. "He can't order me to do that. Killing a fairy goes against every law in the Book. I won't do it."

"Sool knows he can't officially order you to use terminal force on a fairy. What he's doing here is making an unofficial recommendation. The kind that could have a major effect on your career. It's a tricky one, Holly. Best-case scenario, this all blows over somehow."

Artemis voiced the opinion that they all held. "That's not going to happen. This is no opportunistic snatch. We are dealing with an organized group that knew what they were after. These people were at Barcelona and now here. They have an agenda for their demon, and unless they're military, I would bet it involves going public for large amounts of money. This will be bigger than the Loch Ness monster, Bigfoot, and the yeti all rolled into one."

Foaly sighed. "You're in a fix, Holly. The best thing that could happen for you right now would be a nice nonlethal injury to take you out of the game."

Holly remembered her old mentor's words. *It's not about what's best for us*, Julius Root had told her once. *It's about what's best for the People.*

"Sometimes it's not about us, Foaly. I'll figure this out somehow. I do have help, right?"

"That's right," confirmed the centaur. "It's not as if it's the first time we've saved the fairy world."

Foaly's confident tone made Holly feel better, even if he was hundreds of miles underground.

Artemis interrupted them. "You two can swap war stories later. We can't afford to miss a word that these people say. If we can beat them to their destination, it could be an advantage."

Artemis was right. This was not a time for drifting. Holly ran a quick systems check on her helmet instruments, then pointed her visor at the humans below.

"You getting this, Foaly?" she asked.

"Clear as crystal. Did I tell you about my new gas screens?"

Artemis's sigh rattled through the speakers.

"Yes, you did. Now be quiet, centaur. We're on a mission, remember."

"Whatever you say, Mud Boy. Hey, look—your *girlfriend* is saying something."

Artemis had a vast mental reserve of scathing comebacks at his disposal, but none of them covered *girlfriend* insults. He wasn't even sure if it was an insult. And if it was, who was being insulted? Him or the girl?

* * *

𝒟 ◌ ෴ 🜾 ෴ ⚸ ៰ • 🜾 ៰ • ⚸ • 🜾 ៝ 🝐 ៰ • ⊕ ◌

The girl spoke French as only a native could.

"Technically," she said, "the only crime we are guilty of is fare-dodging, and perhaps not even that. Legally speaking, how can you kidnap something that is not supposed to exist? I doubt anyone ever accused Murray Gell-Mann of kidnapping a quark, even though he knowingly carried a billion of them around in his pocket." The girl chuckled gently, causing her glasses to slip down again.

No one else laughed, except an eavesdropping Irish boy two hundred miles away at Fontanarossa International Airport, about to board the last Alitalia flight to Rome. Rome, Artemis reasoned, would be a lot more central than Sicily. Wherever the demon was headed, Artemis could get there faster if he flew from Rome.

"That wasn't bad," Artemis commented, then relayed the joke to Butler. "Obviously there are differences in the scenarios, but it's a joke, not a quantum physics lecture."

Butler's left eyebrow cranked up like a drawbridge. "Differences in the scenarios, that's just what I was thinking."

Back on board the bullet train, one of the men, the one with the miraculously healed leg, shifted on the leatherette upholstery.

"What time do we get into Nice, Minerva?" he said.

This single sentence was a goldmine of information for the listening Artemis. Firstly, the girl's name was Minerva, presumably named for the Roman goddess of wisdom. So far, a very apt name indeed. Secondly, their destination was Nice, in the South of France. And thirdly, this girl seemed to be in charge. Extraordinary.

The girl, who had been smiling still at her *quark* joke, switched to irritated mode.

"No names, remember? There are ears everywhere. If a single person uncovers a single detail of our plan, everything we have worked for could be ruined."

Too late, Mud Girl, thought Captain Holly Short, from her luggage rack. Artemis Fowl already knows too much about you. Not to mention my own little guardian angel, Foaly.

Holly snapped a close-up of the girl's face.

"We have a mug shot and a first name, Foaly. Is that enough for you?"

"Should be," replied the centaur. "I got stills of the males too. Give me a while to run them through my database."

Below her, the second man from Barcelona unzipped the fake top from the golf bag.

"I should check on my *clubs*," he said. "See if they're settled okay. If they've started to move about, I might put in something to keep them still."

All of which would have been perfectly acceptable code had there not been a camera pointed right at them.

The man reached into the bag, and after a moment's feeling around, pulled out a small arm and checked the pulse.

"Fine. Everything's fine."

"Good," said Minerva. "Now, you should get some sleep. We have a long journey ahead of us. I will stay awake for a while because I feel like reading. The next person can read in four hours."

The three men nodded, but nobody lay down. They just sat there, staring at the golf bag as if there were a demon in it.

Artemis and Butler picked up a lucky connection to Nice with Air France, and by ten they had checked into the Hotel Negresco and were enjoying coffee and croissants on the Promenade des Anglais.

Holly was not so lucky. She was still perched on a luggage rack on board a train. Not the same luggage rack. This was her third rack, all together. First they'd had to change in Rome, then again in Monte Carlo, and now finally they were headed for Nice.

Artemis was speaking into his little finger, which transmitted the vibrations to the fairy phone in his palm.

"Any hints as to the exact final destination?"

"Nothing yet," replied a tired and irritated Holly. "This girl is controlling the adults with a rod of iron. They're afraid to say anything. I am sick of lying on this rack. I feel like I have been lying on racks for a year. What are you two doing?"

Artemis put his decaf cappuccino down gently, so as not

to rattle the saucer. "We're at the Nice Library trying to dig up anything on this Minerva person. Perhaps we can find out if she has a villa near here."

"Glad to hear it," said Holly. "I had visions of you two drinking tea at the beach while I sweat it out here."

Twenty yards from where Artemis was sitting, waves swirled along the beach like emerald paint poured from a bucket.

"Tea? At the beach? No time for luxuries, Holly. There is important work to be done." He winked at Butler.

"Are you sure you're at the library? I thought I heard water."

Artemis smiled, enjoying the exchange. "Water? Surely not. The only thing flowing here is information."

"Are you grinning, Artemis? For some reason I get the feeling that you're wearing that smug smile of yours."

Foaly cut into the line. "Pay dirt, Holly. It took a while, but we tracked down our mystery girl."

Artemis's smile vanished. All business now. "Who is she, Foaly? To be honest, I am amazed that I don't already know her."

"The girl is Minerva Paradizo, twelve years old, born in Cagnes sur Mer, in the South of France. The man is her father, Gaspard Paradizo. Fifty-two. Cosmetic surgeon, of Brazilian descent. One more child, a boy, Beau, five years old. The mother left a year ago. Lives in Marseille with the ex-gardener."

Artemis was puzzled. "Gaspard Paradizo is a cosmetic surgeon? Why did it take so long to find these two? There must have been records, pictures."

"That's just it. There were no pictures on the net. Not even a local paper snapshot. I've got the feeling that somebody has systematically wiped out every e-trace of this family they could find."

"But nobody can hide from you, eh, Foaly?"

"That's right. I ran a deep probe and came across a ghost image on a French TV archive page. Minerva Paradizo won a national spelling bee when she was four. Once I had the name, then it was easy to retrieve all the other wipes. Your *girlfriend* is quite something, Artemis. She has already completed high school, and is currently studying for two distance learning degrees. Quantum physics and psychology. I suspect that she also has a doctorate in chemistry, under an assumed name."

"What about the other two men?" asked Holly, moving the conversation on before Foaly could get in another *girlfriend* crack.

"The Latin one is Juan Soto. Head of Soto Security. He seems to be a legitimate security operative. Not much expertise, hardly any training. Nothing to worry about."

"And the sniper?"

"The crutch guy is Billy Kong. A real nasty piece of work. I'm sending the file to your helmet." In seconds the mail alert dinged in Holly's ear and she opened the file in her visor. A 3-D photo of Kong revolved slowly in the top-left corner of the visor, while his criminal record scrolled down before her eyes.

Artemis cleared his throat. "I don't happen to have a helmet, Foaly."

"Oh yes, little Master Lo-tech," said Foaly, his voice dripping with condescension. "Shall I read it for you?"

"If your mighty brain can bear to use simple vocalization."

"Okay. Billy Kong. Grew up in a circus, lost an eye in a fight with a tiger . . ."

Artemis sighed. "Please, Foaly, we don't have time for jokes."

"Sure," retorted the centaur. "Like you're in the library. Okay then, the truth. Born Jonah Lee, Malibu, early seventies. Family originally from Taiwan. Mother, Annie. One older brother, Eric, killed in a gang fight. The mother moved them both back to Hsin-chu, south of Taipei. Kong moved to the city and became a petty thief. He had to leave in the nineties when a row with an accomplice turned into a murder charge. Kong used a kitchen knife on his friend. There's still a warrant out for him there, under the name Jonah Lee."

Holly was surprised. Kong seemed harmless enough. He was a slight man with spiked, highlighted hair. He seemed more like a member of a boy band than a close-up man.

"Moved to Paris and changed his name," continued

Foaly. "Took up martial arts. He's had facial surgery, but not enough to escape my computer."

Artemis lowered his phone hand and talked to Butler. "Billy Kong?"

The bodyguard drew a sharp breath. "Ruthless man. He has a small well-trained crew. They hire themselves out as bodyguards to people who live dangerously. I heard he went legit and was working for a doctor in Europe."

"Kong is on the train," said Artemis. "He was the man with the fake crutch."

Butler nodded thoughtfully. Kong was infamous in underworld circles. The man had no morals, and would happily perform any task, however distasteful, for the right price. Kong only had one rule: never quit until the job was done.

"If Billy Kong is involved, things just got a lot more dangerous. We need to rescue that demon as quickly as possible."

"Agreed," said Artemis, raising the phone. "Do we have an address, Foaly?"

"Gaspard Paradizo owns a chateau on the Vence side of Tourrettes sur Loup, twenty minutes from Nice."

Artemis finished his cappuccino in a single gulp. "Very well. Holly, we shall meet you there."

Artemis stood, straightening his suit jacket. "Butler, old friend, we need some surveillance equipment. Do you know anybody in Nice who might oblige?"

Butler flipped open a wafer-thin cell phone. "What do you think?"

Tourrettes sur Loup

Tourrettes sur Loup is a small artisans' village perched on the lower slopes of the Alps Maritime. The Paradizo chateau was farther up the slopes, on a flattened peak below the snow line.

The chateau was originally nineteenth century but had undergone extensive renovation. The walls were solid stone, the windows were reflective and probably bulletproof, and there were cameras everywhere. The road leading to the chateau was typical of the region; narrow and tightly looped. There was an observation tower on the building's southern corner, which afforded any sentry a three hundred and sixty degree view of any avenue of approach. Several men patrolled the grounds close to the main building, and the gardens were dotted with grassy dunes, but did not provide a shred of cover.

Artemis and Butler were concealed in a line of bushes on the adjacent slope. Butler studied the chateau through high-powered binoculars.

"You certainly can pick them," noted the bodyguard. "I think I saw this place in a Bond movie once."

"No problem for you, surely?"

Butler frowned. "I'm a bodyguard, Artemis. A human

bulletproof vest. Breaking into fortified castles is not my speciality."

"You have rescued me from more secure locations than this one."

"True," agreed the bodyguard. "But I had intel, an inside man. Or I was desperate. If I had to walk away from here, it wouldn't trouble me unduly, so long as you were walking away with me."

Artemis patted his arm. "We can't walk away, old friend."

Butler sighed. "I suppose not." He handed Artemis the binoculars. "Now, start at the western corner and sweep east."

Artemis raised the binoculars to his eyes, then adjusted the focus. "I see two-man patrols."

"Soto's private security company. No weapons showing, but they have bulges below their jackets. Basic training, I imagine. But with more than twenty of them on and around the premises it would be very difficult to overpower them all. And even if I did, the local police would be here in minutes."

Artemis moved the binoculars a few degrees. "I see a little boy wearing a cowboy hat, driving a toy car."

"Paradizo's son, Beau, presumably. Nobody pays much attention to him. Move on."

"Sensors in the eaves?"

"I've actually researched that particular model. The very latest sealed security pods. Close circuit, infrared,

motion sensors, night vision. The works. I've been meaning to upgrade Fowl Manor."

There were small speakers on spikes dotted around the chateau.

"A sound system?"

Butler snorted. "I wish. Those are waffle boxes. They transmit interference. Our directional microphones are useless here. I doubt if even Foaly could pick up anything inside that building."

Holly shimmered into visibility beside them. "You're right. Foaly's pulled one of our shrouded satellites out of orbit to get a look at this place, but it's going to be several hours before the chateau is inside its footprint."

Butler took his hand off his gun butt. "Holly, I wish you wouldn't appear like that. I'm a bodyguard. I get jumpy."

Holly smiled, punching him on the leg. "I know, big man. That's why I do it. Think of me as on-the-job training."

Artemis barely glanced up from the binoculars. "We need to find out what's happening in there. If only we could get a man inside."

Holly frowned. "I can't go into a human dwelling without permission. You know the rules. If a fairy enters a human dwelling without an invitation, they lose their magic, and that's after a few hours of painful vomiting and cramps."

After the battles at Taillte, Frond, the king of the fairy

People, had tried to keep mischievous fairies away from human dwellings by imposing magical *geasa*, or rules, on fairies. He had used his warlocks to construct a powerful spell to impose his will. Anyone attempting to break these rules would become deathly ill, and lose their magic.

"What about Butler? You could lend him a sheet of Foaly's cam-foil. He'd be as good as invisible."

Holly shook her head. "There's a laser pyramid all over the grounds. Even with cam-foil, Butler would break the beams."

"Mulch, then? He's a criminal, long past the allergic reaction stage. Cramps and vomiting wouldn't affect him."

Holly scanned the grounds with her X-ray filter. "This place is built on solid rock, and the walls are three feet thick. Mulch could never burrow in there unnoticed." Her X-ray vision fell on the skeleton of a small boy driving his little electric car. She raised her visor to see Beau Paradizo zigzagging through the guards unmolested.

"Mulch couldn't get in there," she said, smiling. "But I think I know someone who could."

CHAPTER 6: DWARF WALKS INTO A BAR

The Lower Elements

Mulch Diggums strolled through Haven's Market District, feeling more relaxed with every step. The Market District was a lowlife zone, as much as you could have a lowlife zone on a street that boasted two hundred cameras and a permanent LEP cabin on the corner. But even so, criminals outnumbered civilians here eight to one.

My kind of people, thought Mulch. *Or at least they used to be before I threw in with Holly.*

It wasn't that Mulch regretted teaming up with Holly, but sometimes he did miss the old days. There was something about thievery that made his heart sing. The thrill of the snatch, the euphoria of easy money.

Don't forget the despair of prison, his practical side

reminded him. *And the loneliness of life on the run.*

True. Crime wasn't all fun and games. It had minor downsides, like fear, pain, and death. But Mulch had been able to ignore those for a long time, until Commander Julius Root had been killed by a criminal. Until then it had all been a game. Julius was the cat, and he was the elusive mouse. But with Julius gone, returning to a life of crime would seem like a slap in the face to the commander's memory.

And that's why I like this new job so much, concluded Mulch happily. I get to run around behind the LEP's back and consort with known criminals.

He had been watching talk shows in the Section 8 lounge when Foaly had come cantering in. Truth be told, Mulch liked Foaly. They knocked sparks off each other whenever they met, but it kept both of them on their toes, or hooves, whichever the case may be.

In this instance, there had been no time for tomfoolery, and Foaly had brusquely explained the situation aboveground. They did have a plan, but it hinged on Mulch's ability to find the pixie smuggler, Doodah Day, and bring him back to Section 8.

"That's going to take some doing," noted Mulch. "The last time I saw Doodah, he was scraping dwarf gunge off his boots. He doesn't like me very much. I'm going to need leverage."

"You tell that pixie that if helps us out he's a free fairy.

I'll go into the system myself and wipe his record."

Mulch raised his shaggy eyebrows. "It's that important?"

"It's that important."

"I saved this city," grumbled the dwarf. "Twice, in fact! Nobody ever wiped my record. This pixie goes on one mission, and poof, he walks. What do I get? Seeing as we're handing out wishes."

Foaly stamped a hoof impatiently. "You get your exorbitant consultant's fee. Whatever. Just get on this. Do you have any way to track Mr. Day down?"

Mulch whistled. "It's going to be devilishly tough. That pixie will have gone to ground after this morning. But I have certain skills. I can do it."

Foaly glowered at him. "That's why you get paid the big bucks."

In fact, finding Doodah was not going to be quite as devilishly difficult as Mulch had pretended. The last thing Mulch had done before waving a cheery good-bye to Doodah Day was to slip a tracker pill down his boot.

The tracker pills had been a gift from Foaly. He liked to pass redundant equipment to Holly to help her keep the agency afloat. The pills were made from a baked adhesive gel that started to melt as soon as you popped it from its foil case. The gel stuck to whatever it was touching and adopted its color. Inside was a tiny transmitter that emitted harmless radiation for up to five years. The tracking system was not very sophisticated. Each pill left its signature on the individual foil cases, so the case glowed whenever it detected the signature radiation. The brighter the glow, the closer the pill.

Idiotproof, Holly had quipped, issuing the pills.

And idiotproof they were proving to be. Barely ten minutes after leaving Section 8, Mulch had tracked Doodah Day to the Market District. By the dwarf's reckoning, his quarry was somewhere within a twenty-yard radius. The most likely place was the fish bar across the street. Pixies loved fish. Especially shellfish. Especially-especially protected shellfish, such as lobster. Which was why Doodah's smuggling skills were so much in demand.

Mulch crossed the street, adjusted his expression to fearsome, and barged into Happy as a Clam as if he owned the place.

The bar was ostensibly a dive. The floor was bare boards, and the air stank of week-old mackerel. The menu was written on the wall in what looked like fish blood, and the only customer appeared to be asleep in a bowl of chowder.

A pixie waiter glared at Mulch from behind a knee-high counter.

"There's a dwarf bar down the street," he said.

Mulch flashed him a toothy grin. "Now that's not very hospitable. I could be a customer."

"Not likely," said the waiter. "I never saw a dwarf pay for a meal yet."

$\mathcal{R} \oplus \cdot \ominus \triangleright \heartsuit \text{)} \theta \oplus \cdot \mathcal{R} \triangleright \mathcal{P} \cdot \Theta \ominus \theta \theta \cdot \text{)}$

It was true. Dwarfs were scroungers by nature.

"You got me," admitted Mulch. "I'm no customer. I'm looking for someone."

The waiter gestured at the almost deserted restaurant. "If you don't see him, he ain't here."

Mulch flashed a very shiny LEP temporary deputy badge that Foaly had issued. "I think I might take a closer look."

The waiter ran out from behind his counter. "*I* think you might need a warrant to take one more step, cop."

Mulch brushed him aside. "I'm not that kind of cop, pixie."

Mulch followed the transmitter's signal through the main restaurant down a shabby corridor and into the restrooms, which were even shabbier. Even Mulch winced, and *he* burrowed in mud for a living.

One cubicle had an out-of-order sign on the door. Mulch squeezed into the pixie-size space and quickly located the secret door. He wormed his way through into a far more salubrious room than the one he had just left. There was a velvet-lined cloakroom box, staffed by a rather surprised pixie in a pink dress.

"Do you have a reservation?" she asked haltingly.

"More than one," replied Mulch. "For starters, do you think it's a good idea to put the secret entrance to an illegal restaurant in a bathroom? It didn't fool me, and I think I've lost my appetite."

138

Mulch did not wait for an answer. Instead he bowed under a low lintel into an opulent main restaurant. Here, dozens of pixies were tucking into steaming plates of shellfish. Doodah Day was alone at a table for two, cracking a lobster with a hammer as if he hated it.

Mulch walked over, ignoring the glares from other diners.

"Thinking about someone?" he asked, lowering himself into a tiny pixie chair.

Doodah glanced up. If he was surprised, he hid it well.

"You, dwarf. I'm imagining that this claw is your fat head."

Doodah brought the hammer down hard, splattering Mulch with white lobster meat.

"Hey, watch it! That stinks."

Doodah was livid. "That stinks! That stinks! I've taken three showers. Three! And I can't get the stink of your mouth offa me. It follows me like my own personal sewer. You see I'm eating alone. Usually I got me a tableful of buddies, but not today. Today I smell like dwarf."

Mulch was unperturbed. "Hey, easy, little guy. I could get offended."

Doodah waved the hammer. "You see anyone in here caring how you feel? Offended or otherwise."

Mulch took a deep breath. This was going to be a hard sell.

"Yeah, okay, Doodah. Point made. You're a real wise

guy. A ticked off wise guy. But I got an offer for you."

Doodah laughed. "You got an offer for me? I got an offer for you. Why don't you get your dwarf stink outta here before I crack your teeth with this hammer?"

"I get it," said Mulch testily. "You're a tough little guy, and mean, too. And a dwarf would have to be crazy to mess with you. Generally, I would sit here for a couple of hours, trading insults. But today I'm busy. A friend of mine is in trouble."

Doodah smiled broadly, raising a glass of wine in a mock toast. "Well, dwarf, here's hoping it's that slippery elf, Holly Short. 'Cause there's nobody I would rather see up to her pointy ears in something dangerous."

Mulch showed his teeth, but he wasn't smiling.

"Actually, I've been meaning to talk to you about that. You attacked my friend with a multi-mixer. Nearly killed her."

"Nearly," said Doodah, raising a finger. "Just scared her is all. She shouldn't have been chasing me. I just smuggle a few crates of shrimp. I don't kill anyone."

"Just drive."

"That's right. Just drive."

Mulch relaxed. "Well, Doodah, lucky for you, your driving skill is the very thing stopping me from unhinging my jaw and chewing on you like one of those shrimp balls you got there. And this time, who knows which end you'd come out."

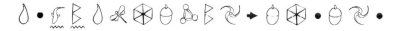

The bravado instantly drained from Doodah's face.

"I'm listening," he said.

Mulch reined in his teeth. "Okay. So you can drive anything, right?"

"Absolutely anything. I don't care if Martians built it, Doodah Day can drive it."

"Good, because I got an offer for you. I'm not particularly happy about it, but I have to run it past you anyway."

"Go for it, Stinky."

Mulch groaned internally. Their little band of adventurers needed another smart-ass like they needed ten years of bad luck.

"I need you for one day, to drive one vehicle, for one trip. You do that and you have amnesty."

Doodah was impressed. It was an impressive deal.

"So all I gotta do is drive and you wipe the slate?"

"Apparently."

Doodah tapped his forehead with a lobster claw. "This is too easy; there's gotta be a catch."

Mulch shrugged. "Well, it's going be aboveground, and there'll be a lot of armed Mud Men chasing after you."

"Yeah?" Doodah grinned through a mouthful of lobster juice. "But what's the catch?"

⊙ ⎔ ⧫ • ⊗ ⬠ • ⚎ ⬡ ⚸ ⚶ • ⚶ • ⚜ ⋎ ⧫

CHAPTER 7: **BOBO'S RUN**

The Chateau Paradizo, Southern France

By the time Mulch and Doodah landed outside Tourrettes sur Loup, the dwarf was a nervous wreck.

"He's crazy," he gibbered, tumbling from the hatch of a tiny titanium pod, which had been landed expertly on a flat patch not much bigger than a postage stamp. "The pixie is crazy! Give me your gun, Holly. I'm going to shoot him."

Doodah Day appeared in the hatch and hopped nimbly to the ground. "That ship is fantastic," he said in Gnommish. "Where can I get one?"

His grin withered and died when he noticed that the thing he had previously believed to be a tree moved and spoke in one of the primitive Mud Man tongues.

"This would be Doodah Day, I presume. He makes a lot of noise, doesn't he?"

• 🜁🜂🜃🜄 • 🦀🜅🌙🜆 • 🜇🜈🜉🜊🍂 • 🜋

"Arkkkk!" said Doodah. "Big Mud Man."

"Yes, he is," said another Mud Man, or maybe a Mud Boy. This one was smaller, but somehow seemed even more dangerous.

"You speak Gnommish?" asked the terrified pixie, in case the big one would eat him for not being polite.

"Yes," said Artemis. "I do, but Butler is not so fluent. So, English, if you wouldn't mind."

"Sure thing. Not a problem," said Doodah, grateful that he still had the tiny spark of magic left in his brain necessary to fuel his gift of tongues.

Doodah and Mulch had flown across the lower peaks of the Alps Maritime in a pod built for riding the magma flares from the earth's core. These chutes had rudimentary shields, but they were not intended for aboveground travel. Doodah's instructions had been to ride the hotshots to a small port near Bern, Switzerland, then strap on a pair of wings and low-fly the rest of the way. But once Doodah got behind the pod's wheel, he decided that it would be much faster if they did the second leg on board the tiny ship.

Holly was impressed. "You fly pretty well for a smuggler. Those pods handle like a three-legged pig."

Doodah slapped a titanium fin fondly. "She's a good girl. You just need to treat her right."

Mulch was still shaking. "We came this close! This close to being incinerated. I lost count after the first dozen times."

Doodah chortled. "That's not all you lost, dwarf. Someone is going to have to swab the decks in there."

Holly looked Doodah in the eyes. Okay, they were making small talk, but there was a little history between them.

"You could have killed me, pixie," said Holly evenly, giving the little smuggler a chance to explain himself.

"I know. I nearly did. That's why it's time for me to get out of the business. Review the situation. Take a long hard look at my priorities."

"Horse manure," tutted Holly. "I don't believe a word."

"Me neither," said Doodah. "That's my parole-board spiel. With the big eyes and the wobbly lip, works every time. But seriously, I'm sorry about the multi-mixer thing, officer. I was desperate. But you were never in danger. These hands are pure magic on a wheel."

Holly decided to let it go. Nursing a grudge would only make a difficult mission next to impossible. And anyway, now Doodah would have a chance to make it up to her.

Butler lifted Mulch to his feet.

"How are you doing there, Mulch?"

Mulch glowered at Doodah. "I will be doing fine once my head stops spinning. That ship is only built for one, you know. I've had that little monkey in my lap for the past few hours. Every time we went over a bump, he butted me under the chin."

Butler winked at his dwarf friend. "Well, look at it this

144

way. You had to take a ride in his environment, but now he
has to take a ride in yours."

Doodah caught the end of that sentence. "Ride? What
ride? Who has to take a ride?"

Mulch rubbed his hairy palms together. "I am going to
enjoy this."

They lay down side by side in a low ditch overlooking
the chateau. The land sloped gently downward and was
dotted with the twisted forms of ancient olive trees. The
surface soil was dry and loose, but reasonably tasty,
according to Mulch.

"The Alpine water is pretty good," he explained,
spitting out a mouthful of pebbles. "And the olives give the
clay a nice tang."

"That's very nice," said Artemis patiently. "But all I
really want to know is can you make it to the septic tank?"

"Septic tank?" said Doodah nervously. "What are we
talking about septic tanks for? I ain't going into no septic
tank. Forget the deal."

"Not into the tank," corrected Artemis. "Behind it. The
tank is the only cover before the chateau itself."

Holly was scanning the terrain with her visor. "The tank
is buried as close to the house as possible. After that it's
just rock. But you have a nice thick vein of soil as far as that
point. What you need to do is lure that boy in the cowboy
hat in behind the tank with a bar of chocolate, then
Doodah takes his place."

⊕ • ⚛ ☽ ⊕ • ⚛ �ᗷ ၄ ⚙ • � ᐧ ᐁ ◊ • ဌ ⚳ ◊

"Then what? That toy car isn't going anywhere fast."

"It doesn't need to, Doodah. All you have to do is drive inside the house and wind this around any video cable you see."

Holly handed Doodah a cable tie with tiny spikes along its length. "This is loaded with fiber optics. Once it's in place, we own their surveillance."

"Can we rewind to the bar of chocolate?" said Mulch. "Does anyone have one?"

"Here," said Artemis, handing him a flat bar in a green wrapper. "Butler bought this in the village. It's very low quality, not seventy percent cocoa, or fair trade, for that matter, but it will do."

"So what about after the kid eats the chocolate?" asked Mulch. "What do I do with a kid?"

"You are not to injure him," said Holly. "Just entertain him for a minute."

"Entertain him? How am I supposed to do that?"

"Use your dwarf talents," suggested Artemis. "Young children are inquisitive. Eat some rocks. Pass wind. Little Beau will be fascinated."

"Couldn't I just shoot him?"

"Mulch!" said Holly, horrified.

"I don't mean kill him. Just knock him out for a few minutes. Kids like naps. I'd be doing him a favor, really."

"Knocking him out would be ideal," admitted Holly.

146

"But I don't have anything safe, so you'll have to keep him busy for five minutes tops."

"I am a charmer, I suppose," said Mulch. "And if worst comes to worst, I can always eat him." He grinned widely at Holly's shocked expression. "I'm kidding. Honest. I'd never eat a Mud Kid, they're too bony."

Holly elbowed Artemis, who was beside her on the bank. "Are you sure about this?"

"It was your basic idea," replied Artemis. "But, yes, I am sure. There are other options, but we don't have the time. Mulch has always displayed initiative. I feel certain he won't let us down. As for Mr. Day, his freedom is on the line. A strong incentive to perform."

"Enough of the chatter," said Mulch. "I'm starting to burn, here. You know how sensitive dwarf skin is." He stood and unbuttoned the bum-flap on the seat of his pants. (Where else would a bum-flap be?) "Okay, pixie. Hop on."

Doodah Day seemed genuinely frightened. "Are you sure?"

Mulch sighed. "Sure I'm sure. What are you afraid of? It's just a rear end."

"Yeah, maybe. But it's smiling at me."

"Perhaps it's happy to see you. You don't want to be there if it gets angry."

Holly punched Mulch on the shoulder.

"That is a really bad habit," complained Mulch, rubbing

his arm. "You should see someone about your anger issues."

"Could you please quit the bum talk? We're on a tight schedule here!"

"Okay. Get on, pixie. I promise it won't bite."

Butler lifted the tiny pixie onto Mulch's back.

"Just don't look down," advised the bodyguard. "You'll be okay."

"Easy for you to say," grumbled Doodah. "You're not the one riding the whirlwind. You never mentioned this in the restaurant, Diggums."

Artemis pointed at the pixie's backpack. "Do you really need that, Mr. Day? It's not very streamlined."

Doodah held on to the strap. "Tools of the trade, Mud Boy. They go where I go."

"Very well," said Artemis. "A word of advice. Get in and out as fast as you can."

Doodah rolled his eyes. "Wow, that's great advice. You should write a book."

Mulch chortled. "Good one."

"And avoid his family," continued Artemis. "Especially the girl Minerva."

"Family. Minerva. Got it. Now let's go if we're going, before I lose my nerve."

The dwarf unhinged his jaw with wince-worthy cracks and dived headfirst into the mound of earth. It was something to see, scythe-like jaws chomping through the dirt, excavating a tunnel for the dwarf and his passenger.

Doodah's eyes were tightly shut, and his expression was one of absolute shock.

"Oh, gods," he said. "Let me off. Let me . . ."

Then they were gone, lost under a blanket of vibrating earth. Holly elbowed her way atop the mound, following their progress through her visor.

"Diggums is fast," she proclaimed. "I'm surprised we ever caught him."

Artemis lay beside her. "I hope he's fast enough. The last thing we need is for Minerva Paradizo to add a dwarf and a pixie to her fairy collection."

Mulch felt good underground. This was a dwarf's natural habitat. His fingers absorbed the rhythms of the earth, and they calmed him. His coarse beard hairs, which were actually a series of sensors, dug into the clay, worming into cracks, sending out pings and reporting back to Mulch's brain. He could feel rabbits digging half a mile to his left. Maybe he could snag one on the way back, for a snack.

Doodah hung on for dear life. His face was a rictus of desperation. He would have screamed but that would have meant opening his mouth. And that was out of the question.

Just below Doodah's toes, Mulch's behind churned out a rapid-fire mixture of dirt and air, driving the pair deeper into the tunnel. Doodah could feel the heat from the reaction spreading up his legs. Every now and then the pixie's boots dropped too close to the dwarf's rear exhaust, and Doodah would have to jerk them up or lose a toe.

It only took Mulch a minute to reach the septic tank. He eased himself from the earth, blinking mud from his eyes with thick corkscrew dwarf lashes.

"Spot on," he mumbled, spitting out a wriggling worm.

Doodah hauled himself over the dwarf's head, clamping a hand over his own mouth to stop himself from screaming. After several deep breaths he calmed down sufficiently to hiss at Mulch.

"You enjoyed that, didn't you?"

Mulch rehinged his jaw, then released a final burst of tunnel gas, which popped him out of the earth.

"It's what I do. Let's say we're even for the pod ride."

Doodah disagreed. "Let's say I still owe you one for swallowing me."

The bickering would probably have continued, in spite of the urgency of their mission, had not a little boy in a electric toy car come trundling around the corner of the tank.

"Hello. I am Beau Paradizo," said the driver. "Are you monsters?"

Doodah and Mulch froze momentarily, then remembered the plan.

"No, little boy," said Mulch, glad he still had the tiny

spark of magic necessary to speak French. He tried to smile endearingly, something he didn't spend a lot of time practicing in the mirror. "We are the chocolate fairies. And we have a special gift for you." He waved the chocolate bar, hoping the theatrical presentation would make the cheap candy seem more impressive than it was.

"Chocolate fairies?" said the boy, climbing from his car. "Sugar-free chocolate, I hope. Because I get hyper with sugar, and Daddy says that God knows I'm already hyper enough without it, but he still loves me."

Mulch glanced at the label. Eighteen percent sugar.

"Yep. Sugar free. Would you like a square?"

Beau took the entire bar and demolished it in less than ten seconds.

"You fairies stink. Especially you, hairy. You stink worse than the blocked toilet in Aunty Morgana's. Stinky fairy."

Doodah laughed. "What can I tell you. The kid tells it like it is, Mulch."

"Do you live in a blocked toilet, Mr. Fatty Chocolate Fairy?"

"Hey," said Mulch brightly. "How about a nap? Would you like a nap, kid?"

Beau Paradizo punched Mulch in the stomach. "I had a nap, stupid. More chocolate! Now!"

"No punching! I don't have more chocolate."

Beau punched him again. "I said more chocolate! Or I'm going to call the guards. And Pierre will reach down your throat and pull out your guts. That's what he does. He told me."

Mulch sniggered. "I'd like to see him reach into my insides."

"Really?" Beau asked brightly. "I'll get him!" The little boy sprinted for the corner of the tank. He moved with surprising speed, and Mulch's instincts took over for his brain. The dwarf leaped toward the boy, unhinging as he went.

"Pierre!" shouted Beau once, but not a second time, because Mulch had enclosed him in his mouth. All except the cowboy hat.

"Do not swallow!" hissed Doodah.

Mulch worked the boy around his cheeks for a few seconds, then spat him out. Beau was dripping wet and sound asleep. Mulch wiped the child's face before the dwarf spittle could harden.

"Sedative in the saliva," he explained, hooking up his jaw. "It's a predator thing. You didn't fall asleep yesterday, because I didn't do your head. He'll wake up completely refreshed. I'll peel this stuff off when it hardens."

Doodah shrugged. "Hey, do I care? I didn't like him anyway."

A voice drifted over the tank. "Beau? Where are you?"

"That must be Pierre. You better get moving, lead him away from here."

Doodah poked his head above the embankment. A large

man was headed their way. Not as large as Butler, true, but plenty big enough to squash the pixie under a single boot. The man wore a black security jumpsuit with a matching hat. A pistol grip poked from between the buttons. The man squinted toward the tank.

"Beau? Is that you?" he said in French.

"Oui. C'est moi," replied Doodah, in a warbling falsetto.

Pierre was not convinced. The voice had sounded more like a talking piglet than a child. He kept coming, reaching inside his jumpsuit for the gun.

Doodah bolted for the electric car. On the way he picked up Beau's cowboy hat and jammed it onto his head. Pierre was barely a dozen steps away now, and quickening his pace.

"Beau? Come here now. Minerva wants you in the house."

Doodah slid over the hood into the car, hillbilly style. He could tell from a single glance that this toy wouldn't do much more than walking speed, which would be zero use to him in an emergency. He pulled a flat black panel from his bag and suckered it onto the little car's plastic dash. This was a Mongocharger, something no self-respecting smuggler would leave home without. The Mongocharger was equipped with a strong computer, omnisensor, and a clean nuclear battery pack. The omnisensor hacked into the toy car's tiny chip and took over its workings. Doodah pulled a retractable spike cable from the Mongocharger's base and plunged the tip into the car's own power cable beneath the dash. Now the toy car was nuclear powered.

Doodah revved the accelerator.

"That's more like it," he said, satisfied.

Pierre came around the right side of the tank. This was good because Mulch and the dozing Beau were on his blind side. It was bad because Pierre was directly behind Doodah.

"Beau?" said Pierre. "Is something wrong?" His gun was out, pointed at the ground.

Doodah's foot hovered over the accelerator but he couldn't punch it now. Not with this goon staring down his neck.

"Nothing's wrong . . . eh . . . Pierre," he trilled, keeping his face hidden under the cowboy hat's brim.

"You sound strange, Beau. Are you ill?"

Doodah tipped the accelerator, inching forward.

"No. I'm fine. Just doing funny voices, the way human kids do."

Pierre was still suspicious. "Human kids?"

Doodah took a chance. "Yes. Human kids. I'm an alien today, pretending to be a human, so go away or I will reach down your throat and pull out your guts."

Pierre stopped in his tracks, thought for a moment, then remembered. "Beau, you scoundrel. Don't let Minerva hear you talking like that. No more chocolate if you do."

"Pull out your guts!" repeated Doodah for good measure, accelerating gently across a gravel bed onto the driveway.

The pixie pulled a stick-on convex mirror from his pack and stuck it to the windshield. He was relieved to see that Pierre had holstered his weapon and was headed back to his post.

Even though it went against all his smuggler's instincts, Doodah kept his speed down on the driveway. His teeth knocked together as he drove over the uneven granite flagstones. A digital readout informed him that he was utilizing one hundredth of one percent of the engine's new power. Doodah remembered just in time to mute the Mongocharger. The last thing he needed was the computer's electronic voice complaining about his driving skills.

There were two guards in front of the main doors. They barely glanced down as Doodah swept past.

"Howdy, sheriff," said one, grinning.

"Chocolate," squeaked Doodah. From the little he knew about Beau, it seemed the appropriate thing to say.

He tapped the accelerator to bump himself over the lintel, then drove slowly across a streaked marble floor. The tires spun for grip on the sleek stone, which was a bit worrying—it could cost crucial seconds in the event that he had to make a quick getaway. But at least the corridor was wide enough for a U-turn if one became necessary.

Doodah motored down the hallway, past rows of

towering potted palms and several bright abstract works of art, until he came to the corridor's end. There was a camera mounted over an archway, pointed directly at the front hall. A cable snaked out from the box and into a conduit, which ran down to the base of the wall.

Doodah pulled his little car up to the conduit and hopped out. So far, his luck was holding. Nobody had challenged him. This human security was lame. In any fairy building he would have been laser-scanned a dozen times by now. The pixie yanked a section of conduit away, revealing the cable beneath. It took him mere seconds to twist the length of loaded fiber optics around the video cable. Job done. Smiling, Doodah climbed back into his stolen car. This had been a sweet deal. Amnesty for five minutes' work. Time to go home and enjoy a life of freedom, until he broke the rules again.

"Beau Paradizo, you little brat. Come over here right now!"

Doodah froze momentarily, then checked his mirror. There was a girl behind him, glaring his way, hands on hips. This, he guessed, would be Minerva. If memory served, he was supposed to keep far away from Minerva.

"Beau. It's time for your antibiotic. Do you want to have that chest infection forever?"

Doodah started the car and rolled it toward the arch and out of the Mud Girl's sight line. Once around the corner, he could floor the accelerator.

156

"Don't you dare drive away from me, Bobo."

Bobo? No wonder I'm driving away, thought Doodah. Who would drive toward someone calling them Bobo?

"Eh . . . chocolate?" said the pixie hopefully.

It was the wrong thing to do. This girl knew her brother's voice when she heard it, and that wasn't it.

"Bobo? Is there something wrong with your voice?"

Doodah swore under his breath.

"Ches inflec-chun?" he said.

But Minerva wasn't buying it. She pulled a walkie-talkie from her pocket and took rapid strides toward the car.

"Pierre, can you come in here, please? Bring André and Louis." And then to Doodah. "Just stay there, Bobo. I have a nice bar of chocolate for you."

Sure, thought Doodah. Chocolate and a concrete cell.

He considered his options for a second, and came to a conclusion. The conclusion was: *I would rather escape quickly than get captured and tortured to death.*

I am out of here, thought Doodah, and floored the accelerator, sending several hundred horsepower shuddering down the fragile driveshaft. He had maybe a minute before the car fell apart, but by then he could be far away from this Mud Girl and her transparent promises of chocolate.

The car took off so fast that it left an image of itself where it had been.

Minerva stopped dead. "What?"

There was a corner coming up quick. Doodah pulled the wheel in as far as he could, but the vehicle's turning circle was too wide.

"Gotta bounce it," said Doodah through gritted teeth.

He leaned hard left, eased up on the accelerator, and hit the wall side-on. At the moment of impact he shifted his weight and stepped on the gas. The car lost a door, but shot out of the corner like a stone from a sling.

Beautiful, thought Doodah as soon as his head stopped ringing.

He had maybe seconds now before the girl could see him again, and who knew how many guards stood between him and freedom.

He was in a long straight corridor, opening onto a sitting room. Doodah could see a wall-mounted television and the top rim of a red velvet sofa. There must be steps down into the room. Not good. This car only had one more impact left in it.

"Where is Bobo?" shouted the girl. "What have you done with him?"

No point in subtlety now. Time to see what this buggy could do. Doodah jammed his foot on the accelerator then made a beeline for a window behind the velvet sofa. He patted the dash.

"You can do it, you little junk box. One jump. Your chance to be a thoroughbred."

The car didn't answer back. They never did. Though sometimes in times of extreme stress and oxygen deprivation, Doodah imagined they shared his cavalier attitude.

Minerva came around the corner. She was running hard and screaming into a walkie-talkie. Doodah heard the words *apprehend, necessary violence*, and *interrogation*. None of which boded well for him.

The toy car's wheels spun on a long rug, then caught. The rug was shunted backward like a length of toffee from a roller. Minerva was bowled over, but kept talking as she went down.

"He's headed for the library. Take him down! Shoot if necessary."

Doodah grimly held on to the wheel, keeping his line. He was going out that window, closed or not. He entered the room at seventy miles per hour, flying off the top step. Not bad acceleration for a toy. There were two guards in the room, in the act of drawing their weapons. They wouldn't shoot, though. It still appeared as though the car was being driven by a child.

Suckers, thought Doodah. Then the first bullet crashed into the chassis. Okay, maybe they would shoot the car.

He flew in a gentle arc toward the window. Two more bullets took plastic chunks from the bodywork, but it was too late to stop the tiny vehicle. It clipped the lower frame, lost a fender, and tumbled out through the open window.

♅|•♐♄♏♄♌•♏♆♆•☸☽♂♁♄

Someone really should be filming this, thought Doodah, as he clenched his teeth for impact.

The crash shook him all the way from his toes to his skull. Stars danced before Doodah's eyes for a moment, then he was in control again, careering toward the septic tank.

Mulch was waiting, his wild halo of hair quivering with impatience.

"Where have you been? I'm running out of sunblock."

Doodah did not waste time with an answer. Instead he extricated himself from the all but demolished car, prying off his Mongocharger and mirror.

Mulch pointed a stubby finger at him. "I have a few more questions."

A bullet fired from the open window ricocheted off the septic tank, throwing up concrete splinters.

"But they can wait. Hop on."

Mulch turned, presenting Doodah with his back, and more besides. Doodah jumped on, grabbing thick hanks of Mulch's beard.

"Go!" he shouted. "They're right behind me!"

Mulch unhinged his jaw and went into the clay like a hairy torpedo.

But fast as he was, he and Doodah wouldn't have made it. Armed guards were two paces away. They would have seen the gently snoring Beau and riddled the moving tunnel mound with bullets. They probably would have tossed in a few grenades for good measure. But they didn't, because at that precise moment, all hell broke loose inside the chateau.

As soon as Doodah had twisted the loaded fiber optics around the video cable, hundreds of tiny spikes had punctured the rubber, making dozens of strong contacts with the wiring inside.

Seconds later in Section 8 HQ, information came flooding into Foaly's terminal. He had video, alarm systems, waffle boxes, and communications all flashing up in separate windows on his screen.

Foaly cackled, cracking his knuckles like a concert pianist. He loved those old fiber-optic twists. Not as fancy as the new organic bugs, but twice as reliable.

"Okay," he said into a reed mike on his desk. "I'm in control. What kind of nightmares would you like to give the Paradizos?"

In the South of France, Captain Holly Short spoke into her helmet microphone. "Whatever you have. Storm troopers, helicopters. Overload their communications, blow out their waffle boxes. Set off all the alarms. I want them to believe they are under attack."

Foaly called up several phantom files on his computer. The phantoms were one of his own pet projects. He would lift patterns from human movies—soldiers, explosions, whatever—and then use them universally in whatever scene he chose. In this case he sent a squad of French army

special forces, the Commandement des Opérations
Spéciales, or COS, to the Paradizo's close-circuit system.
That would do nicely for starters.

Inside the chateau, the Paradizo chief of security, Juan
Soto, had a little problem. His little problem was that a
couple of loose shots were being popped off in the house.
This can only be seen as a little problem in relation to the
very big problem that Foaly was sending his way.

Soto was speaking into a radio.

"Yes, Miss Paradizo," he said, keeping his voice calm. "I
realize that your brother may be missing. I say *may be*
because that *may be* him in the toy car. It sure looks like
him to me. Okay, okay, I take your point. It is *unusual* for
toy cars to fly that far. It could be a malfunction."

Soto resolved to have strong words with the two idiots
who had actually fired on a toy car at Minerva's command.
He did not care how smart she was, no child was giving
orders like that on his watch.

Even though Miss Minerva was nowhere near the
security center and could not see him, Chief Soto adopted
a stern face for the lecture he was about to give.

"Now, Miss Paradizo, you listen to me," he began. Then
his expression changed completely as the security system
went ballistic.

"Yes, Chief, I'm listening."

The chief held on to his radio with one hand, with the

other he flicked numerous switches on his security console, praying for malfunction. "There seems to be a full squad of COS converging on the chateau. My God, there are some in the house. Helicopters, the rooftop cameras are picking up helicopters." Transmissions suddenly squawked through the band monitor. "And we have chatter. They're after you, Miss Paradizo, and your prisoner. My God, the alarms have all been tripped. Every sector. We're surrounded! We need to evacuate. I can see them in the tree line. They have a tank. How did they get a tank up here?"

Outside, Artemis and Butler watched the chaos Foaly had created. Sirens ripped through the Alpine air, and security men sprinted to ordained spots.

Butler lobbed a few smoke grenades onto the grounds to add to the effect.

"A tank," said Artemis wryly into his fairy phone. "You sent them a tank?"

"You've hacked into the audio feed?" said Foaly sharply. "Just what else can that phone of yours do?"

"It can play solitaire and minesweeper," replied Artemis innocently.

Foaly grunted doubtfully. "We'll talk about this later, Mud Boy. For now, let's concentrate on the plan."

"Excellent suggestion. Do you have any phantom guided missiles?"

* * *

The security chief nearly fainted. The radar had picked up two tracks spiraling from the belly of a helicopter.

"Mon Dieu! Missiles. They're firing smart bombs at us. We must evacuate now."

He flicked open a Perspex panel, revealing an orange switch below. With only a moment's hesitation, he pressed the orange switch. The various alarms were immediately cut off and replaced by a single continuous whine. The evac alarm.

The moment this was sounded, the guards changed course and headed for their assigned vehicles or principals, and the nonsecurity residents of the chateau began gathering data or whatever was most precious to them.

On the eastern side of the house, a series of garage doors opened, and six black BMW four-wheel drives sprang into the courtyard like cougars. One had blacked-out windows.

Artemis studied the situation through binoculars.

"Watch the girl," he said into the tiny phone in his palm. "The girl is the key. I'm guessing hers is the vehicle with the tinted windows."

The girl, Minerva, appeared through patio doors, speaking calmly into a walkie-talkie. Her father trailed beside her, dragging a protesting Beau Paradizo by the hand. Billy Kong came last, bending slightly under the weight of a large golf bag.

164

"Here we go, Holly. Are you ready?"

"Artemis! I'm the field agent here," came the irritated reply. "Stay off my band unless you have something to contribute."

"I was just thinking—"

"*I* was just thinking that *you* should change your middle name to *Control Freak*."

Artemis glanced across at Butler, who was lying beside him and couldn't help overhearing the entire exchange.

"Control freak? Can you believe that?"

"The nerve of some people," replied the bodyguard without taking his eyes off the chateau.

To their left, a small patch of earth began to vibrate. Mud grass and insects were thrust upward in a sudden gush, followed by two heads. One dwarf and one pixie.

Doodah climbed over Mulch's shoulders and collapsed onto the ground.

"You people are crazy," he panted, plucking a beetle from his shirt pocket. "I should be getting more than amnesty for this. I should be getting a pension."

"Quiet, little man," said Butler calmly. "Phase two of the plan is about to start, and I wouldn't want to miss it because of you."

Doodah blanched. "Neither would I. Want you to miss it, that is. Because of me."

Outside the chateau's garage, Billy Kong popped one of the BMW's trunks and hefted the golf bag inside. It was the car with the tinted windows.

Artemis opened his mouth to issue an order, then closed it again. Holly probably knew what to do.

She did. The driver's door clunked open a fraction, apparently all on its own, then closed again. Before Minerva or Billy Kong could do more than blink in surprise, the 4x4 started up and laid down a twenty foot layer of rubber, skidding toward the main gate.

"Perfect," said Artemis under his breath. "Now, Miss Minerva Paradizo, would-be criminal mastermind, let us see exactly how smart you are. I know what I would do in this situation."

Minerva Paradizo's reaction was a bit less dramatic than one might expect from a child who has just had her prize possession stolen. There were no tantrums or foot stamping. Billy Kong defied expectations also. He did not so much as draw a weapon. Instead he squatted on his hunkers, ran his fingers through his manga hair, and lit a cigarette, which Minerva promptly plucked from his lips and squashed underfoot.

Meanwhile, the 4x4 was getting away, barreling toward the main gates. Perhaps Minerva was confident that the reinforced steel barrier would be sufficient to halt the BMW in its tracks. She was wrong. Holly had already weakened the bolts with her Neutrino.

One tap from the vehicle's grille would be more than sufficient to barge the gates out of the way.

If it got that far. Which it did not. After she had crushed Kong's cigarette, Minerva took a remote control from her pocket, tapped in a short code, then hit the SEND button. In the BMW's cab, a tiny charge detonated in the air-flow system, releasing a cloud of sevofluorane, a potent sleeping gas. In seconds, the vehicle began to weave, ramping the driveway bushes and cutting a swath through the manicured lawn.

"Problems," said Butler.

"Hmm," said Artemis. "A gas device, I would guess. Fast acting. Possibly cyclopropane or sevofluorane."

Butler knelt, drawing his pistol. "Should I stroll in there and get them?"

"No. You shouldn't."

The BMW was careering wildly now, following the dips and slopes of the grounds' topography. It destroyed a mini-golf green, pulverized a gazebo, and decapitated a centaur statue.

Hundreds of miles belowground, Foaly winced.

The vehicle finally came to rest in a lavender bed, nose down, rear wheels spinning, spitting out hunks of clay and uprooted long-stemmed purple flowers like missiles.

Nice action, thought Mulch, but he kept the notion to himself, fully aware that this might not be the time to stretch Butler's patience.

Butler was raring to go. His gun was out, and the tendons in his neck were stretched, but Artemis held him back with a touch to the forearm.

"No," he said. "Not now. I know your impulse is to help, but now is not the time."

The bodyguard jammed his Sig Sauer handgun back into its holster, scowling. "Are you sure, Artemis?"

"Trust me, old friend."

And of course, Butler did, even though his instincts were not so sure.

Inside the grounds, a dozen security guards were warily approaching the vehicle, led by Billy Kong. The man moved like a cat, on the balls of his feet.

On his signal, the men rushed the car, reclaiming the golf bag and hauling an unconscious Holly from the front seat. The elf was cuffed with plastic ties and hauled across the garden to where Minerva Paradizo and her father stood waiting.

Minerva removed Holly's helmet and knelt to examine her pointed ears. Through his binocular lenses, Artemis could clearly see that Minerva was smiling.

It had been a trap. All a trap.

Minerva tucked the helmet under her arm, then walked briskly back toward the house. Halfway there, she stopped and turned. Shielding her eyes from the sun's glare, she scanned the shadows and peaks of the surrounding hillsides.

☿ ◉ • ⚘ • ⚔ ⚵ ⚵ ◊ ⚙ ⚶ • ⚘ ☖ ⚲ ⚵ •

"What's she looking for?" Butler speculated aloud.

Artemis did not wonder. He knew exactly what this surprising girl was after.

"She's looking for us, old friend. If that were your chateau, perhaps you might wonder where a spy would conceal himself."

"Of course. And that's why I picked this spot. The ideal location would have been farther up the hill, in that cluster of rocks, but that would also have been the first spot any security expert would booby-trap. This would be my second choice, and so, my first choice."

Minerva's gaze swept past the rock cluster and rested on the line of bushes where they were hiding. She couldn't possibly see them, but her intellect told her that they were there.

Artemis focused on the girl's pretty face. It amazed him that he could appreciate Minerva's features even as his friend was being hauled into captivity. Puberty was a powerful force.

Minerva was smiling. Her eyes were bright and they taunted Artemis across the distance between them. She spoke to them in English. Artemis and Butler, both expert lip-readers had no difficulty interpreting her short sentence.

"Did you get that, Artemis?" asked Butler.

"I got it. And she got us."

Your move, Artemis Fowl, Minerva had said.

Butler sat back in the ditch, slapping mud from his elbows.

"I thought you were one of a kind, Artemis, but that girl is a smart one."

"Yes," said Artemis, musing. "She's a regular juvenile criminal mastermind."

Belowground, in Section 8 headquarters, Foaly groaned into his microphone.

"Great," he said. "Now there are two of you."

CHAPTER 8: SUDDEN IMPACT

Inside Chateau Paradizo

Nº1 was having a lovely dream. In the dream, his mother was holding a surprise party for him, in honor of his graduation from warlock college. The food was scrumptious. The dishes were cooked, and most of the meat was already dead.

He was reaching for a beautifully presented basted pheasant in a basket of woven herb bread ropes, just like the one described in three of *Lady Heatherington Smythe's Hedgerow*, when suddenly the vision retreated into the far distance, as though reality itself were being stretched.

Nº1 tried to follow the feast, but it drew farther and farther away, and now his legs wouldn't work, and Nº1 couldn't understand why. He looked down and saw to his horror that everything from his armpits down had turned to stone. The stone virus was spreading upward across his chest and along his neck. N°1 felt the urge to scream, and he was suddenly terrified that his mouth would turn to stone before he could. To be petrified forever and hold that scream inside would be the ultimate horror.

N°1 opened his mouth and screamed.

Billy Kong, who had been lounging on a chair, watching, snapped his fingers at a camera on the ceiling.

"The ugly one is awake," he said. "And I think it wants its mother."

N°1 stopped screaming when his breath ran out. It was a bit of an anticlimax, really, starting out with a lusty howl and petering off to a reedy whine.

Okay, thought N°1. I am alive and in the land of men. Time to open my eyes and find out just how deep in the pig dung I actually am.

N°1 cracked his eyes open warily, as though he might see something big and hard heading for his face at high speed. What he did see was that he was in a small bare room. There were rectangular lights on the ceiling that threw out the light of a thousand candles, and most of one wall was taken up by a mirror. There was a human, possibly a child, perhaps a female, with a ridiculous mane of blond curls and an extra finger on each hand. The creature was wearing a ludicrously impractical toga-type

arrangement and spongy-soled shoes with lightning bolts embossed on the sides. There was another person in the room. A slouching, leering, thin man, who tapped a staccato rhythm on his leg. Nº1's eyes were drawn to the second human's hair. There were at least half a dozen colors in there. The man was a peacock.

Nº1 decided that perhaps he should raise his empty hands to show that he wasn't carrying a weapon, but it's difficult to do that when you are tied to a chair.

"I'm tied to a chair," he said apologetically, as though it were his fault. Unfortunately, he said this in Gnommish and in the demon dialect. To the humans it sounded like he was trying to dislodge a particularly annoying blockage from his throat.

Nº1 resolved not to talk again. Doubtless, he would say the wrong thing, and the humans would have to ritually execute him. Thankfully, the female seemed eager to chat.

"Hello, I am Minerva Paradizo, and this man is Mr. Kong," she said. "Can you understand me?"

It was all gibberish to Nº1. Not a single recognizable word from the text of *Lady Heatherington Smythe's Hedgerow*.

He smiled encouragingly to show he appreciated the effort.

"Do you speak French?" asked the blond girl, then switched languages. "How about English?"

N°1 sat up. That last bit was familiar. Strange inflections, surely, but the words themselves were from the book.

"English?" he repeated.

This was the language of Lady Heatherington Smythe. Learned at her mother's knee. Explored in the lecture halls of Oxford. Used to profess her undying love for Professor Rupert Smythe. N°1 loved the book. He sometimes believed that he was the only one who did. Even Abbot didn't seem to appreciate the romantic bits.

"Yes," said Minerva. "English. The last one spoke it well enough. French, too."

Manners must be appreciated somewhere outside a book, N°1 had always thought, so he decided to give them a go.

He growled, which was the polite demon way of asking to speak in front of your betters. This must not be how humans interpreted it, because the skinny human jumped to his feet, pulling out a knife.

"No, kind sir," said N°1 hurriedly, cobbling together a couple of sentences from Lady Heatherington. "Prithee sheath thine weapon. I bring joyous tidings only."

The skinny human was confounded. He spoke English as well as the next American, but this little runt was spouting some kind of medieval nonsense.

Kong straddled N°1, holding the knife to his throat.

"Talk straight, ugly," said the man, deciding to give Taiwanese a go.

"I wish I could understand," said N°1, shaking. Unfortunately, he said this in Gnommish. "What I . . . eh . . . meanest to say is . . ."

It was no good. Quotes from Lady Heatherington that he could generally shoehorn into any occasion just weren't coming under pressure.

"Talk straight or die!" shrieked the human into his face.

N°1 shrieked right back at him. "How can I talk straight, you son of a three-legged dog? I don't speak Taiwanese!"

All of this was said in perfect Taiwanese. N°1 was stunned. The gift of tongues was not one demons possessed. Except the warlocks. More proof.

He intended to ponder this development for a few moments, now that the knife-wielding human had backed off, but suddenly the beauty of language exploded inside his brain. Even his own tongue, Gnommish, had been severely culled by the demons. There were thousands of words that had been dropped from regular use on the basis that they did not relate to killing things or eating them, and not necessarily in that order.

"Cappuccino!" shouted N°1, surprising everyone.

"Excuse me?" said Minerva.

"What a lovely word. And 'maneuver.' And 'balloon.'"

The skinny man pocketed his knife. "Now he's talking.

If he's anything like the videos you showed me of the other one, we'll never get him to shut up."

"'Pink!'" exclaimed N°1 delightedly. "We don't have a word for that color in the demon commonspeak. Pink is considered undemonlike, so we ignore it. It's such a relief to be able to say pink!"

"Pink," said Minerva. "Fabulous."

"Tell me," said N°1. "What is a cotton candy? I know the words, and it sounds . . . scrumptious . . . but the picture in my head cannot be accurate."

The girl seemed pleased that N°1 could talk, but slightly miffed that he had forgotten his situation.

"We can talk about cotton candy later, little demon. There are more important things to discuss."

"Yes," agreed Kong. "The demon invasion, for example."

N°1 rolled the sentence around in his head. "Sorry, my gifts must not be fully developed. The only meaning I have for 'invasion' is a hostile entry of an armed force into a territory."

"That's the one I mean, you little toad."

"Again, I'm a little confused. My new vocabulary is telling me that a toad is a froglike creature. . . ." N°1's face fell. "Oh. I see, you're insulting me."

Kong scowled at Minerva. "I think I preferred him when he spoke like an old movie."

"I was quoting scripture," explained N°1, enjoying the shape of these new words in his mouth. "From the

sacred book *Lady Heatherington Smythe's Hedgerow*."

Minerva frowned, looking at the ceiling as she thought back in time. "Lady Heatherington Smythe. Why is that familiar?"

"*Lady Heatherington Smythe's Hedgerow* is the source of all our human knowledge. Lord Abbot brought it back to us." N°1 bit his lip, shutting off his own babbling. He had said too much already. These humans were the enemy, and he had given them the blueprint to Abbot's plans. *Blueprint*. Nice word.

Minerva clapped her hands once sharply. She had found the memory she was looking for.

"Lady Heatherington Smythe. My goodness, that ridiculous romance! Remember, Mr. Kong?"

Kong shrugged. "I don't read fiction. Manuals mostly."

"No, remember the video footage of the other demon. We let him have a book; he carried it around like a security blanket."

"Ah, yes. I remember that. Stupid little goat. Always toting around that stupid book."

"You know, you're repeating yourself," said N°1, chattering nervously. "There are other words for *stupid*. 'Dim,' 'dense,' 'slow,' 'thick,' just to name a few. I can do Taiwanese if you prefer."

A knife appeared in Kong's hand as if from nowhere.

"Wow," said N°1. "That's a real talent. A 'bravura,' in fact."

Kong ignored the compliment, flipping the knife so he was holding the blade.

"Just shut up, creature. Or this goes between your eyes. I don't care how valuable you are to Miss Paradizo. To me, you and your kind are simply something to be wiped off the face of the earth."

Minerva folded her arms. "I will thank you, Mr. Kong, not to threaten our guest. You work for my father, and you will do what my father tells you to do. And I am pretty sure my father told you to keep a civil tongue in your head."

Minerva Paradizo may have been a precocious talent in many areas, but because of her age, she had limited experience. From her studies, she knew how to read body language, but she did not know that a skilled martial artist can train himself to control his body so that his real feelings are hidden. A true disciple of the discipline would have noted the subtle tightening of the tendons in Billy Kong's neck. This was a man holding himself in check.

Not yet, his stance said. *Not yet.*

Minerva returned her attention to N°1.

"*Lady Heatherington Smythe's Hedgerow*, you say?"

N°1 nodded. He was afraid to speak in case his runaway mouth leaked any more information than it already had.

Minerva spoke now to the large mirror. "You

remember that one, Papa? The most ridiculous fluffy romance you are ever likely to avoid like the plague. I loved it when I was six. It's all about a nineteenth-century English aristocrat. Oh, who's the author . . . Carter Cooper Barbison. The Canadian girl. She was eighteen when she wrote it. Did absolutely no research. She had nineteenth-century nobles speaking like they were from the fifteen hundreds. Absolute trash, so obviously a worldwide hit. Well, it seems our old friend Abbot brought it home with him. The cheeky devil has managed to sell it as gospel truth. It seems he has the rest of the demons spouting Cooper Barbison as though she were an evangelist."

Nº1 broke his no-speaking vow. "Abbot? Abbot was here?"

"*Mais oui,*" said Minerva, resting her palms on her knees. "How do you think we knew where to find you. Abbot told us everything."

A voice boomed through a wall-mounted speaker. "Not everything. His figures were flawed. But my young genius Minerva figured it out. I'll get you a pony for this, darling. Whatever color you like."

Minerva waved at the mirror. "Thank you, Papa. You should know by now that I don't like ponies. Or ballet."

The speaker laughed. "That's my little girl. What about a trip to Disneyland Paris? You could dress as a princess."

"Perhaps after the selection committee," said Minerva with a smile. The smile was slightly forced, though. She did not have time for Disney dreams at the moment. "After I am sure of the Nobel nomination. We have less than a week to question our subjects and organize secure travel to the Royal Academy in Stockholm."

Nº1 had another important question. "And *Lady Heatherington Smythe's Hedgerow*? It's not true?"

Minerva laughed delightedly. "True? My dear little fellow. Nothing could be further from the truth. That book is a cringe-worthy testament to teenage hormonal fabrication."

Nº1 was stunned. "But I studied that book. For hours. I acted out scenes. I made costumes. Are you telling me that there is no Heatherington Hall?"

"No Heatherington Hall."

"And no evil Prince Karloz?"

"Fiction."

Nº1 remembered something. "But Abbot came back with a crossbow, just like in the book. That's evidence."

Kong joined the discussion; after all, this was his area of expertise. "Crossbows? Ancient history, toad. We use things like these now." Billy Kong drew a black ceramic handgun from a holster tucked in his armpit. "This little beauty shoots fire and death. We've got much bigger ones, too. We fly around the world in our metal birds and rain down exploding eggs on our enemies."

Nº1 snorted. "That little thing shoots fire and death? Flying metal birds? And I suppose you eat lead and blow golden bubbles, too."

Kong did not respond well to cynicism, especially from a little reptilian creature. In one fluid motion he flicked the safety off his weapon and fired three shots, blowing apart the headrest of Nº1's seat. The imp's face was showered with sparks and splinters, and the sound of the shots echoed like thunder in the confined space.

Minerva was furious. She began screaming long before anyone could hear her.

"Get out of here, Kong. Out!"

She kept screaming this, or words to this effect, until their ears stopped ringing. When Minerva realized that Billy Kong was ignoring her commands, she switched to Taiwanese.

"I told my father not to employ you. You are an impulsive and violent man. We are conducting a scientific experiment here. This demon is of no use to me if he is dead, do you understand, you reckless man? I need to communicate with our guest, so you must leave because you obviously terrify him. Go now, I warn you, or your contract will be terminated."

Kong rubbed the bridge of his nose. It was taking every shred of patience he had not to dispose of this whining infant right now, and take his chances with her security.

But it would be foolhardy to risk everything because he could not keep his temper for a few more hours. For now, he would have to content himself with some more insolence.

Kong took a small mirror from his trouser pocket and plucked at the gelled strands of his hair.

"I will go now, little girl, but be careful how you speak to me. You may come to regret it."

Minerva spread the fingers of her right hand into a W.

"Whatever," she said in English.

Kong pocketed his mirror, winked at N°1, and left. N°1 did not feel comforted by that wink. In the demon world, you winked at your opponent in pitched battle to make clear your intention to kill him next. N°1 got the distinct impression that this spiky-haired human had that same intention.

Minerva sighed, took a moment to compose herself, then resumed her interview with the prisoner.

"Let's start at the beginning. What is your name?"

N°1 supposed that was a safe question to answer. "I have no real name, because I never warped. I used to worry about that, but now I seem to have a lot more to worry about."

Minerva realized that her questions would have to be quite specific.

"What do people call you?"

"You mean human people? Or other demons?"

• 𝇌 ♁ ⚛ 𝈫 𝈁 ⟑ • ∪ ♁ ☽ 𝈁 𐊄 • ⚲ ◊ ◉ ⟑

"Demons."

"Oh . . . right. They call me N°1."

"N°1?"

"That's right. It's not much of a name, but it's all I have. And I console myself with the fact that it's better than N°2."

"I see. Well then, N°1, I suppose you would like to know what's going on here."

N°1's eyes were wide and pleading. "Yes, please."

"Two years ago, one of your pride materialized here. Just popped up in the middle of the night on the statue of D'Artagnan in the courtyard. He was lucky not to be killed, actually. D'Artagnan's sword pierced one of his arms. The tip broke off inside."

"Was the sword silver?" asked N°1.

"Yes. Yes it was. We realized later that the silver anchored him to this dimension; otherwise he would have been attracted to his own space and time. The demon was, of course, Abbot. My parents wanted to call the gendarmes, but I persuaded them to bring the poor half-dead beast inside. Papa has a small surgery here that he uses for his more paranoid patients. He treated Abbot's burns, but we missed the silver tip until a few weeks later when the wound became infected and Papa did an X-ray. Abbot was quite fascinating to observe. Initially, and for many days, he flew into psychotic rages whenever a human approached him. He tried to kill us all, and vowed that his army was coming to exterminate humankind from the face of the earth. He conducted long arguments with himself. It was more than split personality. It was as if there were two people in one body. A warrior and a scientist. The warrior would rage and thrash, then the scientist would write calculations on the wall. I knew that I was on to something important here. Something revolutionary. I had discovered a new species, or rather, rediscovered an old one. And if Abbot really was going to bring a demon army, then it was up to me to save lives. Human and demon. But of course, I am merely a child so no one would listen to me. But if I could record this and present it to the Nobel Committee in Stockholm, I could win the physics prize and establish demons as a protected species. Saving a species would give me a certain satisfaction, and no child has ever won the prize before, not even the great Artemis Fowl."

Something had been puzzling N°1. "Aren't you a little young to be studying other species? And you're a girl, too. That pony offer made by the magic voice box sounded pretty good."

Minerva had obviously come across this attitude before. "Times are changing, demon," she snapped. "Children are a lot smarter than they used to be. We're writing books, mastering computers, tearing apart scientific myths. Did you know that most scientists won't even acknowledge the existence of magic? Once you add magic into the energy

equation, nearly all the current laws of physics are shown to be seriously flawed."

"I see," said N°1, not convincing anyone.

"I am exactly the right age for this project," added Minerva. "I am young enough to believe in magic, and old enough to understand how it works. When I present you in Stockholm, and we put forward our thesis on time travel and magic as elemental energy, it will be a historic moment. The world will have to take magic seriously, and make ready for the invasion!"

"There is no invasion," protested N°1.

Minerva smiled, as a kindergarten teacher would at a fibbing child. "I know all about it. Once Abbot's warrior personality became dominant, he told us about the Battle of Taillte and how the demons would return and wage a terrible war with the Mud Men, as he called us. There was a lot of blood and hacking of limbs involved."

N°1 nodded. That sounded like Abbot.

"That's what Abbot believed, but things have changed."

"I explained that to him. I explained that he had been flitting through time and space for ten thousand years, and that we had come a long way since then. There are more of us than there used to be, and we didn't use crossbows anymore."

"You didn't? You don't?"

"You saw Mr. Kong's gun. That's only a tiny example of the kind of weaponry we have. Even if your entire pride of

185

demons arrived all together, armed to the teeth, it would take about ten minutes to have you all locked up."

"Is that what you're going to do? Lock us up?"

"That was the plan, yes," admitted Minerva. "As soon as Abbot realized that the demons could never beat us, he changed his tactics. He voluntarily explained the mechanics of the time tunnel to me, and in return I gave him books to read and old weapons to examine. After a few days' reading, he asked to be called Abbot, after General Leon Abbot in the book. I knew that once I presented Leon Abbot in Stockholm, it would be easy to get funding for an international task force. Whenever a demon popped up, we could tag him with silver and house him in an artificial demon community for study. The Central Park Zoo was my preferred location."

N°1 ran the word "zoo" through his new lexicon. "Aren't zoos for animals?"

Minerva gazed at her feet. "Yes. I am rethinking that, especially having met you. You seem quite civilized, not like that Abbot person. He *was* an animal. When he arrived, we tended his wounds, nursed him back to health, and all he could do was try to eat us, so we had no choice but to restrain him."

"So you're not going to lock us up in a zoo any-more?"

"Actually, I don't have a choice. Judging by my calculations, the time tunnel is unraveling at both ends and deteriorating along the shaft. Soon, any calculations will be unreliable, and it will be impossible to predict where or when demons will materialize. I'm afraid, N°1, that your pride doesn't have long left before it disappears altogether."

N°1 was stunned. This was more information than anyone could absorb in one day. For some reason the demoness with the red markings flashed into his mind. "Isn't there any way to help? We are intelligent beings, you know. Not animals."

Minerva stood and paced, stretching one of her corkscrew curls.

"I have been giving this some thought. There's nothing that can be done without magic, and Abbot told me the warlocks all died in the transition."

"It's true," said N°1. He did not mention that he might be a warlock himself. Something told him that this was valuable information, and it was not a good idea to reveal too much valuable information to a person who had tied you to a chair. He had said too much already.

"Maybe if Abbot had known about the time spell, he wouldn't have been so eager to get back to Hybras," mused Minerva. "Papa told him that there was a silver chip in his arm, and that very night he dug it out with his nails and disappeared. We have the whole thing on tape. I have wondered every day if he'd managed to make it home."

"He made it," said N°1. "The time spell took him right

back to the beginning. He never said anything about this place. Just turned up with the book and the crossbow, claiming to be our savior. It was all lies."

"Well then," sighed Minerva, and she seemed genuinely sorry. "I don't have a single idea about how to save the pride. Maybe your little friend in the next room can help when she wakes up."

"What little friend?" asked N°1, puzzled.

"The one who knocked out Bobo, my brother. The little creature we captured trying to rescue you," explained Minerva. "Or more accurately, trying to rescue an empty golf bag. She looks like a magical creature. Maybe she can help."

Who would want to rescue a golf bag? wondered N°1.

The door opened a crack, and Juan Soto's head appeared in the gap.

"Minerva?"

"Not now," snapped Minerva, waving at the man to go away.

"There's a call for you."

"I'm not available. Take a number."

The security guard persisted; he stepped into the room, one hand cupped over the mouthpiece of a cordless phone.

"I think you might want to talk to this person. He says his name is Artemis Fowl."

Minerva gave Soto her full attention.

"I'll take it," she said, reaching for the phone.

* * *

The LEPrecon field helmet is an amazing piece of equipment. The Section 8 field helmet, on the other hand, is a miracle of modern science. To compare the two would be akin to comparing a flintlock to a laser-sighted sniper rifle.

Foaly had taken full advantage of his almost unlimited budget to indulge his every tech-head fantasy and stuff the helmet with every piece of diagnostic, surveillance, defense, and just plain cool equipment he could cram in there.

The centaur was vocally proud of the entire package. But if forced to pick just one add-on to brag about, he would go for the bouncing bags every time.

Bouncing bags in themselves were not a recent addition. Even civilian helmets had gel bags in between their outer and inner shells that provided a bit of extra buffering in case of a crash. But Foaly had replaced the helmet's rigid outer shell with a more yielding polymer and then swapped the electro-sensitive gel for tiny electro-sensitive beads. The beads could be controlled with electronic pulses to expand, contract, roll, or group, providing the helmet with a simple but highly effective propulsion system.

"*This little marvel can't fly, but it can bounce wherever you want it to,*" Foaly had said earlier, when Holly was signing out her equipment. "*Only commanders get the flying helmets. I wouldn't recommend them, though; the engine's field has been known to straighten perms. Not that I'm saying you have a perm. Or need one, for that matter."*

While Nº1 was being interrogated by Minerva, Foaly was flexing his fingers over the remote controls for Holly's Section 8 helmet. At the moment, the helmet was locked in a wire mesh strongbox at the rear of the security office.

Foaly liked to sing a little ditty while he worked. In this instance the song was the Riverbend classic: "If It Looks Like a Dwarf, and Smells Like a Dwarf, Then It's Probably a Dwarf (Or a Latrine Wearing Dungarees)." This was a relatively short title for a Riverbend song, which was the fairy equivalent of human Country & Western.

"When I got an itch I can't scratch,
When there's a slug in my vole stew,
When I got sunburn on my bald patch,
That's when I remember you . . ."

Foaly had considerately switched off his mike, so Artemis would not have the chance to object to his singing. In fact, he was using an extremely old hardwired antenna to send his signal, in the hope that no one in Police Plaza would pick up on his transmission. Haven City was in lockdown, and that meant no communications with the surface. Foaly was knowingly disobeying Commander Ark

Sool's orders, and he was quite enjoying himself while doing it.

The centaur donned a set of V-goggles through which he could see everything in the helmet's vista. Not only that, but the goggles' PIP facility gave him rear and side views from the helmet's cameras. Foaly already had control of the chateau's security systems; now he wanted to have a little peek through their computer files, something he could not do from Section 8 HQ, especially not with the LEP waiting to pounce on any signal coming out of the city.

The helmet was naturally equipped with wireless omnisensor capabilities, but the closer he could get to an actual hard drive, the quicker the job could be completed.

Foaly pressed a combination key command on his V-keyboard. To anyone watching, it would have seemed like the centaur was playing an invisible piano, but in fact the V-goggles interpreted the movements as keystrokes. A small laser pencil popped out of a hidden compartment just above the right ear cushion of Holly's helmet.

Foaly targeted the wire mesh box's locking mechanism.

"One second burst. Fire." Nothing happened, so Foaly swore briefly, turned on his microphone, and tried it again.

"One second burst. Fire."

This time, a red beam pulsed from the pencil's tip, and the lock melted into metallic mush.

Always good to have the equipment switched on, thought Foaly, glad that no one had witnessed his mistake, especially Artemis Fowl.

Foaly targeted a desktop computer at the far side of the office with a glare and three blinks.

"Compute bounce," he ordered the helmet, and almost immediately an animated dotted arrow appeared on the screen, dipping once to the floor and then rising to the computer desk.

"Execute bounce," said Foaly, and smiled as his creation rolled into life. The helmet hit the floor with a basketball ping, then bounced across the room, directly onto the computer desk.

"Perfect, you genius," said Foaly, congratulating himself. Sometimes his own achievements brought a tear to his eye.

I wish Caballine could have seen that, he thought. And then, *Wow, I must be getting serious about this girl.*

Caballine was a centaur he had bumped into at a gallery downtown. She was a researcher with PPTV by day and a sculptor by night. A very smart lady, and she knew all about Foaly. Apparently, Caballine was a big fan of the mood blanket, a multi-sensor massage and homeopathic garment designed by Foaly specifically for centaurs. So they talked about that for a half hour. One thing led to another, and now he found himself jogging with her every evening. Whenever there wasn't an emergency.

Which there is now! he reminded himself, turning his attention back to work.

The helmet was sitting next to the human computer keyboard, with its omnisensor pointed directly at the hard drive.

Foaly stared at the hard drive and blinked three times, selecting it on the screen.

"Download all files from this and any networked computers," instructed the centaur, and the helmet immediately began to suck information from the Apple Mac.

After several seconds, an animated bottle on the V-goggles screen was filled to the brim, and burped. Transfer completed. Now they could find out exactly how much information these humans had, and where they were getting it from. But there was still the matter of back-up files. This group could have burned their information onto CDs, or even sent it by e-mail or stored it on the Internet.

Foaly used the virtual keyboard to open a data-charge folder and send a virus into the human computer. The charge would completely wipe out any computers on the network, but before that, it would run along any Internet pathways explored by these humans and completely burn the sites. Foaly would have liked to have been a bit more delicate about it, and just erase fairy-related files, but he couldn't afford to take chances with this mysterious group. The mere fact that they had avoided detection for so long was proof that they were not to be trifled with.

This was a major virus to lob into a human system. It would probably crash thousands of sites, including Google and Yahoo, but Foaly didn't see that he had a choice.

On Foaly's screen, the data charge appeared as a red flickering flame that chuckled nastily as it dived into the omnisensor's data stream. In five minutes, the Paradizo's hard drives would be burned beyond repair. And as an added bonus, the charge would also attach itself to any storage devices within the sensor's range that bore the network's signature. So any information stored on CDs or flash drives would disintegrate as soon as someone tried to load them. It was potent stuff, and there wasn't a firewall or antivirus that could stop it.

Artemis's voice issued from two gel speakers in jars on the desk, interrupting his concentration.

"There's a wall safe in the office. It's where Minerva keeps her notes. You need to burn anything inside it."

"Wall safe," replied Foaly. "Let's see."

The centaur ran an X-ray scan on the room and found the safe behind a row of shelving. Given the time, he would have liked to have scanned all the contents, but he had a rendezvous to keep. He sent a concentrated laser beam the width of a length of fishing line into the belly of the safe, reducing the contents to ash. Hopefully he was destroying more than the family jewels.

The X-ray scan revealed nothing else promising, so Foaly sent the helmet beads spinning, toppling Holly's helmet off the desk. In a display of keyboard virtuosity, Foaly used the laser to carve a section from the base of the office door while the helmet was in midair. In two choreographed bounces, the helmet was through the section and into the corridor outside.

Foaly grinned, satisfied.

"Never even touched the wood," he said.

The centaur called up a blueprint for the Chateau Paradizo and superimposed it over a grid on his screen. There were two dots on the grid. One was the helmet, and the other was Holly. It was time the two were reunited.

As he worked, Foaly unconsciously sang a verse of the Riverbend dirge.

"When my lucky numbers run out of luck,
When I'm stuck in the hole I tumbled into,
When my favorite dawg gets squashed by a truck,
That's when I think me some thoughts of you."

On the planet's surface, Artemis winced as the song twanged through his tiny phone and along his thumb.

"Please, Foaly," he said in pained tones. "I'm trying to negotiate on the other line."

Foaly whinnied, surprised. He'd forgotten about Artemis.

"Some people ain't got no Riverbend in their souls," he said, switching off his microphone.

Billy Kong decided that he'd have a little word with the new prisoner. The female. If indeed she was female. How was he supposed to know for sure what class of a creature it was? It looked like a girl, but maybe demon girls weren't the same as human ones. So Billy Kong thought he might ask *it* what exactly *it* was, among other things. If the creature decided not to answer, Kong didn't mind. There were ways to persuade people to talk. Asking them nicely was one way. Giving them candy was another. But Billy Kong preferred torture.

Back in the early eighties, when Billy Kong was still plain old Jonah Lee, he had lived in the California beach town of Malibu with his mother, Annie, and big brother, Eric.

Annie worked two jobs to keep her boys in sneakers, so Jonah got left with Eric in the evenings. That should have worked out fine. Eric was sixteen and old enough to look after his kid brother. But like most sixteen-year-olds, he had more on his mind than little brothers. In fact, babysitting Jonah was seriously interfering with his social life.

The problem was, as Eric saw it, that Jonah was an outdoorsy kind of boy. As soon as Eric took off to hang out with his friends, Jonah would ignore his big brother's orders and head out into the California evening. And out-doors in the city was no place for an eight-year-old. So what Eric needed to do was devise a scheme that kept Jonah indoors, and allowed Eric to roam free.

He came upon the perfect strategy quite by accident one night, returning home after a late-night argument with his girlfriend's other boyfriend and his brothers.

For once, Jonah had not ventured out, and was plonked in front of the TV, watching a horror show on hacked cable. Eric, who had always been impulsive and reckless, had taken to sneaking around with the girlfriend of a local gangster. Now word had leaked out, and the gang was after him. They had roughed him up a bit already, but he had gotten away. He was bloody and tired, but still kind of enjoying himself.

"Lock the doors," he'd called to his little brother, startling him out of his TV stupor.

Jonah jumped to his feet, eyes widening as he noticed Eric's bloodied nose and lip.

"What happened to you?"

Eric grinned. He was that kind of person—exhausted, battered, but buzzing with adrenaline.

"I got . . . There was this bunch of . . ."

And then he stopped, because the spark of an idea was ricocheting around in his head. He must look pretty beat up. Maybe he could use this to keep little Jonah indoors while Mom was working.

"I can't tell you," he said, dragging a smear of blood across his face with one sleeve. "I've sworn an oath. Just bolt the doors and close the shutters."

Usually Jonah didn't have time for his brother's theatrics, but tonight there was blood and horror on the TV, and he could hear footsteps pounding up the driveway.

"Dammit, they've found me," swore Eric, peeking through a shutter.

Little Jonah grabbed his brother's sleeve. "Who's found you, Eric? You gotta tell me."

Eric appeared to consider it.

"Okay," he said finally. "I belong to a . . . uh . . . secret society. We fight a secret enemy."

"What, like a gang?"

"No," said Eric. "We fight demons."

"Demons?" said little Jonah, half skeptical, half scared out of his wits.

"Yeah. They're all over California. By day, they're normal guys. Accountants and basketball players, stuff like that. But at night they peel off their skin and go hunting kids. Under-tens."

"Under-tens? Like me."

"Like you. Exactly like you. I found these demons chewing on a couple of twin girls. Maybe eight years old. I killed most of 'em, but a few must've followed me home. We gotta stay real quiet and they'll go away."

Jonah rushed for the phone. "We should call Mom."

"No!" said Eric, snatching the phone. "You want to get Mom killed? Is that what you want?"

The idea of his mother dying started Jonah crying. "No. Mom can't die."

"Exactly," Eric said gently. "You gotta leave the demon-slaying to me and my boys. When you're fifteen, then you get to be sworn in, but until then, this is our secret. You stay in the house and let me do my duty. Promise?"

Jonah nodded, blubbering too much to say the word.

And so the brothers sat huddled on the sofa while Eric's girlfriend's boyfriend's brothers battered on the windows and called him out.

This is a cruel trick, Eric thought. Maybe I'll just let it run for a couple of months. It'll keep the kid out of trouble until everything dies down.

The deception worked well. Jonah didn't set foot outside the house after dusk for weeks. He sat on the couch with his knees drawn to his chin, waiting for Eric to return with elaborate demon-slaying stories. Every night he feared that his brother would not return, that the demons would kill him.

One night his fears came to pass. The cops said that Eric had been killed by a notorious gang of brothers who had been gunning for him. Something about a girl. But Jonah knew different. He knew the demons had done it. They had peeled off their faces and killed his brother.

* * *

So Jonah Lee, now known as Billy Kong, was going in to see Holly, carrying the weight of his childhood memories. For the sake of his sanity, he had managed to convince himself over the decades that there were no demons, and that his beloved brother had lied to him. This betrayal had messed him up for years, preventing him from forming lasting relationships, and making it a lot easier for him to hurt people. And now this crazy Minerva girl was paying him to help her to hunt down actual demons, and it turns out they *were* real. He had seen them with his own eyes.

At this stage, Billy Kong couldn't tell fact from fiction. A part of him believed that he had had a bad accident, and that all of this was coma hallucinations. All Billy knew for sure was that if there was the slightest chance that these demons were the same ones who'd killed Eric, then they were going to pay. It was revenge he was after.

Holly was not too happy playing the victim. She'd had enough of that in the Academy. Every time the curriculum had thrown up a role-playing game, Holly, as the only girl in that class, had been picked to be the hostage, or the elf walking home alone, or the teller facing a bank robber. She'd tried to object that this was stereotyping, but the instructor had replied that stereotypes were stereotypes for a reason, and get that blond wig on. So when Artemis proposed that she allow herself to get caught, Holly had taken a bit of persuading. Now she was tied to a wooden chair in a dark damp basement room, waiting for some human to come and torture her. The next time Artemis had a plan involving someone being taken hostage, he could play the part himself. It was ridiculous. She was a captain in her eighties and Artemis was a fourteen-year-old civilian, and yet he was dishing out the orders and she was taking them.

That's because Artemis is a tactical genius, said her sensible side.

Oh, shut up, her irritated side responded eloquently.

And then Billy Kong came into the room and proceeded to irritate Holly even further. He glided across the floor like a pale, hair-gelled ghost, circling Holly silently several times before speaking.

"Tell me something, demon. Can you peel off your face?"

Holly met his eyes. "With what? My teeth? Hands tied, moron."

Billy Kong sighed. Lately, everyone under five feet seemed to think it was their prerogative to give him verbal abuse.

"You probably know I'm not supposed to kill you," said Billy, teasing his hair into spikes. "But I often do things that I'm not supposed to."

Holly decided to crack this human's confidence a little.

"I know that, Billy, or should I say, Jonah. You've done a lot of bad things over the years."

Kong took a step back. "You know me?"

"We know all about you, Billy. We've been watching you for years."

This wasn't strictly true, of course. Holly knew no more about Kong than what Foaly had told her. Perhaps she wouldn't have baited him if she'd known about his *demon* history.

To Billy Kong, this simple statement was confirmation of everything Eric had told him. Suddenly the building blocks of his beliefs and understandings toppled and smashed beyond repair.

It was all true. Eric had not lied. Demons walked the earth, and his brother had tried to protect him and paid with his life.

"You remember my brother?" he asked, his voice shaking.

Holly presumed that this was a test. Foaly *had* mentioned a brother.

"Yes. I remember. Derek, wasn't it?"

Kong pulled a stiletto knife from his breast pocket, gripping it so tightly his knuckles whitened.

"Eric!" he shouted, spittle spraying from his mouth. "It was Eric! Do you remember what happened to him?"

Holly suddenly felt nervous. This Mud Man was unstable. It would only take her a second to escape from these bonds, but maybe a second was too long. Artemis

had requested that she remain bound for as long as possible, but from the look on Billy Kong's face, it seemed that staying bound could be a fatal mistake.

"Do you remember what happened to my brother?" asked Kong again, waving the knife like a conductor's baton.

"I remember," said Holly. "He died. Violently."

Kong was thunderstruck. Reeling internally. For several moments he circled the room muttering to himself, which didn't comfort Holly any.

"It's true. Eric never betrayed me! My brother loved me. He loved me and *they* took him!"

Holly took advantage of this lack of focus to escape from the plastic ties binding her wrists. She did this using an old LEP trick taught to her by Commander Vinyáya back in the Academy. She rubbed her wrists against the rough edge, causing two small grazes. When magical sparks erupted from her fingertips to heal the wounds, she siphoned off a few to melt the plastic, enough for her to yank her way out.

When Kong faced Holly again, she was untethered, but concealing the fact.

Kong knelt before her so their eyes were level. He was blinking rapidly, and his pulse beat in a temple vein. He spoke slowly, in a voice fraught with barely repressed madness and violence. He had switched to Taiwanese, his family's first language.

"I want you to peel off your face. Right now."

This, reasoned Kong, would be the final proof. If this demon could peel off her face, then he would stab her in the heart and damn the consequences.

"I can't," said Holly. "My hands are tied. Why don't you peel it off for me? We have new masks now. Disposable. They come off easily."

Kong coughed in surprise, rocking back on his hunkers. Then he steadied himself and reached out shaking hands. His hands did not shake from fear, but from anger and sorrow that he had dishonored his brother's memory by believing the worst of him.

"At the hairline," said Holly. "Just grab and pull. Don't worry if you tear it."

Kong looked up, and they made eye contact. This was all Holly needed to employ the magical fairy *mesmer*.

"Don't those arms feel heavy?" she asked, her voice layered and irresistible.

Kong's brow suddenly creased, and the creases filled with sweat.

"My arms. What? They're like lead. Like two lead pipes. I can't . . ."

Holly pushed the *mesmer* a little harder. "Why don't you put them down. Take it easy. Sit on the floor."

Kong sat on the concrete. "I'm just going to sit for a second. We're still doing the face-peeling thing. But in a second. I'm tired."

"You probably feel like talking."

"You know what, demon. I feel like talking. What should we talk about?"

"This whole group you're involved with, Billy. The Paradizos. Tell me about them."

Kong snorted. "The Paradizos! You're only dealing with one Paradizo here. And that's the girl, Minerva. Her daddy is just a money man. If Minerva wants it, Gaspard pays for it. He's so proud of his little girl the genius that he does whatever she says. Can you believe that she convinced him to keep the whole demon thing quiet until after the Nobel council gets a look at her research?"

This was very good news. "You mean that no one outside this house knows about the demons?"

"Hardly anybody *inside* the house knows. Minerva is paranoid that some other egghead will get ahold of her work. The staff thinks we're guarding a political prisoner who needs his face redone. Only Juan Soto, the chief of in-house security, and myself were told the truth."

"Does Minerva keep records?"

"Records? She writes everything down, and I mean everything. We have records of every demon action, right down to toilet breaks. She's got every twitch on video. The only reason that there's no cameras down here is that we weren't expecting anyone."

"Where does she keep these notes?"

"A little wall safe in the security office. Minerva thinks

I don't know the combination, but I do. Bobo's birthday."

Holly touched a skin-colored microphone pad glued to her throat. "A wall safe in the security office," she said clearly. "I hope you're getting that."

There was no reply. Wearing an earpiece had been too risky, so Holly had had to make do with the mike pad on her neck and an iris-cam suckered like a contact lense over her right eye.

Kong still felt like talking. "You know, I'm going to kill all of you demons. I've got a plan. Real clever, too. Miss Minerva thinks that she's going to Stockholm, but that's never going to happen. I'm just waiting for the right moment. I know that silver is the only thing keeping you in this dimension. So I'm going to send you back, and give you a little present to take with you."

Not if I can help it, thought Holly.

Kong half smiled at her. "Are we doing the face-peeling thing? Can you really do that?"

"Of course I can," said Holly. "Are you sure you want to see it?"

Kong nodded, slack jawed.

"Okay, then. Watch carefully."

Holly raised her hands to her face, and when she took them away, her head had disappeared. Her body and limbs quickly followed suit.

"Not only can I peel off my face," said Holly's voice from thin air, "I can do my entire body."

206

"It's true," croaked Kong. "It's all true."

Then a tiny invisible fist swished through the air, knocking him into unconsciousness. Billy Kong lay on the concrete floor, dreaming that he was Jonah Lee once more, and his brother stood before him saying, *"I told you so, bro. I told you there were demons. They murdered me back in Malibu. So what are you going to do about it?"*

And little Jonah answered: *"I'm working on it, Eric."*

Minerva accepted the phone from the security guard.

"Minerva Paradizo speaking."

"Minerva, this is Artemis Fowl," said a voice in perfect French. "We met once across a crowded room, in Sicily."

"I know who you are, we nearly met in Barcelona, too. And I know it's really you. I memorized your voice pattern and cadence from a lecture you gave on Balkan politics two years ago at Trinity College."

"Very good. I find it strange that I haven't heard of you."

Minerva smiled. "I am not as careless as you, Artemis. I prefer anonymity, until I have something exceptional to be recognized for."

"The existence of demons, for instance," prompted Artemis. "That *would* be exceptional."

Minerva gripped the phone tightly. "Yes, Master Fowl. It would be exceptional. It *is* exceptional. So you can keep your Irish paws off my research. The last thing I need is for some bigheaded teenage boy to hijack all my work at the last second. You had your own demon, but that wasn't enough. You had to try and steal mine, too. The moment I recognized you in Barcelona, I knew you would be after my research subject. I knew you would try to smoke us out, have someone hide in the car. It was the logical thing to do, so I booby-trapped the vehicle. You knocked out my baby brother, too. How could you?"

"Apparently I did you a favor," said Artemis lightly. "Little Bobo is obnoxious by all accounts."

"Is that why you called me? To insult my family?"

"No," replied Artemis. "I do apologize, that was juvenile. I called you to try and make you see sense. There is much more at stake here than a Nobel Prize, not to belittle the prize, of course."

Minerva smiled knowingly. "Artemis Fowl, whatever your pretence, you called me because your plan failed. I have your demon, and you want her back. But if it makes you feel better, please proceed with your good-of-humanity speech."

Outside, on the bluff overlooking Chateau Paradizo, Artemis frowned. This girl reminded him a lot of himself eighteen months ago, when achievement and acquisition were everything, and family and friends were secondary. Honesty, on this occasion, actually was the best policy.

"Miss Paradizo," he said gently. "Minerva. Listen to me for a few moments; you will feel the truth of what I say."

Minerva tutted. "Why is that? Because we're connected?"

"Actually, we are. We are similar people. Both the most intelligent person in whatever room we happen to be in. Both constantly underestimated. Both determined to shine brightest in whichever discipline we pursue. Both dogged by scorn and loneliness."

"Ridiculous," scoffed Minerva, but her protestations rang hollow. "I am not lonely. I have my work."

Artemis persisted. "I know how it feels, Minerva. And let me tell you, no matter how many prizes you win, no matter how many theorems you prove, it will not be enough to make people like you."

"Oh, spare me your amateur psychology lecture. You're not even three years older than I am."

Artemis was injured. "Hardly amateur. And for your information, age is often detrimental to intelligence. I have written a paper on the subject in *Psychology Today*, under the pseudonym Dr. C. Niall DeMencha."

Minerva giggled. "I get it, senile dementia. Very good."

Artemis himself smiled. "You are the first person to get that."

"I always am."

"Me too."

"Don't you find that tiresome?"

"Incredibly. I mean, what is wrong with people? Everybody says that I have no sense of humor, then I construct a perfectly sound pun around a well-known psychological condition, and it is ignored. People should be rolling in the aisles."

"Absolutely," agreed Minerva. "That happens to me all the time."

"I know. I loved that Murray Gell-Mann kidnapping a quark joke that you did on the train. Very clever analogy."

The congenial conversation ground to a frosty halt.

"How did you hear that? How long have you been spying on me?"

Artemis was quietly stunned. He had not meant to reveal that fact. It was most unlike him to chatter on about trifles when there were lives at stake. But he liked this Minerva girl. She was so similar to him.

"There was a security camera in the corridor, on the train. I procured the tape, had it enhanced, and read your lips."

"Hmm," said Minerva. "I don't remember a camera."

"It was there. Inside a red plastic bubble. Fish-eye lens. I apologize for the intrusion of your privacy, but it was an emergency."

Minerva was silent for a moment. "Artemis. We could have a lot to talk about. I haven't talked this much with a boy in . . . well, ever. But I have to finish this project. Can you call me again in six weeks?"

"Six weeks will be too late. The world will be a different place and possibly not a better one."

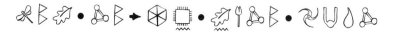

"Artemis. Stop it. I was just beginning to like you, and now we're back to where we started."

"Just give me one more minute," Artemis insisted. "If I can't convince you in a single minute, then I will hang up and leave you to your research."

"Fifty-nine," said Minerva. "Fifty-eight . . ."

Artemis wondered if all girls were so emotional. Holly could be this way, too. Warm one moment and icy the next.

"You are holding two creatures captive. Both sentient. Neither human. If you expose either one to the wider scientific community, then their kind will be hunted down. You will be responsible for the extinction of at least one species. Is that what you want?"

"That's what they want," retorted Minerva. "The first one we rescued threatened to kill us all, and possibly eat us. He said that the demons would return and wipe out the human scourge."

"I know all about Abbot," said Artemis, using what he had learned from Minerva's own surveillance cameras. "He was a dinosaur. Demons could never take on humans now. Judging by my temporal calculations, Abbot was whisked ten thousand years into his own future and then sent back again. Declaring war on demons would be like declaring war on monkeys. In fact, monkeys would be a bigger threat. There are more of them. And anyway, the demons can't even fully materialize unless we shoot them full of silver."

"I am sure they will find a way around that. Or one could get through accidentally, just like Abbot, then open the gates for the rest of them."

"Highly unlikely. I mean, really, Minerva, what are the odds?"

"So, Artemis Fowl wants me to forget all about my Nobel project and turn my demon captives loose."

"Forget the project, certainly," said Artemis, checking his watch. "But I don't think there is any need for you to set your captives free."

"Oh, really? And why is that?"

"Because, I imagine they are already gone."

Minerva spun around to face the spot where N°1 had been sitting. It was empty; her captive demon had disappeared along with his chair. A perfunctory sweep told her the entire room was empty, except for her.

"Where is he, Artemis?" she screamed into the phone. "Where is my prize?"

"Forget about all of this," said Artemis softly. "It's not worth it. Take it from someone who has made your mistakes. I will call you soon."

Minerva squeezed the phone as though it were Artemis's neck.

"You tricked me!" she said, the truth suddenly dawning on her. "You *allowed* me to capture your demon!"

But Artemis did not reply. He had reluctantly closed his fist on the conversation. Generally, outsmarting someone

gave him a warm and fuzzy feeling, but hoodwinking Minerva Paradizo just made him feel like a sneak. It was ironic that he felt like a bad guy, now that he was almost a good guy.

Butler glanced across at him from his perch on the knoll.

"How did that go?" he asked. "Your first lengthy conversation with a girl your own age."

"Fabulous," said Artemis, his voice dripping with sarcasm. "We're planning a June wedding."

CHAPTER 9: **TURNED TABLES**

Chateau Paradizo

When Holly Short had opened the door of her makeshift basement cell, she had found her helmet bouncing on the spot in front of her with a 3-D image of Foaly's face projected onto it.

"That is really creepy," she said. "Couldn't you just text me?"

Foaly had included a 3-D help program in Holly's helmet's computer. It came as no surprise to Holly that he had given the help module his own features.

"I've lost some weight since this model was constructed," said Foaly's image. "I've been jogging. Every evening."

"Focus," Holly ordered.

Holly dipped her chin and Foaly bounced the helmet onto her head. She sealed it tight.

"Where is the demon?"

"Straight up the stairs. Second door on the left," answered Foaly.

"Good. You've wiped our patterns from the security system?"

"Of course. The demon is invisible, and you can't be picked up, no matter what kind of lens they use."

Holly jumped up the human-size steps. It would have been easier to fly, but she had left her wings outside, along with her suit computer. There had been no need to risk placing them in human hands, other than Artemis's. And even that had taken a little thinking about.

She hurried along the corridor, past the first door on the left, and crept through the open doorway of the second, taking in the situation with a quick scan of the room.

The demon was secured on a chair, and the human girl was on the phone facing away from him. There was a large two-way mirror on the wall. Holly used her thermal scan to ascertain that the adjoining room had one occupant, a large male. He appeared to be talking on his cell phone, not facing the demon's cell.

"Should I stun the girl?" asked Foaly hopefully. "She knocked you out with sleeping gas." He was quite enjoying playing with his new toy. It was like a first-person computer game.

"I wasn't actually unconscious," said Holly, her words contained by the helmet's seal. "I was holding my breath. Artemis had told me that she would use gas. The first thing I did was vent the vehicle."

"What about that Mud Man next door?" persisted Foaly. "I can focus the laser through the glass. It's quite clever, really."

"Shut up or you will pay for it when I get home," warned Holly. "We only shoot in an emergency."

Holly skirted Minerva, careful to avoid brushing against the Mud Girl or treading on a loose board. A single creak now could scupper all their plans. She squatted before the little demon, who did not seem too worried about his plight. What he was actually doing was listing off words, and having a little giggle after every one.

"'Cornucopia,' oh, very good," he said. And then. "'Sanitary.' I like that one. Hee-hee."

Marvelous, thought Holly. This demon obviously lost a few brain cells in the transfer. She used voice command to type a text on her visor.

"Nod if you can read this," the text read. To the demon, the words appeared floating in space before him.

"'Nod if you can . . .'" he mouthed, then stopped and began nodding furiously.

"Stop nodding!" sent Holly. "I am an elf. One of the

216

First Family of fairies. I am here to rescue you. Do you understand?"

No response, so Holly sent a command. "Nod once if you understand."

A single nod from the demon.

"Good. All you need to do is stay very still and quiet."

Another nod. The little demon was catching on.

Foaly had transferred his image to the inside of Holly's visor.

"Ready?" asked the centaur.

"Yep. You keep an eye on the Mud Man next door. If he turns around, then you can stun him."

Holly wiggled her hand up her right sleeve, pincering a sheet of foil between her index and middle fingers. This is not as easy as it sounds, when a fairy is shielded and vibrating at speeds faster than the human eye could follow. It was made easier by the Section 8 suit, which reduced the amount of vibration necessary. Holly pulled out and unfolded a large square of cam-foil that automatically projected a fair approximation of what should be behind it. Each bead on the cam-foil was actually a fairy-made multifaceted diamond that could reflect accurately no matter what the viewing angle was.

She backed up close to N°1, then held up the sheet of foil. The foil was equipped with multisensor techno-logy, so it was a simple matter for Foaly to wipe N°1 from the projection. To Minerva it would seem that

her demon captive had simply vanished. To Nº1 it would seem like nothing whatsoever was happening, and that this was the lamest rescue in the history of rescues.

Seconds later, Minerva turned quickly to face them.

Nº1 nodded hello, and was amazed to find that Minerva could not see him.

"Where is he, Artemis?" the girl screamed into her phone. "Where is my prize?"

Nº1 thought about saying *I'm right here!* but decided against it.

"You tricked me!" squealed Minerva. "You *allowed* me to capture your demon!"

Finally the penny drops, thought Holly. Now go and search the chateau like a good girl.

Minerva obligingly stalked out of the room, yelling for her father. Next door, Papa Paradizo, hearing his daughter's screams, closed his phone, and began to turn . . .

Foaly activated the helmet laser and shot him in the chest. He tumbled to the floor and lay in a heap, his chest heaving with the slow breaths of the unconscious.

"Sweet," crowed the centaur. "Did you see that? Not so much as a smudge on the glass."

"He was heading for the door!" objected Holly, dropping the cam-foil.

"He was coming to the glass. I had to stun him."

"We will talk about this later, Foaly. I do not like your new gung-ho attitude."

"Caballine likes me to be masterful. She calls me her stallion."

"Who? Listen, just stop talking!" hissed Holly, melting N°1's bonds with two sharp laser bursts.

"Free!" exclaimed the imp, jumping to his feet. "Liberated. Unbound. Without restrictions."

Holly shut off her shield and revealed herself to N°1.

"I hope that's a helmet," said N°1.

Holly touched a button and her visor slid up. "Yes. I am a fairy, just like you. Only from a different family."

"An elf!" exclaimed N°1 delightedly. "An actual elf. I hear you cook your food, and like music. Is that true?"

"Occasionally, when we're not trying to escape from murderous humans."

"Oh, they're not murderous, pugnacious, homicidal, or even bellicose."

"Maybe not the one you met. But there's a guy with funny hair in the basement. And believe me, when he wakes up he's going to be murderous and all those other things you mentioned."

N°1 remembered Billy Kong; he had no desire to meet him again.

"Very well, elf. What next?"

"Call me Holly."

"I am N°1. So what next, Holly?"

"Next, we escape. There are friends waiting for us . . . eh . . . N°1."

• ⚜ ꝋ ⊛ • ⋃ ⟩ ◊ • ⊙ ♗ ◊ • ⚸ • ꝋ ♗ ◊

"Friends?" said N°1. He knew the word, of course, but never imagined it could apply to him. It was a warming notion, even in these dire straits.

"What do I do?"

Holly wrapped the cam-foil around him like a shawl.

"Keep this on. It will cover most of you."

"Amazing," said N°1. "A cloak of invisibility."

Foaly moaned in Holly's ear. "A cloak of invisibility? That is a highly sensitive piece of field equipment. What does he think? Some warlock pulled it out of his armpit?"

Holly ignored the centaur, something that was becoming a habit.

"Hold the foil close with one hand. Hang on to my belt with the other. We need to get out of here quickly. I only have enough magic left for a few minutes' shielding. Ready?"

N°1's anxious features peeped out from the shawl of invisibility.

"Hold the foil. Hang on to the belt. Got it."

"Good. Foaly, watch our backs. Let's move out."

Holly shielded, then hurried out the open door, pulling N°1 behind her. The corridor was lined with tall potted plants and lush oil paintings, including a Matisse. Holly could hear the humans shouting in adjacent rooms. There was activity all around them, and it could only be seconds before some Mud Men spilled into this corridor.

Nº1 struggled to keep up, his little legs stumbling along behind the super-fit elfin captain. It seemed impossible that they could escape. All around was the clatter of approaching footsteps. Nº1, slightly distracted, snagged his toe on the cam-foil and trampled it underfoot. The foil's electronics crackled and died. The demon was as visible as a bloodstain on a patch of snow.

"We lost the foil," said Foaly.

Holly clenched her fingers. She missed her handgun.

"Okay. Nothing to do but make a run for it. Foaly, you have free rein, if you'll pardon the horse analogy."

"Finally," whinnied the centaur. "I added a gamepod joystick to my controls. A bit unorthodox, but very accurate. We've got hostiles converging from all sides. My advice is to take the direct route. Go to the end of the corridor and follow our friend Doodah's path out the window. Butler will cover you once you're in the open."

"Okay. Hold on, Nº1. Whatever happens, don't let go."

The first threat came from ahead. Two security guards rounded the corner, guns extended.

Ex-police, Holly guessed. *Covering the diagonals*.

The men were shocked to see Nº1. Obviously they were not in the need-to-know loop.

"What the hell?" said one.

The other kept his nerve. "Hold it right there."

Foaly hit them both in the chest with fat laser bursts. The energy sank through their clothes and they slid down the wall.

"Unconscious," panted N°1. "Comatose, cataleptic, out for the count." He realized that this vocabulary spouting was a good way to deal with stress.

"Stress. Pressure, strain, and anxiety."

Holly dragged them both onward, toward the still-open window. More guards came from the side corridors, and Foaly dispatched them efficiently.

"I should get bonus points for this," he said. "Or at the very least a free life."

There were two more guards in the sitting room, sneaking an espresso. Foaly dropped them where they stood, and then flashed out a fan laser burst to evaporate the coffee before it hit the rug.

"It's Tunisian," he explained. "Very difficult to get coffee out. Now they can just suck up the grains."

Holly stepped down into the room.

"Sometimes I think you don't quite get the gravity of field missions," she said, skirting a massive velvet sofa.

N°1 stumbled down the human-size steps after his rescuer. In spite of all his new vocabulary, the imp was not quite sure how he was feeling.

Scared, of course. Big Mud Men with fire weapons and

222

all that. Excited, too. Being rescued by some kind of elf superhero, who was invisible, too. Pain in the leg, don't forget that. The angry human had shot him in the leg, with a silver bullet, no doubt. But N°1 realized that one feeling was missing from the melting pot. One that had been strong within him for as long as he could remember. Uncertainty. In spite of the frantic antics unfolding all around, he felt more at home on this planet than he ever had on Hybras.

A bullet whistled past his ear.

Then again, maybe Hybras hadn't been so bad.

"Wake up, Foaly!" admonished Holly. "You're supposed to be watching our backs."

"Sorry," said the centaur, swiveling the laser and strobing the doorway. The female guard smiled broadly then collapsed. On the ground she began singing a nursery rhyme about doggies and their bones.

"Bizarre," said Foaly. "That guard is singing."

"Often happens," grunted Holly, clambering onto the windowsill. "The laser knocks out some functions, but sometimes awakens others."

Interesting, thought the centaur. A happy gun. Certainly worth investigating.

Holly reached down and grasped N°1's wrist, pulling him over the sill. She was dismayed to see that her own arms were not as invisible as she would have hoped. Her magic was wearing thin. Shielding was a real power siphon. She would flicker into visibility soon, whether they were safely away or not.

"Nearly there," she said.

"Just across the wide-open green space, is it?" said N°1, displaying a real gift for sarcasm.

"I like him," said Foaly.

They tumbled out onto the lawn. The alarm was well and truly raised now, and guards poured from the various doors like beads from a ruptured beanbag.

"Go crazy, Foaly," said Holly. "And take out their vehicles, too."

"Yes sir, ma'am," said Foaly, and began firing.

Holly ran flat out, pulling the imp behind her. There was no time to consider his physical abilities; either he kept up or he got dragged. The laser pencil on her helmet flashed out burst after burst, swiveling in wide arcs to cover the approaching guards. Holly felt the weapon's heat on the crown of her head and resolved to mention the helmet's supposedly revolutionary cooling system to Foaly, if they ever made it out of this.

The centaur was too busy for chat now. All Holly could hear through her headset was grunting and whinnying as Foaly concentrated on his job. He was not concerned about pinpoint accuracy anymore; there were too many things to shoot. He sent out scything fans of energy that socked half a dozen guards per burst. The guards would be perfectly fine in half an hour, though some might experience headaches, hair loss, irritability, loss of bowel control, and other assorted side effects for a few days.

Foaly targeted the four-wheel drives next, firing several pulses into each petrol tank. The BMWs exploded in sequence, turning spectacular fiery cartwheels. The force of the blast cupped Holly and Nº1 like a giant hand, scooting them on their way a little faster. Holly's helmet protected her from the noise, but poor Nº1's head would ring for quite a while.

Thick black smoke billowed from cracked engines and prowled across the tended garden, more effective than any smoke grenade. Holly and Nº1 raced just ahead of the smoke line toward the main gates.

"Gates," Holly panted into her microphone.

"I see them," said Foaly, melting the wrought-iron barriers right off their hinges. They collapsed to the ground with a big bell bong.

A rented MPV skidded to a halt outside the pillars, and the passenger door slid open.

Artemis was inside, reaching out to Nº1.

"Come on," he said urgently. "Get in."

"Arrgh!" said Nº1. "A human!"

Holly leaped inside the vehicle, dragging Nº1 with her.

"It's okay," she said, switching off her shield to conserve the little magic that was left. "He's a friend."

Nº1 clung to Holly's back, trying not to throw up. He

glanced toward the front of the MPV to where Butler sat.

"What about him? Please tell me he's a friend, too."

Holly grinned, climbing into a seat. "Yes, he's a friend. The very best."

Butler yanked the gearshift into drive. "Buckle up, boys and girls. We're about to be in a car chase."

The sun was setting as Butler expertly steered the car around the natural chicanes of the Route de Vence. The road had been hewn from the mountainside, with stone villas teetering above and the Gorges du Loup yawning below. It took a skilled driver to negotiate the bends at speed, but Butler had once driven an Al Fahd armored vehicle through a crowded Cairo market, so the Alpine roads were not too much of a challenge for him.

As it turned out, there was no car chase. The Paradizo fleet lay in flaming, mangled, inverted heaps in the Chateau driveway. There was not so much as a moped left intact to tail the getaway car.

Butler checked the rearview mirror constantly, and only allowed himself a satisfied grin when they passed through the toll station at Cagnes sur Mer.

"We're clear," he pronounced, accelerating into the motorway's fast lane. "There's not a vehicle left intact on the estate, including little Beau's toy car."

Artemis smiled, giddy with success. "Perhaps we should have left them Mr. Day's marvelous booster."

☽ ◌ ∞ ◌ ∞ ⚹ ◌ • ◌ ◌ • ⚹ • ⚘ ⍓ ☊ ◌ • ⊗ ◌

Holly noticed that N°1 was happily examining his seat belt.

"Buckle up," she said, slotting the buckle into its catch.

"Buckle," said N°1. "Clasp, clip, fastener. Why are you with these humans?"

"They're going to help us," Holly explained gently.

N°1 had a million questions, and knew exactly how to phrase every one of them. But for the moment, words took a backseat to pictures, and N°1's square impish jaw dropped farther and farther as he stared through the tinted glass, absorbing the wonders of the modern motorway.

Holly took the opportunity to catch up with events.

"Doodah and Mulch got away okay?"

"Yes," confirmed Artemis. "Foaly was anxious to have the shuttle returned, as he had taken it without clearance. We shouldn't be more than a few hours behind them. By the time you get to the shuttleport, the shutdown should be lifted. I wouldn't be surprised if you've earned yourself a medal, Holly. Job spectacularly well done."

"There are still loose ends."

"True. But nothing an LEP mindwipe team can't take care of. There is no physical evidence that anything other than humans caused this devastation."

Holly leaned back against the seat. "I'm forgetting something."

"You're forgetting the demons. Their spell is disintegrating. Their island will be lost in time. Will be, or has been. They drift in and out of time, making contact like a bouncing ball."

Nº1 picked up on one word. "Disintegrating?"

"Hybras is doomed," said Artemis frankly. "Your home will shortly be dragged through the time tunnel along with everything on it. When I say *shortly*, I mean at our end. At your end it could have already happened, or maybe it will happen in a million years." He extended his hand. "And by the way, my name is Artemis Fowl."

Nº1 took the hand, nibbling the forefinger as was the demon custom.

"I am Nº1. Imp. Isn't there something we can do to save Hybras?"

"Hardly," replied Artemis, retrieving his finger and checking it for bite marks. "The only way to save Hybras is to bring it back to Earth under controlled circumstances. Sadly, the only people who could have done that were the warlocks, and they are all dead."

Nº1 chewed his lip. "Em, well, I'm not too sure, but I might be a warlock. I can speak in tongues."

Artemis sat forward, straining his seat belt. "Speaking in tongues could be merely an aptitude. What else can you do?"

"Again, not positive about this, but I may have, possibly, turned wood to stone."

"The gargoyle's touch. Now that is interesting. You know, Nº1, there's something about you. Those markings.

You seem familiar to me." Artemis frowned, irritated that he couldn't quite place the memory. "We haven't met before, I would certainly remember. Nevertheless, there is something . . ."

"These markings are quite common, especially the forehead hex. Demons often think they know me. Now, about saving Hybras?"

Artemis nodded. "Of course. The best course of action is to get you belowground. I only dabble in magical theory; Foaly has live experts just dying to examine you. I feel confident that the LEP can come up with a plan to save your island."

"Really?"

Butler interrupted from the front of the car, saving Artemis from answering.

"We have a bit of a situation at Chateau Paradizo," he said, tapping the screen of a compact laptop suckered to the dashboard. "Maybe you'd better take a look."

The bodyguard passed the computer over his shoulder. The screen was divided into a dozen boxes, the security feed from Chateau Paradizo still being supplied by Foaly's data twist.

Artemis balanced the laptop on his knees, his bright eyes flickering across the screen.

"Oh, dear," he said thoughtfully. "This is not good."

Holly swapped seats, so she could see the screen.

"Not good at all," she said.

Nº1 was not too worried about the computer. As far as he was concerned, it was just a little box.

"Not good," he mused, accessing the dictionary in his head. "A synonym for 'bad.'"

Artemis did not look up from the screen. "That's exactly right, Nº1. This is bad. *Very* bad."

CHAPTER 10: KONG THE KING

Chateau Paradizo

Minerva Paradizo was simply furious. That odious Fowl boy had somehow stolen her research subject from right under her nose. And after all the money Papa had spent on security, even hiring that despicable Mr. Kong. Sometimes Minerva wondered if all males were boors, except Papa, of course.

The grounds were a mess. Master Fowl had left quite a trail of destruction in his wake. The cars were so much scrap metal. The lawns were plowed deep enough to plant vegetables, and the stink of smoke and oil had penetrated every corner of every room of the chateau. Only a hurried phone call to the police station in Vence and a few improvised fabrications about a generator accident had prevented the arrival of a police car.

Once the fires were under control, Minerva called a staff meeting on the patio. Juan Soto, the security chief; her father, Gaspard; and of course, Billy Kong, were in attendance. Mr. Kong seemed more agitated than usual.

"Demons," muttered the Malibu native. "True, all true. I have a responsibility to my brother. Finish what he started."

If Minerva had been paying attention to Billy Kong's words, she might have noticed a touch of the ominous about them, but Minerva was busy worrying about her own problems. And in Minerva's opinion, her own problems were far more important than anyone else's.

"Can we focus here, everyone? You may have noticed that my project is in crisis."

Gaspard Paradizo had just about had it with Minerva's project. So far, he had indulged her to the tune of one and a half million euros, but now his entire estate had been trashed. It really was too much.

"Minerva, *cherie*," he said, smoothing back his silver hair. "I think we need to take a step back from this. Perhaps quit while we're not too far behind."

"Quit, Papa? Quit? While Artemis Fowl conducts a parallel project? I think not."

Gaspard spoke again, this time with a little iron in his tone. "You think not, Minerva?"

Minerva blushed. "Sorry, Papa. I am infuriated, that's

all. This Irish boy swans in here with his troops, and just like that, ruins all our work. It is unbearable, no?"

Gaspard was seated, as they all were, at a wrought-iron table on the rear patio overlooking the pool. He pushed back his chair and circled the table to his daughter's seat. From her vantage point there was a spectacular view over the wooded gorge and down into Antibes. Nobody was very interested in the view on this evening.

"I think, Minerva," he said, hunkering down beside her, "that we have gone too far in this matter. There are otherworldly forces at work here. Danger follows these creatures, and I can no longer allow you to place yourself, or others, in harm's way. We fought a noble fight, and I am so proud of you that my heart may burst; but now this must become a government matter."

"It can't, Papa," argued Minerva. "We have no records. No sources. Nothing. All our computer files and disks were destroyed. They drilled the safe and burned everything in it. I think Artemis Fowl even crashed Google and Yahoo. It's hopeless. How would it look, a little girl turning up at the department of defense chattering on about monsters in the basement? I need evidence."

Gaspard stood, his knees cracking. "Evidence, little one? These are not criminals. I watched you talk with our visitor. He was alert, intelligent, he had done nothing wrong. He was not an animal. It is one thing to present the Nobel committee with proof of an invasion through time, but quite another to hound innocent, sentient creatures."

"But, Papa!" Minerva pleaded. "One more try. I need a month to rebuild my time tunnel model, then I can make a materialization prediction."

Gaspard kissed his daughter on the forehead. "Look into your heart, my little genius. What does it tell you to do?"

Minerva scowled. "Look into my heart? Honestly, Papa, I am not a Care Bear."

"Please, *cherie*," said her father. "You know I love you, and I respect your genius, but just for once, couldn't we go with the pony option? Couldn't I just get Justin Timber-guy to play at your birthday party?"

Minerva fumed for several moments, but she knew Papa was right. She had no business detaining intelligent creatures. It was cruelty, nothing less. Especially when they intended no harm. But she could not just give up. Minerva silently resolved that Artemis Fowl would be her next project. She would find out all about the Irish boy, and what he knew of demons.

"Very well, Papa," she sighed. "For you, I will forego my Nobel prize. This year, at any rate."

Next year will be different, she thought. When I know what Artemis Fowl knows. There are whole worlds just beyond my grasp.

Gaspard embraced his daughter warmly. "Good. It is for the best."

⊳ • 🦀🐎🌙 • 🐚🐎🍵🪰⊳ ⊠ • ⚜ • 🦋⚜🍵

The French surgeon returned to his seat. "Now, Mr. Soto, damage report."

The Spanish security chief consulted his clipboard. "I have only a preliminary report, Monsieur Paradizo. I suspect we will be finding damage for many weeks. The vehicles are completely destroyed. Thankfully, we do have war-zone insurance, so we should have new cars within five working days. There is shrapnel in the pool. One piece pierced the skimmer and the wall, so we have a leak and no filtration. I know a man in Tourrettes sur Loup. Very reasonable, and he can keep his mouth shut."

"How about the men?"

Soto shook his head. "I don't know what they hit us with. Some kind of ray gun. Like Martians. Anyway, most of the men are up and about. A few have headaches. No other side effects, except for Thierry, who has spent the past half an hour in the bathroom. We hear the odd scream—"

Suddenly Billy Kong emerged from his mumbling daydream, slamming his palm onto the glass-topped iron table.

"No. This will not do. Absolutely not. I need another demon."

Gaspard frowned. "That unhappy experiment is over. I should never have allowed it. I was blinded by pride and ambition. There will be no more demons in this house."

"Unacceptable," said Kong, as though he were the

employer and not the employee. "Eric's work must be completed. I owe him that much."

"Now listen here, Mister," said Soto sternly. "What you find unacceptable is hardly an issue. You and your men were subcontracted to do a job, and that job does not include pronouncements on what is acceptable and what is not."

As he spoke, Kong checked his hair in the small mirror he carried everywhere. "You need to understand a few things, Paradizo. First, you are not in charge here. Not really. Not since my men and I joined your little group. Secondly, I don't generally work on this side of the law. My speciality is taking whatever I want by any means necessary. I only signed on for babysitting duty because I owe these demons a little payback. A lot of payback, actually. I know little Minerva just wanted to take photos of her guests and ask them a lot of psych questions, but I have my own plan for them. Something a little more painful."

Gaspard turned his head toward Soto. "Mr. Soto. Do you have a response to this outrageous statement?"

"I do indeed," blustered Juan Soto. "How dare you speak to Monsieur Paradizo in this fashion. You are an employee here, that is all. As a matter of fact, you are no longer an employee. Your contract is terminated. You have one hour to vacate your room and be off the premises."

Billy Kong's grin was as dangerous as a shark's. "Or else what?"

"Or else my guards will remove you. I would remind

you that there are only four men in your group and five times that number in mine."

Kong winked at him. "Perhaps. But my four are the best."

He flipped his jacket lapel to reveal a small clip-on microphone.

"I am moving up the schedule," he said into the mike. "Open the horse."

Soto was puzzled. *What was this idiot talking about? Horses?*

"Where did you get that microphone? Is that from the strongbox? Channels are to be kept clear for official transmissions."

But Minerva caught the *Iliad* reference. *Opening the horse* could only refer to the Wooden Horse of Troy. Kong had planted traitors in the camp.

"Papa," she said urgently. "We must leave."

"Leave? This is my house. I have agreed to almost everything you have asked of me, *cherie*, but this is ridiculous. . . ."

Minerva pushed back her chair and raced around the table.

"Please, Papa. We are in danger here."

Soto tutted. "Mademoiselle is in no danger. My men will protect you. Perhaps the strain of the day has made you irritable. Maybe you should take a nap."

Minerva scowled in frustration. "Can't you see what is

happening here? Mr. Kong has given a signal to his men. Possibly they are already in charge. He has come among us as a wolf in sheep's clothing."

Gaspard Paradizo was well aware of his daughter's intelligence. "Soto? Is this possible?"

"Impossible!" declared Juan Soto, but behind his enraged blush was a tinge of pallor. Something about Kong's grinning calmness unnerved him. And, truth be told, he was not quite the soldier that his résumé had declared him to be. True, he had spent a year with the Spanish peacekeeping force in Namibia, but he'd been attached to a journalist for the entire tour and had never participated in any action. He had got by in this job with mere bluster and a rudimentary knowledge of weaponry and tactics. But if someone were to come along who actually knew what he was talking about . . .

Soto reached to his belt, snicking off a walkie-talkie.

"Impossible," he repeated. "But to reassure you, I will double the guard and instruct my team to be on alert." He clicked the talk button. "Report in pairs. From the top."

Soto released the button, filling the air with static. The empty hiss seemed more ominous than a ghost's howl. This went on for several seconds. Soto tried valiantly to maintain a jaunty confidence, but was betrayed by a bead of sweat rolling down his forehead. "Equipment mal-function," he said weakly.

Billy Kong shook his head.

〰️⊗ • 𝄫 ⊚◗ • 〰️⊗ ⚹✿ • ⚹ • ⚙🕯️🦴𝄫

"Two shots," he said into his lapel mike.

Barely a second later, two sharp cracks echoed across the estate.

Kong grinned. "Confirmation," he said. "I'm in control here."

Soto had often wondered how he would react if faced with actual danger. Earlier, when he had believed that they were under siege, he had panicked slightly, but followed procedure. This was different.

Soto went for his gun. A practiced pistol man could do this without looking down. Soto was not practiced enough. By the time he glanced toward his holster, Kong had already leaped onto the table and knocked Soto unconscious.

The security chief keeled over backward with a dainty sigh.

Kong sat atop the table, elbows resting on knees.

"I need that demon back," he said, casually drawing a stiletto blade from a secret pocket in the sleeve of his jacket. "How do we find him?"

Gaspard Paradizo smothered Minerva in his arms, protecting every inch of his daughter.

"If you hurt her, Kong . . ."

Billy Kong rolled his eyes. "No time for negotiations, doctor."

He twirled the blade between his fingertips, then snapped his wrist, flicking the stiletto at Gaspard. The weapon's handle thunked against the doctor's forehead, and he fell away from Minerva like a discarded coat.

Minerva knelt, cradling her father's head. "Papa? Wake up, Papa." For a moment she was a little girl; then her intellect kicked in. She checked her father's pulse and tapped the point of impact with her index and middle fingers.

"You are lucky, Mr. Kong, not to be facing a murder charge."

Kong shrugged. "I've faced them before. It's amazing how easy it is to elude the authorities. It costs exactly ten thousand dollars. Three for the face job, two for new papers, and five for a really good hacker to create a computer past for you."

"Nevertheless, one more half revolution of your blade and my father would be dead, and not merely unconscious."

Kong pulled a second blade from his sleeve pocket. "There's still time. Now, tell me how we go about finding our little friend."

Minerva stood, facing Kong, her fists clenched defiantly.

"Listen to me, idiot. That demon is gone. I have no doubt that his benefactors plucked the silver bullet from his leg as soon as they had him in the car. He is back on his island. Forget about him."

Kong frowned. "It makes sense. That's what I would do. Well, okay then, when is the next materialization?"

Minerva should have been terrified. Her ability to do anything besides chatter and sob should have deserted her. After all, her father was lying unconscious, and the man who had put him in that state was sitting on her patio table brandishing a knife. But Minerva Paradizo was no ordinary twelve-year-old. She had always displayed remarkable composure in times of stress. So even though she *was* scared, Minerva was more than capable of communicating her scorn to Billy Kong.

"Where have you been for the past thirty minutes?" she asked, then snapped her fingers. "Of course, asleep. I believe you people call it *neutralized*. And by a tiny demoness too. Well, let me fill you in on what's happened. Our entire operation has been *neutralized*. I have no research, no calculations, and no subject. I am starting from scratch. In fact, I wish I was starting from scratch. Starting from scratch would be a dream come true. Last time I was handed the time tunnel calculations, this time I have to work them out by myself. Now, don't get me wrong, I could do it. I am a genius, after all, but it will take at least seventeen months. At the very least. *Comprenez-vous*, Monsieur Kong?"

Billy Kong understood, all right. He understood that this little pain in the rear was trying to blind him with science.

"Seventeen months, eh? How long if you had some incentive?"

$$\mathcal{X} \oplus \bullet \ominus \triangleright \rotatebox{180}{\mathcal{C}} \mathbb{D} \, \S \oplus \bullet \, \mathcal{X} \triangleright \mathcal{Z} \bullet \S \ominus \S \S \bullet \Diamond$$

"Incentive won't change the laws of science."

Kong leaped down from the table, landing soundlessly on the balls of his feet. "I thought that was your speciality, changing the laws of science. Wasn't this project all about proving how every other scientist in the world is a dummy, except you?"

"It's not that simple. . . ."

Kong began flipping his knife and catching it without so much as a glance at the blade. End over end it twirled, a silver fan in the air. Hypnotic.

"I'm making it simple. I think you *can* get me a demon, and I think you can do it in less than seventeen months. So here's what I am going to do." He leaned down and heaved Juan Soto's chair upright. The security chief slumped forward onto the table.

"I am going to hurt Mr. Soto. Simple as that. There is nothing you can do to stop that from happening. This is a demonstration of my earnestness. It connects you with the reality of your situation. And then you know I mean business. So after that, you start talking. And if you don't start talking, then we move on to lucky contestant number two."

Minerva had no doubt that contestant number two was her father.

"Please, Mr. Kong, there is no need for any of this. I am telling you the truth."

"Oh, it's *please* now, is it?" said Kong in mock surprise.

"And *Mr. Kong*, too. What happened to *idiot* and *moron*?"

"Don't kill him. He's a nice man. He has a family."

Kong grabbed a bunch of Soto's hair and yanked his head back. The chief's Adam's apple stuck out like a plum.

"He's an incompetent," snarled Kong. "Look how easily your demon escaped. See how simple it was for me to take over."

"Let him live," pleaded Minerva. "My father has money."

Kong sighed. "You're just not getting it, are you? For a smart girl you can be pretty stupid a lot of the time. I don't want money. I want a demon. Now stop talking and pay attention. There is no point in trying to negotiate."

Minerva's heart sank as she realized just how far out of her depth she actually was. In less than an hour she had crossed over to a world of darkness and cruelty. And her own arrogance had led her to it.

"Please," she said. She struggled to maintain her composure. "Please."

Kong adjusted his grip on the knife. "Don't look away now, little girl. Watch and remember who's boss."

Minerva could not avert her eyes. Her gaze was trapped by this terrible tableau. It was like a scene from a scary movie, complete with its own sound track.

Minerva frowned. Real life did not have a sound track. There was music coming from somewhere.

The somewhere proved to be Kong's trouser pocket. His polyphonic phone was playing the "Toreador Song" from *Carmen*. Kong pulled the phone from his pocket.

"Who is this?" he snapped.

"My name is not important," said a youthful voice. "The important thing is that I have something you want."

"How did you get this number?"

"I have a friend," replied the mystery caller. "He knows all the numbers. Now, to business. I believe you're in the market for a demon?"

Minutes earlier, Butler had pulled off the motorway at the airport exit and had crammed himself into the backseat beside Artemis and Holly. They had watched the drama unfold in Chateau Paradizo on their tiny laptop.

Artemis gripped his knees tight. "I can't allow this. I won't allow it."

Holly placed a hand over his. "We have no choice, Artemis. We're clear now. This is not our fight. I can't risk exposing N°1."

Artemis's frown cut a line from his furrow to the bridge of his nose.

"I know. Of course. But still, how can this not be my fight?" He glanced sharply at Butler. "Will Kong kill those men?"

"Without a doubt," replied the bodyguard. "In his mind, it's already done."

Artemis rubbed his eyes, suddenly fatigued. "I am responsible, indirectly. I can't have a man's death on my conscience. Holly, you do what you have to do, but I need to save those people."

"Conscience," said N°1. "What a lovely word. The *sh* in the middle."

It was plain that the imp was not actually listening to the conversation, just picking up on certain words. The incongruity of this simple statement made Artemis look across toward the demon. His eyes rested for a moment on N°1's chest markings. And suddenly he knew where he had seen them before. A plan hit him like a bolt of lightning.

"Holly, do you trust me?"

Holly groaned. "Artemis, don't ask me that. I just know one of your outrageous plans is coming."

"Do you trust me?"

"Yes," Holly sighed. "I do. More than anyone."

"Well then, trust me to get us all out of this. I will explain later."

Holly was torn. This decision could affect the rest of her life, and the imp's too. And the effect could be to shorten them dramatically.

"Okay, Artemis. But I'll be watching."

Artemis spoke into his ring-phone. "Foaly, can you put me through to Mr. Kong's cell phone?"

"Not a problem," replied the centaur from Section 8 headquarters. "But it's going to be the last thing I do for you. Sool has tracked my line out. In thirty seconds

I'm going to be shut down, and you'll be on your own."

"I understand. Put me through."

Butler gripped Artemis's shoulder. "If you call him, then he has the upper hand. Kong will want to choose where to meet."

"I know where we should meet. I just have to convince Mr. Kong that the rendezvous point is his idea." Artemis closed his fist, covering the phone. "Quiet. It's ringing."

"Who is this?" snapped Kong.

"My name is not important," said Artemis. "The important thing is that I have something you want."

"How did you get this number?"

"I have a friend," replied the mystery caller. "He knows all the numbers. Now, to business. I believe you're in the market for a demon?"

"So, you must be the great Artemis Fowl. Minerva's idol. I am so sick of you smart kids. Why can't you just boost cars or steal stuff like normal kids?"

"We *do* steal stuff. Just *bigger* stuff. Now, are you interested in my demon or not?"

"I could be," said Kong. "What do you have in mind?"

"A straight trade. I pick a public place, and we swap. My demon for your girl."

"You're not picking anything, kid. I pick the rendezvous point. You called me, remember? What do you want with this girl anyway?"

"Her life," said Artemis simply. "I do not like murder, or

murderers. You and your crew walk out of there with one hostage, and we do a swap. It's a simple transaction. Don't tell me you've never released a hostage before."

"I'm an old hand, kid. I've been picking up ransoms for years."

"Good. I'm glad we can do business. Now why don't you name your preferred location. I'll be wearing a burgundy tie. Pay attention to that. There are a hundred and one ways this could go wrong. If it does, the police could tie one of us up for a long time."

In the getaway car, Holly frowned quizzically at Artemis. It wasn't like him to chatter. He calmed her with a look and a wave of his hand.

"Okay," said Kong. "I just thought of somewhere. You know Taipei 101?"

"In Taiwan?" said Artemis. "One of the world's tallest buildings? You are not serious. That's on the far side of the world."

"I am deadly serious. Taipei is my second home. I know it well. You will have a tough enough time getting there by the deadline, so there will be no tricks. We will exchange on the observation deck at twelve noon, two days from now. If you don't show, then the girl takes the express elevator down. If you see what I mean."

"I see. I'll be there."

"Good. Don't come alone. Bring the ugly guy with you, or the female. I don't care, I only need one."

"We have already released the female."

"Okay. The guy then. You see how easy it is to deal with me. I'm a reasonable man, unless I'm crossed. So don't cross me."

"Don't worry," said Artemis. "I won't."

And he said it with such conviction that, if you didn't know him, you would absolutely believe it.

CHAPTER 11: **A LOΠG WAY DOWΠ**

Taipei, Taiwan

Taipei 101 is among the tallest buildings in the world. Some say it is the tallest, if the sixty foot spire can be counted, but others argue that a spire is not a building, and so Taipei 101 can technically only be called the tallest *structure* in the world. In any event, there were four buildings in construction, two in Asia, one in Africa, and the fourth in Saudi Arabia, with their sights set on the world's tallest building crown. So Taipei's claim to fame could be a fleeting one.

Artemis and company landed at Chiang Kai-shek International Airport barely three hours before the deadline in a rented Lear jet. And though Butler was a registered pilot, qualified for day and night flying on

⊕ • ⁂ ☽ ⊕ • 👁 ▷ ୫ 🦀 • ❘ 👁 👁 ◊ • 🐚 🦒 ◊

various aircraft, it was Artemis who flew most of the way.

Flying helped him think, he claimed. Also, no one would interrupt while he put the finishing touches to his audacious plan. Artemis was fully aware of the risks involved with this particular scheme. The pivotal element was purely theoretical and the rest was highly risky.

He briefed the others on the details in the back of a rented Lexus on the forty-minute drive from the airport to downtown Taipei. The entire group looked drained, even though they had eaten and rested on the plane. Only N°1 was in high spirits. Everywhere he looked there were new wonders to be gaped at, and he could not imagine that anyone would be able to injure him while he was under Butler's protection.

"The bad news is that we are running close to the deadline," said Artemis. "So there will be no time to set a trap."

"And the good news, Artemis?" said Holly grumpily. She was grumpy for a few reasons. She was dressed as a human girl because Artemis had asked her to save her magic for when it would be needed. She had managed to boost her magical energy by burying a sealed acorn she kept around her neck, but there had been no full moon so her power reserves were limited. Also, she was completely shut off from the People, and to top it all off, she had no doubt that Ark Sool would have her up on charges if any of them did manage to survive the trade-off. After all, she had brought N°1 halfway across the world instead of escorting him safely to Haven City.

"The good news is that Kong can't be too far ahead of us, so it is unlikely he had time to set up any traps either."

The Lexus entered the Xinyi District, and Taipei 101 rose from the cityscape like a giant bamboo shoot. The buildings around it seemed to shrink back in awe.

Butler craned his head back to see the top of the sixteen hundred–plus feet building. "We never do anything small, do we? Why can't we for once have a meeting in a Starbucks?"

"I didn't pick this building," said Artemis. "It picked us. Fate has brought us here."

He tapped Butler on the shoulder, and the bodyguard pulled over into the first space he could find. It took several minutes. Taipei morning traffic was thick and slow-moving and spewed smoke like an irritated dragon. Many of the thousands of pedestrians and cyclists had smog masks strapped across their faces.

When the vehicle stopped, Artemis continued his briefing.

"Taipei 101 is a miracle of modern engineering. The architects took their inspiration from the humble bamboo. But this shape alone does not keep the skyscraper steady in the event of an earthquake or high winds, so the designers built it on a frame of concrete-filled steel-boxed super columns, and installed a seven hundred–ton steel ball as a mass damper pendulum to absorb the force of the wind. Ingenious. The pendulum swings instead of the building. It's become quite the tourist attraction. You can even watch it from the observation deck. The owners have covered the damper with six inches of solid silver, which have been etched by the famous Taiwanese artist Alexander Chou."

"Thanks for the fine-art lesson," interrupted Holly. "Now how about you let us in on your plan. I want to get this over with and take off this ridiculous tracksuit. It's so shiny, I feel sure I can be picked up on satellite."

"I don't much like this outfit either," complained N°1, who was dressed in an orange floral muumuu. Orange, he had decided, was definitely not for him.

"Your outfit is the least of your worries," noted Holly. "I'm guessing that we're about to hand you over to a bloodthirsty hit man, eh, Artemis?"

"That we are," confirmed Artemis. "But only for a few seconds. There will be little or no danger to you. And if my suspicions are correct, it is just possible that we may save Hybras."

"Go back to me being in danger for a few seconds," said N°1, his thick brow folding in a frown. "In Hybras, a few seconds can last a very long time."

"Not here," said Artemis, in what he hoped was a reassuring tone. "Here *a few seconds* is how long it will take you to open your hand."

N°1 experimentally opened his fingers a couple of times. "That's still pretty long. Any way to cut it down?"

"Not really. If we do, it means sacrificing Minerva."

"Well, she did tie me to a chair." N°1 glanced around at the shocked faces. "What? I'm joking. Of course I'll do it. But no more orange. Please."

Artemis smiled, but it did not quite reach his eyes. "Very well, no more orange. Now, the plan. It is in two parts. If the first part doesn't work, then the second is redundant."

"Redundant," said N°1 almost unconsciously. "Not needed, superfluous."

"Exactly. So I'll explain that when necessary."

"What about the first part?" asked Holly.

"In the first part, we meet a vicious hit man and his band of thugs, and he will expect us to hand over N°1."

"So what do we do?"

"We hand over N°1," said Artemis. He turned to the slightly nervous imp. "How do you like the plan so far?"

"Well, I don't like the first bit and I don't know the last bit. So I'm really hoping the middle bit is exceptional."

"Don't worry," said Artemis. "It is."

Taipei 101

The group took a high-speed elevator from Taipei 101's cavernous lobby to the observation floor. Holly and N°1 had technically been given permission to enter the building by a small plaque over the main door that simply urged visitors to come and go as they pleased. And seeing as she did not feel the urge to throw up in the elevator, Holly guessed that the plaque counted as an invitation.

"Toshiba elevators," said Artemis, reading from a pamphlet he had picked up at information. "These are the fastest elevators in the world. We are moving at fifty-five feet per second, so it shouldn't take much more than half a minute to reach the eighty-ninth floor."

Artemis consulted his watch when the doors dinged open.

"Hmm. Right on time. Impressive engineering. I may get one of these for the house."

They stepped out into the observation area, which had a restaurant at the far end. From this lofty vantage point, visitors could walk all the way around the building and shoot video of the panoramic view. From this height it was even possible to see China across the Taiwan Strait.

For a moment the group forgot their worries and allowed themselves to be awestruck by the grace of this enormous structure. The sky outside the window blended almost seamlessly with the sea on the horizon. N°1 was especially dumbfounded. He turned in small circles, the muumuu swishing around his legs.

"Less of the pirouetting, little man," advised Butler, the first to get his mind back on the job. "You're showing your legs. And pull that bonnet down over your face."

N°1 obliged, though he was not happy with the bonnet. It was shapeless and saggy, and made his head look like a bag of laundry.

"Good luck, Holly," said Artemis into thin air. "We will meet you on the twenty-third floor."

"Get this done as quickly as you can," Holly whispered into his ear. "I don't have enough magic for a long shield. I'm barely invisible as it is."

"Understood," said Artemis from the side of his mouth.

The small band walked slowly toward the bar area and took a table below the enormous mass damper suspended a few feet above the eighty-eighth floor. The seven hundred-ton ball was a sight to behold, like an indoor moon, its surface etched with traditional Yuanzhumin drawings.

"This is the legend of Nian," explained Artemis casually, while Butler scanned the room. "A ferocious beast that would feed on human flesh each New Year's eve. To scare Nian away torches were lit and firecrackers were set off, because Nian was known to fear the color red. Thus the splashes of red paint. It seems likely from the pictures that Nian was actually a troll. Chou must have based his work on contemporary accounts."

A waitress came to their table.

"*Li ho bo*," said Artemis. "Can we have a pot of oolong tea. Organic if you have it."

The waitress blinked at Artemis, then looked up at Butler, who was still standing.

"You are Mr. Fowl?" she asked, in excellent English.

"*I* am *Master* Fowl," said Artemis, tapping the table for attention. "Do you have something for me?"

The waitress passed him a napkin.

"From the gentleman at the bar," she said.

Artemis glanced down the arc of the metal railing and buffer system that kept patrons away from the mass damper, and more important, kept the mass damper away from them.

Billy Kong was seated a dozen tables down, waggling his eyebrows in their direction. He was not alone. No one else was eyebrow waggling, but three men were at the table with him, and several others were dotted around the bar area. Minerva was on Kong's knee. He held her fast by the forearm. Her shoulders were tense but there was defiance in the set of her mouth.

"Well?" Artemis said to Butler.

"At least twelve," replied the bodyguard. "Billy must have friends in Taiwan."

"None of them invisible, thank goodness," said Artemis, opening the napkin.

Send the creature to the reserved table, read the message on the napkin. *I will send the girl. No tricks or people will get hurt.*

He passed the napkin to Butler. "What do you think?"

Butler gave the message a summary glance. "I think he

won't try anything here. Too many cameras. If security doesn't get him on film, a tourist will. If Kong goes for a double cross, it will be outside."

"And by then it should be too late."

"So we hope."

The waitress returned with a bamboo tray, bearing a clay pot of tea and three glasses. Artemis took his time pouring himself some of the steaming liquid.

"How are you feeling, Nº1?"

"My leg hurts a bit."

"The painkiller is wearing off. I'll ask Butler to give you another shot later. Are you ready to go? Everything will be fine, I assure you."

"All I have to do is open my hand?"

"As soon as we're in the elevator."

"That's it. Do you want me to distract the bad man with some witty banter, like you do with Holly?"

"No. That won't be necessary. Just open your hand."

"Should I look scared?"

"That would be appropriate."

"Good. Shouldn't be a problem."

Butler was functioning in full-action mode. Generally, he reined himself in, walking with a slight stoop to avoid drawing attention. But now he stood tall and tensed, ready to spring into action. His gaze was fierce, and muscles bulged in his neck. He caught Billy Kong's gaze and zeroed in on his eyeballs. Even across a crowded room, the hostility was palpable. A couple of psychically sensitive bystanders suddenly felt anxious and cast their eyes about for the nearest restroom.

When he was finished staring down Billy Kong, Butler knelt to give final instructions to N°1.

"All you have to do is walk down to that table with the reserved sign. Wait until Minerva gets there, then continue on to Kong. If they hustle you out straightaway, count to twenty then open your hand. If they wait for us to leave, open your hand when the elevator doors have closed. Understand?"

"I understand everything. In any language you care to speak in."

"Are you set?"

N°1 took a deep breath. He could feel his tail vibrating anxiously. He had been in a bit of a daze since the time tunnel. How could anyone take all of this in? Skyscrapers, for heaven's sake. Buildings that actually scraped the sky.

"I'm set," he said.

"Off you go, then. Good luck."

N°1 began his long lonely walk back into captivity. Scores of humans thronged around him, excited, sweating, chewing things, pointing machines at one another.

Those would be cameras, I suppose.

The noon sun flashed through the ceiling-to-floor windows, catching on the silver of the mass damper, lighting it up like a disco ball. The tabletops loomed just above head height. Waiters and waitresses bustled past with loaded trays. Glasses fell, children screamed.

Too many people, thought N°1. I miss demons. Even Abbot. Well, okay, maybe not Abbot.

N°1 reached the reserved table. He had to stand on tippytoes to see the folded piece of card with the word printed on it. He lifted the flap on his bonnet to get a clear look. He was beginning to realize that a muumuu and bonnet were not typical Mud Child garb, as Artemis had told him.

This is a terrible disguise. I look like a freak. Surely someone will see that I am not human. I wish I could shield, like Holly.

Unfortunately, even if N°1 could control his burgeoning magical powers, shielding had never been a weapon in the demon warlock arsenal.

N°1 took a step to the right, squinting past the glare of the giant mass damper. Minerva was on her way down, taking small careful steps toward the reserved table. Behind her, Kong leaned forward in his seat, toes tapping with excitement and anticipation. He was like a dog on a leash with the scent of a fox in his nose.

Minerva arrived. She lifted the brim of N°1's bonnet to check it was him.

"It's not my bonnet," said N°1. "And this is certainly not my muumuu."

Minerva took his hand. Before the abduction she had been eighty percent genius and twenty percent twelve-

〰 symbols 〰

year-old girl. Now it was about fifty-fifty. "I'm sorry for everything. For tying you up, and the rest. I thought you would try to eat me."

"We're not all savages," said Nº1. "And my wrists did hurt for ages. But I forgive you, I suppose. As long as your tying-up days are over."

"Over. Yes. I promise." Minerva looked over Nº1's head toward Artemis's table. "Why is he helping me? Do you know?"

Nº1 shrugged. "I'm not sure. Holly, our friend, said it was something about puberty. Apparently you're pretty, though to be honest, I can't see it myself."

Their conversation was interrupted by a whistle from farther down the bar. Billy Kong was growing impatient. The ex-Paradizo employee beckoned Nº1 on with his index finger.

"I should go. Leave. Depart."

Minerva nodded. "Okay. Be careful. I will see you soon. Where is it? In your hand?"

"Yes," said Nº1 automatically, then, "how did you know?"

Minerva walked on slowly. "Genius. Can't help it."

This place is littered with genii, thought Nº1. I just hope Mr. Kong isn't another one.

He continued on his way, being careful to keep his feet and hands inside the muumuu. The last thing he wanted to do was cause a panic by exposing his gray stumpy digits.

Although, perhaps the humans would bow down and adore him. After all, he was incredibly handsome compared to their own gangly males.

Billy Kong was all smiles when N°1 reached the table. On *his* face, a smile looked like the first symptom of a disease. His hair was spiked in perfect points. Even in the middle of a kidnapping, Kong still made time for his hair. Good grooming says a lot about a person.

"Welcome back, demon," he said, grabbing a hank of the muumuu. "So nice to see you. If it is you. . . ."

"If it is me?" said N°1, confused. "Me is all I can be."

"Excuse me if I don't take your word for it," snorted Kong, tugging back the bonnet frill for a quick peek at N°1's face. "If that Fowl kid is half as smart as I've heard, then he's sure to be trying something."

Kong examined the imp's face, poking the plate on his forehead, pulling back his lips to check the pink gums and square white teeth. Finally he traced the rune on N°1's forehead with his finger to make sure it wasn't painted on.

"Satisfied?"

"Pretty much. I guess little Artemis didn't have time to do a switch. I ran him too hard."

"You ran us all too hard," complained N°1. "We had to fly here in a machine. I saw the moon close up."

"You're breaking my heart, demon. After what you did to my brother, you're lucky to be alive. Something I hope to remedy in the next few minutes."

N°1 twisted his head to catch a glimpse of the elevators. Artemis, Butler, and Minerva were two steps away from the doors.

"Don't look at them. They can't help you. Nobody can help you."

Kong clicked his fingers, and a muscular man joined them at the table. He was hefting a large metal suitcase.

"In case you're wondering, this is a bomb. You know what a bomb is, don't you?"

"Bomb," said N°1. "Explosive. Incendiary device." His eyes widened. "But that could hurt someone. A lot of someones."

"Exactly. Not humans, though. Demons. I am going to strap this on to you, set the timer, then send you back to your island. The blast should at the very least put a big dent in the demon population. You won't be crossing over here for your little nighttime hunts for quite a while."

"I won't do it," said N°1, actually stamping his foot.

Kong laughed. "Are you sure you're a demon? From what I hear, the last one was more . . . demonic."

"I am a demon. A warlock demon."

Kong leaned close enough for N°1 to smell his citrus aftershave. "Well, little Mr. Warlock, maybe you can turn this bomb into a bunch of flowers, but I doubt it."

"I don't have to do anything, because you can't make me go back to Hybras."

Kong took a set of handcuffs from his pocket. "On the

contrary. I know exactly what to do. I picked up a thing or two in the Chateau. All we have to do is dig that silver slug out of your leg, and Hybras will suck you home."

N°1 glanced again toward the elevator. The doors were closing on his new friends.

"You mean this silver slug?" he asked, showing Kong what had been concealed in his hand.

"He took it out," breathed Billy Kong. "Fowl took out the slug."

"Took it out," agreed N°1. "Extracted. Removed."

Then he dropped the silver nugget and disappeared.

Holly had been crouched on the mass damper watching events unfold. So far, everything had gone according to plan. Minerva had reached Artemis, and Butler had hustled them both to the elevator. At the other end of the bar, Billy Kong was doing his whole grinning-psycho bit. When this was all over, that Mud Man would have to be mind-wiped. There would be quite a few loose ends to clear up, actually. Not by her, though; she was not LEP anymore. After this she would be lucky to be Section 8.

Holly tapped a button on her wrist computer, zooming in on N°1. The imp raised his left hand. The signal. This was it. Time to test theories. It was either hello again or good-bye forever.

Artemis's plan was a risky one because his calculations were theoretical, but it was the only chance to save the demon island. And Artemis had been right so far. If Holly had to rely on someone's theories, she would prefer those theories to be Artemis Fowl's.

As Holly watched N°1 drop the silver slug and disappear, she could not resist snapping a photo of Kong's face with her helmet camera. His reaction was priceless. They would have a good laugh over that later.

Then she activated her wings, rising above the giant silver ball, watching for signs.

Seconds later, a faint blue electrical rectangle began spinning at the silver ball's crown, exactly where Artemis had known it would. N°1 was coming back. Just as Artemis had predicted.

Such a large mass of silver within ten feet should interrupt N°1's journey home. It should cause a momentary materialization at the summit, where the damper's energy field is most concentrated. You, Holly, have to be there to make sure this momentary materialization becomes more permanent.

On the mass damper, N°1's shape was visible inside the glowing rectangle. He seemed a little confused, as though half asleep. One arm snaked through into this world, grasping at reality. It was enough for Holly. She darted down and clamped a silver bracelet around N°1's gray wrist. The ghostly fingers wiggled, then solidified. Solidity sped along N°1's arm like gray paint, rescuing him from limbo. In seconds, where there had only been space, now crouched a shivering creature.

"Did I go?" asked the little imp. "Am I back?"

"Yes and yes," said Holly. "Now stay quiet and still. We have to get you out of here."

The mass damper swung slowly, dissipating the wind power buffeting Taipei 101. Holly leaned into the sway, grabbed hold of N^o1, and took off vertically, careful to keep her cargo shielded by the seven hundred ton silver ball.

The next floor up was another observation deck, but it was closed for renovation. A single workman was slicing carpet for a corner section, and he did not seem surprised to see a muumuu-clad imp come sailing over the railing.

"Hey," he said. "It's an imp in a muumuu. You know something, imp?"

N^o1 landed on the floor with a thump. "No," he said cautiously. "Tell me something."

"I am not a bit surprised to see you," said the man. "In fact, you are so unremarkable, that I am going to forget all about you as soon as you've gone."

N^o1 picked himself up, straightening his bonnet. "You've had a talk with him, I see."

Holly switched off her shield and speckled into view. "I gave him a blast of the *mesmer*." She peered over the railing, down into the restaurant. "Come here, N^o1. You'll enjoy this."

N^o1 placed his fingers against the glass. Kong and his cronies were creating chaos below, blundering toward the elevators. Kong was particularly perturbed, barging tourists from his path and overturning tables.

"We probably don't have time for this," said N°1.

"Probably not," agreed Holly. Neither fairy moved.

"Hey, look," said the workman. "Another fairy. How utterly unremarkable."

Only when the Toshiba elevator doors had closed behind Billy Kong and his crew, did Holly turn to leave.

"Where to now?" asked N°1, wiping a happy tear from his eye.

"Now we go to stage two," replied Holly, pressing the button for the elevator. "Time to save Hybras."

"Never a dull moment," said N°1, scurrying into the metal box. "Hey, my first cliché."

Artemis and Butler had watched Minerva cross the restaurant toward them. She held herself with considerable courage under the circumstances. Her chin was up and she had a determined look in her eye.

"Butler, can I ask you something?" said Artemis.

Butler was trying to keep an eye on every single person in the restaurant.

"I'm a little busy at the moment, Artemis."

"Nothing taxing. Just a 'yes' or 'no' answer. Is it normal, during puberty, to feel these blasted feelings of attraction at stressful times? During a ransom drop, for instance."

266

"She's pretty, isn't she?"

"Extremely. And funny, too—remember that quark joke?"

"I do. We must have a talk about jokes someday. Perhaps Minerva could join us. And in response to your question, it *is* normal. The more stressful the situation, the more your body pumps out the hormones."

"Good. Back to business, then."

Minerva didn't rush. She picked her way around tourists and tables as she walked steadily toward them.

When she drew level, Butler placed a guiding and protective hand on her back.

"Get kidnapped every day, do you?" he growled, steering her toward the elevator.

Artemis followed, glancing back over his shoulder to make sure they were not being pursued. Kong was not even looking at them, so happy was he with his prize.

The elevator opened and the trio stepped inside. On the elevator wall, the floor light was rapidly winking downward.

Artemis held out his hand to Minerva. "Artemis Fowl the Second. Pleased to meet you finally."

Minerva shook his hand warmly. "Minerva Paradizo. Likewise. You gave up your demon for me. I do appreciate it." She blushed slightly.

The elevator slowed to a smooth stop, and the steel doors slid open with barely a hiss.

Minerva peeked out. "This is not the lobby. Why aren't we leaving?"

Artemis stepped out onto the fortieth floor. "Our work here is not finished. I need to get our demon back, and it's about time you knew what you almost went up against."

CHAPTER 12: **HEART OF STONE**

Taipei 101, 40th Floor, Kimsichiog Gallery

Artemis strode through the Kimsichiog Gallery lobby, flanked by Butler and Minerva.

"We're in an art gallery," said Minerva. "Do we really have time for art?"

Artemis halted, surprised. "There's always time for art," he said. "But we're here for a very special piece of art."

"Which is?"

Artemis pointed at painted silk banners hanging at regular intervals from the ceiling. Each banner was emblazoned with a single dramatic spiraling rune.

"I follow what is happening in the art world. This exhibition is of particular interest to me. The centerpiece is the remains of a fantastic sculpture. A semicircle of strange dancing creatures. Maybe ten thousand years old. Believed to have been found off the shore of Ireland, and yet here it is, in Taiwan, being exhibited by an American oil company."

"Artemis, why are we here? I need to get home to my father."

"Don't you recognize the rune? Haven't you seen it somewhere?"

Minerva remembered immediately. "*Mais oui! Certainement*. It is the rune from the demon's forehead. The very same."

Artemis snapped his fingers and continued walking.

"Exactly. When I met N°1, I knew his markings looked familiar. It took me a while to remember where I had seen them before, but once I knew, then it occurred to me that maybe this sculpture was not a sculpture at all."

Minerva's brain raced ahead. "It was the ring of warlocks. From the original time spell."

"Precisely. What if they were not blasted into space? What if one of them had had the quick thinking to use the gargoyle's touch, to turn them all to stone?"

"And if N°1 is a warlock, then he is the only one who can reanimate them."

"Very good, Minerva. You catch on quick. Young, quick, and arrogant. You remind me of someone. Who could that be?"

)⊕⊕♊⋓☏ • ℘♉⚹꜀ • ⚹⌅✈ • ⚹ • ◊

"Beats me," said Butler, rolling his eyes.

"But how did you set this up?" the French girl wondered aloud. "The meeting site was Kong's idea. I heard him on the phone."

Artemis smiled at his own cleverness. "While he was thinking about it, I said, 'I'll be wearing a burgundy *tie*. *Pay* attention to that. There are *a hundred and one* ways this could go wrong. If it does, the police could *tie one* of us up for a long time.' Do you see?"

Minerva plucked at a curl thoughtfully. "*Mon Dieu!* You used the power of suggestion. Tie pay. A hundred and one. Tie one."

"Or what Kong's subconscious heard: Taipei 101, Taiwan."

"Brilliant, Artemis. Extraordinary. And coming from me, that means something."

"It was brilliant," said Artemis, with his characteristic lack of modesty. "Allied to the fact that Kong's second home is Taiwan, I was reasonably confident that it would work."

There was a harried-looking man at the gallery's reception desk. He was dressed in a neon-blue suit, and his head was completely shaven, except for a spiral of stubble in the shape of N°1's rune. He spoke in rapid Taiwanese into a Bluetooth headset clipped to his ear.

"No, no. Salmon is not good enough. Squid and lobster are what we ordered. You have them here by eight o'clock, or I will come down there, slice you up, and serve you as sushi instead."

"Trouble with the caterers?" Artemis said pleasantly when the man had disconnected.

"Yes," replied the man. "The exhibition is opening tonight and . . ."

The man stopped because he had looked up to see who he was talking to and spotted Butler.

"Well, wow. Big. I mean hello. I am Mr. Lin, the curator here. Can I help you?"

"We were hoping for a private preview of the exhibition," said Artemis. "Specifically, the dancing figures."

Mr. Lin was so surprised, he could do little more than bluster. "What? A what? Private? No, no, no. Impossible, out of the question. This is important art. Look at my head. Look! I don't just do this for any old exhibition."

"I realize that, but my friend here, the large one, would be extremely happy if you could let us in for a minute."

Mr. Lin opened his mouth to answer, but something down the hall caught his attention.

"What is that? Is that a muumuu?"

Artemis didn't bother to look. "Oh, yes. We have disguised our fairy friend as a child in a muumuu."

Mr. Lin frowned, and the spiral on his head moved. "Fairy friend? Oh, really? Who are you people? Are you from *Pop Art Today*? Is this one of Dougie Hemler's postmodern stunts?"

"No. He's a real fairy. A demon warlock, to be precise. The one behind him, flying, is an elf."

"Flying? You tell Dougie Hemler from me that there's isn't a chance in . . ." Then he spotted Holly hovering over N°1's head. "Oh!"

"Oh!" agreed Artemis. "That's a fair reaction. Now, can we go in? It's extremely important."

"Are you going to ruin the exhibition?"

"Probably," Artemis admitted.

Mr. Lin's lip quivered as he spoke. "Then I can't let you in."

Holly darted forward, collapsing her helmet visor.

"I think you can let us in," she said, her voice layered with magic. "Because these three humans are your oldest friends. You invited them for a sneak preview."

"And what about you two?"

"Don't worry about us. We're not even here. We're just inspiration for your next exhibition. So why don't you buzz us all in."

Mr. Lin flapped a hand at Holly. "Why would I worry about you? You're not even here. Just some silly idea flying around my head. As for you three guys, I am *so* glad you could make it. Why don't you go ahead. That exhibit is going to knock your socks off!"

"You don't need to video us," prompted Holly.

"Why don't you shut down the gallery cameras?"

"I'll just switch off the gallery cameras, give you guys a little privacy."

"Good idea."

The curator had turned his attention to the pile of posters on his desk before the security door closed behind Artemis and his group.

The exhibition hall was ultramodern, with dark wooden floors and slatted blinds. The walls were hung with photographs, giant blow-ups of the dancing figures in the center of the room. The figures themselves were raised on a dais, to make their detail easier to view. There were so many spotlights on the figures that there was barely a shadow on the stone.

N°1 absently pulled off his bonnet, approaching the exhibit in a daze as though *he* had been *mesmerized* and not the curator.

He climbed onto the dais, stroking the stone skin of the first figure.

"Warlocks," he whispered. "Brothers."

The sculpture was beautiful in its detail, and yet horrific in its subject matter. It consisted of four creatures, ranged in a broken semicircle, in the act of dancing or recoiling from something. They were small squat fairies, like N°1, with thrusting jaws, barrel chests, and stumpy tails. Their bodies, limbs, and foreheads were covered with swirling runes. The demons were all holding hands, and the fourth held on to the severed hand of the next in line.

"The circle was broken," said N°1. "Something went wrong."

Artemis climbed onto the dais beside him. "Can you bring them back?

"Bring them back?" said N°1, startled.

"From what I know of the gargoyle's touch, it can transform living things to stone, and back again. You have the touch; can you use it?"

N°1 rubbed his palms nervously. "I may have the touch. You know, *maybe* and that's a big maybe. I turned a wooden skewer to stone, at least I think it was stone. Maybe it was just coated with ash. I was under a lot of pressure. Everybody was watching. You know how it is—maybe you don't. How many of you have even been in imp school. None, right?"

Artemis gripped his shoulder. "You're babbling, N°1. You need to concentrate."

"Yes. Of course. Concentrate. Focus. Think."

"Good. Now see if you can bring them back. It's the only way to save Hybras."

Holly shook her head. "Way to keep the pressure off, genius."

Minerva was circling the exhibit in a daze. "These statues *are* actual demons. They have been among us all this time. I should have seen it, but Abbot looked nothing like this."

Holly landed beside the girl, up close.

"There are entire species that you know nothing about. You almost helped to wipe out one of them. You were lucky. If that *had* happened, a dozen Artemis Fowls would not have been enough to rescue you from the fairy police."

"I see. I said sorry already. Can we move on?"

Holly frowned at her. "Glad to see you've forgiven yourself so quickly."

"Harboring feelings of guilt can have a negative affect on mental health."

"Child geniuses," growled Holly.

"Genii," said Minerva.

On the dais, N°1 was laying hands on one of the petrified demons.

"So, back in Hybras. I just kind of held the skewer and got excited, then it started. I wasn't trying to turn it into stone."

"Could you get excited now?" asked Artemis.

"What? Just like that? I don't know. I feel a bit sick, to be honest. I think the muumuu is giving me a headache. It really is bright."

"Maybe if Butler gave you a fright?"

"It's not the same. I need some real pressure. I know Mr. Butler wouldn't actually kill me."

"I wouldn't be too sure."

"Oh, ha-ha. You're a funny one," said Nº1. "I can see I'm going to have to stay on my toes around you."

Butler was checking his pistol, when he heard noises in the corridor. He ran to the security door and peered out through the small rectangle of toughened glass.

"We've got company," he declared, cocking his pistol. "Kong found us."

The bodyguard put a single round into the electronic lock, frying the chip and sealing the door.

"It's not going to take them long to open that door. We need to wake up those demons and get out of here. Now!"

Artemis squeezed Nº1's shoulder, nodding at the security door.

"That enough pressure for you?"

On the other side of the security door, Kong and his men were halted by the sight of a smoking keypad.

"Dammit," swore Kong. "He busted the lock. We're going to have to shoot our way in. There's no time for planning. Don, you have the case?"

Don held up the suitcase. "Right here."

"Good. If by some miracle there is a demon in there, clip the case onto its little wrist, good and tight. I don't want to miss another chance."

"Will do. We have grenades, boss. We could blow the door."

"No," snapped Kong. "I need Minerva and I don't

want her injured. Anyone hurts her, I hurt them. Understood?"

Everybody understood. Nothing complicated about it.

Inside the gallery, Artemis was getting a little anxious. He had hoped that Kong would leave the building immediately, but the hit man must have spotted one of the exhibition posters in the elevator and come to the same conclusion that Artemis himself had.

"Anything?" he asked N°1, who was vaguely rubbing a statue's arm.

"Not yet. I'm trying."

Artemis patted his shoulder. "Try a little harder. I have no desire to get involved in a firefight in a high-rise building. At the very least we would all end up in a Taiwanese prison."

Okay, thought N°1. Concentrate. Reach into the stone.

He held the stone warlock's finger tightly and tried to feel something. From the little he knew about warlocks, he guessed that this was probably Qwan, the elder magician. The stone figure's head was encircled by a simple band with a spiral motif at the front, the sign of leadership.

How terrible it must have been, N°1 reflected, to see your home dematerialize and be left behind. To know it was all your own fault.

It was not my fault! snapped a voice in N°1's head. *It was*

that stupid demon N'zall. Now are you going to get me out of here or not?

N°1 almost fainted. His breath came in short explosive gasps, and his heart seemed to hike upward in his chest.

Come on, young warlock. Release me! I have been waiting for a long long time.

The voice, the presence, was inside the sculpture. It was Qwan.

Of course it's Qwan. You're holding my hand. Who did you think it was? You're not a simpleton, are you? Just my luck, wait ten thousand years and then a simpleton turns up.

"I am not a simpleton!" blurted N°1.

"Of course not," said Artemis encouragingly. "Just do your best. I will instruct Butler to hold Kong back for as long as he can."

N°1 bit his lip and nodded. If he spoke aloud, it could get confusing. And this situation was confusing enough without him adding to it.

He would try thought-power. Qwan was speaking in his mind, maybe it would work the other way.

Of course it works! Qwan sent. *And what is all that nonsense about cooked food? Just release me from this prison.*

N°1 winced, trying to mentally black out his dreams of a cooked banquet.

I don't know how to set you free, he thought. *I don't know if I can.*

Of course you can, responded Qwan. *You have enough*

magic in you to teach a troll to play an instrument. Just let it out.

How? I have no idea how.

Qwan was silent for a moment while he took a quick peek into N°1's memories.

Oh, I see. You are a complete novice. No training of any kind. Just as well, really; without expert tuition you could have blown up half of Hybras. Very well, I will give you a little nudge in the right direction. I can't do much from here, but maybe I can get your power flowing. It will get easier after this. Once you have been in contact with a warlock, some of his knowledge is passed on to you.

N°1 could have sworn that the stone fingers in his own moved a fraction, but that could just have been his imagination. What was definitely not in his imagination was the sudden feeling of cold loss that sped along his arm. As though life itself were being sucked from him.

Don't worry, young warlock. I'm simply siphoning off a little magic to get the sparks running. It feels terrible, but it will not last.

It did feel terrible. N°1 imagined that dying piece by piece would feel something like this, which in a way was what was happening. And in such a situation the body will try to defend itself by fighting off the intruder. The magic that had lain dormant inside N°1 until recently suddenly exploded in his brain and gave chase to the invader.

To N°1 it felt as though he suddenly had an entire new spectrum of vision. He had been blind before, but now he could see through walls. Of course, it was not really some kind of super vision, it was an understanding of his own abilities. The magic flowed through him like liquid fire, chasing impurities out through his pores. Venting steam through his orifices and setting the runes on his body aglow.

Good boy, sent Qwan. *Now let it go. Chase me out.*

N°1 found that he was able to do exactly that, to control the magical flow. He sent it after Qwan's tendril, through his own fingers, and into Qwan's. The dead feeling was replaced by a buzzing of power. He began to vibrate, and so did the statue, shedding wafers of stone like a dead snakeskin. The old warlock's fingers were solid no more, but living, breathing skin. They held on to N°1 tightly, keeping the connection solid.

That's it, boy. You're doing it.

I am doing it, thought N°1 incredulously. This is really happening.

Artemis and Holly looked on in amazement as the magic spread through Qwan's body, sloughing the stone from his limbs with pistol-shot cracks and orange flame. Life claimed Qwan's hand, then his arm, then his torso. Stone fell from his chin and mouth, allowing the warlock to heave his first breath in ten millennia. Bright blue eyes squinted against the light and shut tightly. And still the magic ran on, blasting every last shard of stone from Qwan's body. But there it stopped. When the sparks of

Nº1's power reached the next warlock in line, they simply fizzled and died.

"What about the others?" asked Nº1. Surely he could free them, too.

Qwan hacked and coughed for several moments before he answered.

"Dead," he said, then collapsed in the rubble.

On the other side of the gallery security door, Kong was emptying a third clip from his machine pistol into the keypad.

"The door won't hold much longer," said Butler. "Any second now."

"Can you slow them down?" asked Artemis.

"Shouldn't be a problem. I don't want to leave any bodies here, Artemis. I imagine the police are already on their way."

"Maybe you could just scare them a bit."

Butler grinned. "My pleasure."

The shooting stopped, and the security door drooped slightly on its hinges. Butler ripped the door open smartly, yanking Billy Kong inside, then jammed the door closed again.

"Hello, Billy," he said, pinning the smaller man to the wall.

Kong was too demented to be scared. He lashed out with a series of blows, any one of which would have been

282

fatal to a normal person. They bounced off Butler like a fly bouncing off a Tiger tank. That's not to say they didn't hurt. Kong's trained hands felt like heated brands where they impacted. Butler's only reaction to the pain was a slight tightening around the corners of his mouth.

"Holly?" he said.

"Pull," said Holly, aiming her Neutrino at a point in space.

Butler catapulted Billy Kong straight up, and Holly plucked him out of the air with a blast from her weapon. Kong spun across the floor, still throwing spasmodic punches.

"The snake's head is out of action," said Artemis. "Let's hope the rest will follow suit."

Minerva decided to take advantage of Billy Kong's unconsciousness to indulge in some payback. She stalked over to her prone kidnapper.

"You, Mr. Kong, are nothing but a thug," she said, kicking him in the leg.

"Young lady," said Butler sharply. "Move away. He may not be completely out."

"If my father has as much as a hair out of place," continued Minerva, oblivious to Butler's warnings, "I will personally ensure that you spend the maximum time in prison."

Kong cracked open an eye. "That's no way to talk to your staff," he croaked, and wrapped steely fingers around her ankle.

Minerva realized that she had made a drastic mistake, and decided that the best course of action was to scream as shrilly as possible. Which she did.

Butler was torn. His duty was to protect Artemis, not Minerva, but through years of working with Artemis and, indeed Holly, he had unconsciously adopted the role of general protector. Whenever somebody was in danger, he helped them to get out of it. And this foolish girl was certainly in danger. Mortal danger.

Why is it, he wondered, that the smart ones always think they're invincible?

And so Butler made a decision, the consequences of which would haunt his dreams and waking hours for years to come. As a professional bodyguard, he knew the futility of second-guessing his own actions, but in the nights ahead he would often sit by the fire, with his head in his hands, and replay the moment in his mind, wishing that he had acted differently. Whatever way he played it out, the results were tragic, but at least they would not have been tragic for Artemis.

So Butler acted. He took four steps away from the door to disentangle Minerva from Kong's grasp. It was a simple thing; the man was barely conscious. He seemed to be operating on some kind of psychotic energy. Butler simply stepped down hard on his wrist, then rapped him sharply between the eyes with the knuckle of his index finger.

• ⚛ ⊙ • ▢ ⊖ ∿ • ◊ ⊖ ⎈ ▢ ❈ • ⚜ ☽ ❈

Kong's eyes rolled back in his head, and his fingers relaxed like the legs of a dying spider.

Minerva stepped out of Kong's range.

"That was very foolish of me. I apologize."

"It's a little late for that," reprimanded Butler. "Now, will you please take cover?"

The entire mini-episode took about four seconds, but in that four seconds a lot happened on the other side of the security door. Don, who was holding the bomb, and had recently been punched for no good reason by his boss, decided to win Kong's favor by bursting into the gallery and taking on the giant in there. He put his shoulder to the door at the exact moment that Butler stepped away from the other side, and to his own surprise went tumbling headfirst into the room, followed quickly by four more of Kong's henchmen, brandishing an assortment of weapons.

Holly, who was covering the door with her Neutrino, was not unduly worried. She *began* to worry when a grenade rolled out of the tangle of men and tapped against her foot. It would be easy enough for her to escape the explosion, but Artemis and N°1 would be well within the blast radius.

Think fast!

There was a solution, but it was costly in terms of equipment. She holstered her weapon, whipped off her helmet, and jammed it down over the grenade, holding it there with her own weight. This was a trick she had employed before with mixed results. She had hoped it wouldn't become a habit.

She squatted there like a frog on a toadstool for what seemed like a long time, but it couldn't have been more than a few seconds. She noticed from the corner of her eye that a thug with a silver case was slapping the man who had rolled the grenade. Perhaps using lethal force had been against orders.

The grenade exploded, blasting Holly into a sharp arc. The helmet absorbed most of the shock, and all of the shrapnel, but there was still enough force to shatter both of Holly's shinbones and fracture one femur. She landed on Artemis's back like a sack of rocks.

"Ow," she said, and passed out.

Artemis and N°1 were attempting to revive Qwan.

"He's alive," said Artemis, checking the warlock's pulse. "Steady heartbeat. He should come out of it soon. You keep a strong contact with him or he could disappear."

N°1 cradled the old demon's head. "He called me a warlock," he said tearfully. "I am not alone."

"Time enough for a talk-show moment later," said Artemis brusquely. "We need to get you out of here."

Kong's men were in the gallery now, and shots were being fired. Artemis was confident that Butler and Holly could take care of a few thugs, but this confidence took a blow when there was a sudden explosion and a battered

Holly landed on his back. Her body was instantly enveloped in a cocoon of blue light. Sparks dropped from the cocoon, like falling stars, pinpointing the most severe injuries.

Artemis crawled out from beneath her, laying his recuperating friend gently on the floor beside Qwan.

Kong's men were now embroiled with Butler, and probably regretting choosing this line of work. He tore through them like a bowling ball into a pack of quivering pins, but with considerably more economy of movement.

One made it past Butler. A tall man with a tattooed neck and an aluminium case. Artemis guessed that this case probably did not contain a selection of Asian spices, and realized that he would have to take action himself. While he was wondering exactly what it was he could do, the man sent him sprawling. By the time he made it back to Holly's side, his friend was sitting up groggily and there was a suitcase handcuffed to her wrist. The man who had delivered the case had returned to the fray, where he had lasted less than a second before Butler took him out of it again.

Artemis knelt by Holly's side. "Are you all right?"

Holly smiled, but it was an effort. "Just about, thanks to the magic. I'm out, though, not a drop left. So I would advise everyone to stay healthy until I can complete my ritual." She shook her wrist, jangling the chain. "What's in the case?"

Artemis looked paler than usual. "I would guess nothing pleasant." He flicked the clips and lifted the lid. "And I would be right. It's a bomb. Big and complicated. They sneaked it past security somehow. Through an area still under construction, probably."

Holly blinked herself alert, shaking her head until the pain woke her up.

"Okay. Bomb. Can you see a timer?"

"Eight minutes. And counting."

"Can you disarm it?"

Artemis pursed his lips. "Perhaps. I need to open the casing and get into the works before I know for sure. It could be a straight detonator, or we could have all kinds of decoys."

Qwan struggled to his elbows, coughing up large globs of dust and spit. "What? I'm flesh and bone after ten thousand years and now you're telling me a bomb is going to blow me to a million pieces?"

"This is Qwan," explained N°1. "He's the most powerful warlock in the magic circle."

"I'm the only one now," said Qwan. "I couldn't save the rest. Just us two left, boy."

"Can you petrify the bomb?" asked Holly.

"It will take several minutes before my magic is up and running. Anyway, the gargoyle's touch only works on organic matter. Plants and animals. A bomb is full of man-made compounds."

Artemis raised an eyebrow. "You know about bombs?"

"I was petrified. Not dead. I could see what was happening around me. The stories I could tell you. You wouldn't believe where tourists stick gum."

Butler was piling unconscious bodies against the security doors.

"We have to get out of here!" he called. "The police are in the hallway."

Artemis stood and took a half dozen steps away from the group, closing his eyes.

"Artemis, this is no time to fall apart," chided Minerva, crawling from behind a display case. "We need a plan."

"Shh, young lady," said Butler. "He's thinking."

Artemis gave himself twenty seconds to rack his brains. What he came up with was very far from perfect.

"Very well. Holly, you must fly us out of here."

Holly did a few sums in her head. "It will take two trips, maybe three."

"No time for that. The bomb must go first. There are a lot of people in this building. I must go with the bomb, as there is a chance I can defuse it. And the fairies must come, too; it is imperative that they are not taken into custody. Hybras would be lost."

"I can't allow this," objected Butler. "I have a duty to your parents."

Artemis was stern with his protector. "I am giving you

a new duty," he said. "Look after Minerva. Keep her safe until we can rendezvous."

"Let Holly fly out over the sea and drop the bomb," argued Butler. "We can mount a rescue mission later."

"It will be too late. If we don't get these fairies out of here, the eyes of the world will be on Taipei. And anyway, the local seas are thronged with fishing boats. This is the only way. I will not allow humans or fairies to die when I might have prevented it."

Butler would not give up. "Listen to yourself. You sound like a . . . like a *good guy*! There's nothing in this for you."

Artemis had no time for emotions. "In the words of HP Woodman, 'Time is ticking on, and so we must be gone.' Holly, tie us to your belt, all except Butler and Minerva."

Holly nodded, still slightly shell-shocked. She reeled out a number of pitons from her belt, wishing she had been issued one of Foaly's Moonbelts, which generated a lo-grav field around everything attached to it.

"Under the arms," she instructed Nº1. "Then clip it back onto the loop."

Butler helped Artemis with his strap. "This is it, Artemis. I've had it, I swear. When we get home I am retiring. I'm older than I look, and I feel older than I am. No more plotting. Promise me?"

Artemis forced a smile. "I am simply flying to the next building. If I cannot defuse the bomb, then Holly can fly it out to sea and endeavor to find a safe spot."

⦁ ◗ ⦚ ⦀ ⦁ ◉ ◗ ⦁ ⬡ ⦚ ⊗ ⧖ ⦁ ⊗ ⌷ ⦁ ⚞ ◖ ◗

They both knew that Artemis was lying. If he could not defuse the bomb, there would be no time to find a safe drop point.

"Here," said Butler, handing him a flat leather wallet. "My picks. So you can at least get into the works."

"Thank you."

Holly was loaded to the chin. N°1 and Qwan clung to her waist, while Artemis was cinched to the front.

"Okay. Everyone ready?"

"I wish my magic would return," grumbled Qwan. "I'd turn myself back into a statue."

"Terrified," said N°1. "Freaking. Planking. Up the creek."

"Colloquialisms," said Artemis. "Very good."

Butler closed the case. "One building across. That's as far as you need to go. Get that panel off and go straight for the explosive itself. Rip out the detonator if you have to."

"Understood."

"Okay. I won't say good-bye, just good luck. I will see you as soon as I can talk us out of here."

"Thirty minutes, if that."

Up to that point Minerva had hung back, looking shamefaced. Now she came forward. "I'm sorry, Artemis. I shouldn't have gone near Mr. Kong."

Butler bodily lifted her aside. "No, you shouldn't have, but there's no time for apologies now. Just stand by the door and look innocent."

"But I—"

"Innocent! Now!"

Minerva obliged, wisely realizing that this was not the time for arguing.

"Okay, Holly," said Artemis. "Lift off."

"Check," said Holly, activating her backpack. The wings struggled with the extra weight for a moment, and there was something about the engine vibration that Holly didn't like, but gradually her rig took the strain and lifted all four of them off the floor.

"Okay," she said. "I think we're good."

Butler nudged the flying group toward a window. This was all so risky, he couldn't believe that he was letting it happen. But there was no time to deliberate. It was do or die.

He reached up and yanked down on the window's security catch. The entire six foot pane swung wide, allowing the high-altitude wind to scream into the building. Suddenly everyone was deafened and under attack from the elements. It was hard to see anyone, and even harder to hear them.

Holly floated the group outside. They would have been whipped away had Butler not held on for a second.

"Go with the wind," he shouted to Holly, releasing his grip. "Make your descent gradual."

Holly nodded. Her wing motor skipped a beat and they dropped six feet. Artemis's stomach lurched.

"Butler," he called, his voice thin and childlike in the wind.

"Yes, Artemis, what?"

"If something goes wrong, wait for me. No matter how it looks, I will return. I will bring them all back."

Butler nearly jumped out after them. "What are you planning, Artemis? What are you going to do?"

Artemis called back, but the wind caught his words, and his bodyguard could only stand, framed by steel and glass, shouting into the wind.

They dropped quickly. A bit more quickly than Holly would have liked.

The wings can't take it, she realized. *Not the weight and the wind. We're not going to make it.*

She rapped a knuckle on Artemis's head. "Artemis!" she shouted.

"I know," shouted the Irish boy. "Too much weight."

If they fell now, the bomb would detonate in the middle of Taipei. That was unacceptable. There was only one thing to do. Artemis had not mentioned this option to Butler, as he knew the bodyguard would reject it no matter how sound his own reasoning.

Before Artemis had time to act on his theory, Holly's wings spluttered, jerked, and died. They fell in ragged free fall, like a sack of anchors, head over heels, dangerously close to the skyscraper wall.

Artemis's eyes were scalded by wind, his limbs were

folded back to breaking point by rushing air, and his cheeks were ballooned to comical proportions, though there was nothing funny about falling hundreds of feet to a certain death.

No! said Artemis's iron core. *I will not let this be the end.*

With a grim and physical determination that he must have picked up from Butler, Artemis raised his arms and grabbed Nº1's arm. The object he sought was right there, almost in his face and yet seemingly impossible to reach.

Impossible or not, I must reach it.

It was like trying to push against the skin of a giant balloon, but push Artemis did.

The ground rushed up from below, smaller skyscrapers jutting up like spears. And still Artemis pushed.

Finally, his fingers closed around Nº1's silver bracelet.

Good-bye, world, he thought. One way or another.

And he ripped the bracelet off, flinging it into air. Now the demonkind were no longer anchored to this dimension. For a second there was no obvious reaction to this, but then, just as they were passing between the first of the lower skyscrapers, a revolving purple trapezoid opened in the sky and swallowed them as neatly as a kid catching a Cheerio in his mouth.

Butler staggered back from the window, trying to process what he had seen. Holly's wings had failed, that much was clear, but then what? What?

It dawned on him suddenly. Artemis must have had a secondary plan; that boy always did. Artemis wouldn't go to the bathroom without a back-up. So they weren't dead. There was a good chance of that. They had just disappeared into the demon dimension. He would have to keep telling himself that until he believed it.

Butler noticed that Minerva was crying. "They're all dead, aren't they? Because of me."

Butler placed a hand on her shoulder. "If they were all dead, it would be because of you. But they're not. Artemis has everything under control. Now, chin up, we have to talk our way out of here, daughter."

Minerva frowned. "Daughter?"

Butler winked, though he felt anything but cheery. "Yes, daughter."

Seconds later, a squad of Taiwanese regular police heaved open the door, flooding the room with blue-and-gray uniforms. Butler found himself looking down the barrels of a dozen police special pistols. Most of these barrels were wobbling slightly.

"No, you dolts," squealed Mr. Lin, threading his way through the policemen, slapping at their gun arms. "Not that one. He is my good friend. Those other ones, the unconscious ones. They are the ones who broke in here; they knocked me down. It is a miracle my friend and his . . ."

"Daughter," prompted Butler.

⊕ ▢ ⚷ ⊕ • ⊘ ⚴ ⚴ ⚲ ⦙ • ⚷ ◗ ⚴ ☽ ⌱ ⚘ • ⊕

"And his daughter were not harmed."

Then the curator noticed his demolished exhibit and faked a faint. When no one rushed to aid him, he picked himself up, went off into a corner, and had a little cry.

An inspector who wore his gun cowboy style ambled across to Butler.

"You did this?"

"No. Not me. We were hiding behind a crate. They blew up the sculpture then started fighting among themselves."

"Do you have any idea why these people would want to destroy a sculpture?"

Butler shrugged. "I think they think they're anarchists. Who knows with these people."

"They have no ID," said the inspector. "Not one of them. I find that a bit strange."

Butler smiled bitterly. After all Billy Kong had done, he would only be prosecuted for property damage. Of course, they could mention the kidnapping, but that would lead to weeks, possibly months, of red tape in Taiwan. And Butler did not particularly want anyone looking too deeply into his past, or indeed the selection of false passports in his jacket pocket.

Then something struck him. Something about Kong from a conversation back in Nice.

Kong used a kitchen knife on his friend, Foaly had said. *There's still a warrant out for him there, under the name Jonah Lee.*

Kong was wanted for murder in Taiwan, Butler realized, and there was no statute of limitations on murder.

"I heard them talking to that one," said Butler, pointing to the supine Billy Kong. "They called him Mr. Lee, or Jonah. He was the boss."

The inspector was interested. "Oh, really. Did you hear anything else? Sometimes the smallest detail can be important."

Butler frowned, thinking about it. "One of them said something, I don't even know what it means. . . ."

"Go on," urged the inspector.

"He said . . . let me think. He said 'You're not such a tough guy, Jonah. You haven't notched your barrel in years.' What does that mean, notching your barrel?"

The inspector pulled a cell phone from his pocket. "It means that man is a murder suspect." He hit ONE, then SPEED DIAL. "Base? Chan here. I need you to run the name Jonah Lee through records, go back a few years." He closed the phone. "Thanks, Mister . . . ?"

"Arnott," said Butler. "Franklin Arnott, New York City." He had been using the Arnott passport for several years. It was genuinely rumpled.

"Thanks Mr. Arnott, you may just have caught a murderer."

Butler blinked. "A murderer! Wow. Do you hear that, Eloise? Daddy caught a murderer."

⚐𝕭 • ◉ ◑𝕭 🦎 • ⚐ • ▢ ◗ 🍴 ⚐𝕭 • ✹ 🔺 •

"Well done, Daddy," said *Eloise*, looking unhappy.

The inspector turned to pursue his inquiries, then stopped.

"The curator said there was another person. A boy. A friend of yours?"

"Yes. And no. He's my son. Arty."

"I don't see him around."

"He just stepped out, but he'll be back."

"Are you sure?"

Butler's eyes lost their focus. "Yes, I'm sure. He told me."

CHAPTER 13: **OUT OF TIME**

The journey between dimensions was more violent than Artemis remembered. There was no time to reflect on various scenery changes, and barely time for his senses to register sights, sounds, or temperature changes. They were ripped from their own dimension and dragged through wormholes of space and time with only their consciousnesses intact. Only once did they materialize for the briefest second.

The landscape was gray, bleak, and pockmarked, and in the distance Artemis could see a blue planet camouflaged by cloud cover.

I'm on the moon, thought Artemis, then they were gone again, drawn by the lure of Hybras.

It was an unnatural feeling, this out-of-body, out-of-mind travel. How am I still aware? thought Artemis. How is any of this possible?

And stranger still, when he concentrated, Artemis could feel the thoughts of the others swirling around him. It was mostly broad emotions, such as fear or excitement, but after a bit of mental twiddling, Artemis detected specific thoughts, too.

There was Holly, wondering if her weapon would arrive intact. Typical soldier. And there was N°1, fretting incessantly, not about the journey itself but about someone who would be waiting for him in Hybras. Abbot. A demon named Abbot.

Artemis reached out and found Qwan floating in the ether. His mind was formidable, juggling complex computations and philosophical puzzles.

You are keeping the mind active, young human.

Artemis's consciousness realized that this thought was directed at him. The warlock had felt his clumsy probe.

Artemis could feel a difference between his mind and the others. They had something different. An alien energy. It was difficult to explain a feeling without senses, but for some reason it seemed to be blue. A blue plasma, electric and alive. Artemis allowed this rich feeling to flow through his mind and was instantly jolted by its energy.

Magic, he realized. *Magic is in the mind.* Now this was something worth knowing. Artemis retreated to his own mind-space, but he took a sample of the blue plasma with him. You never know when a touch of magic would come in handy.

)〡⧖Ɓ⧜ • ⊗⛭♋ • ⬚⧖∪⏛ • ◔Ɓ⊗

They materialized on Hybras, inside the crater itself. Their arrival was accompanied by a flash of displaced energy. The group lay on the soot-blackened slopes, panting and steaming. The ground beneath them was warm to the touch, and the acrid stink of sulphur stung their nostrils. The euphoria of materialization soon dissipated.

Artemis breathed experimentally, the air from his mouth blowing up small dust eddies. Volcanic gas made his eyes water, and flat flakes of ash instantly coated every exposed patch of skin.

"This could be hell," he commented.

"Hell or Hybras," said N°1, climbing to his knees. "I got some of this ash on a tunic before. It never comes out."

Holly was up, too, running a system's check on her equipment.

"My Neutrino is fine. But I can't get a lock on a communications signal. We're on our own. And I seem to have lost the bomb."

Artemis knelt, his knees cracking through the ash crust, releasing the heat below. He glanced at his watch and caught sight of his own face. His hair was gray with ash, and for a second he thought he was looking at his father.

A thought struck him. I look like my father, a father I may never see again. Mother. Butler. I have only one friend left.

"Holly," he said. "Let me look at you."

Holly did not look up from her wrist computer.

"No time right now, Artemis."

Artemis padded across to her, walking gingerly on the thin crust.

"Holly, let me look at you," he said again, holding her shoulders.

Something in Artemis's voice made Holly stop what she was doing and pay attention. This was not a tone Artemis Fowl used very often. It could almost classify as tenderness.

"I just need to make sure you're still you. Things get mixed up between dimensions. On my last trip I switched fingers."

He held up his hand for her to see. "Strange, I know. But you seem to be fine. All present and correct."

Something flashed in the corner of Artemis's eye. There was a metal case half buried in the ash farther up the crater wall.

"The bomb," sighed Artemis. "I thought we'd lost it in transit. There was a flash when we landed."

Qwan hurried across to the bomb. "No. That was energy displacement. Mostly mine. Magic is almost another being. It flows where it will. Some of mine did not flow back to me in time, and ignited on reentry. I am happy to say that the rest of my power is fired up and ready to go."

Artemis was struck by how much of this prehistoric being's language was similar to NASA jargon. No wonder

we don't have a chance against the fairies, he thought. They were solving dimensional equations when we were still knocking stones together.

Artemis helped the warlock heave the bomb from the ash's grip. The timer had been knocked for a loop by the time-jump and now read more than five thousand hours. Finally, a stroke of luck.

Artemis used Butler's picks to examine the bomb's workings. Maybe he could disarm it if he had a few months, a couple of computers, and some laser tools. Without those things, there was about as much chance of him disarming this weapon as there was of a squirrel making a paper airplane.

"This bomb is perfectly operational," he said to Qwan. "Only the timer was affected."

The warlock stroked his beard. "That makes sense. That instrument is relatively simple, compared to the complexity of our bodies. The dimension tunnel would have no trouble reassembling it. The timer is another matter. It will be affected by any time flares we run across here. It could blow at any second, or never."

Not never, thought Artemis. I may not be able to disarm this thing, but I can certainly blow it when I need to.

Holly peered at the deadly device. "Is there any way we can dispose of it?"

Qwan shook his head. "Inanimate objects cannot travel unaccompanied in the time tunnel. We, on the other hand, could get sucked back in at any moment. We need to get some silver on us immediately."

Holly glanced at Artemis. "Maybe some of us want to get sucked back in."

"Maybe you do," said Qwan. "But only under certain conditions. If you just let yourselves go, who knows where you'll end up. Or when. Your natural space and time will attract you, but with the spell deteriorating, you could arrive encased in rock a mile below the surface, or stranded on the moon."

This was a sobering thought. It was one thing to have a quick tourist's look at the surface of the moon. It was quite another to be stuck there forever. Not that you would know anything about it after the first minute.

"So we're stuck here?" said Holly. "Come on, Artemis. You have a plan. You always have a plan."

The others gathered around Artemis. There was something about him that always made people assume that he was the leader. Perhaps it was the way he assumed it himself. Also, in this instance, he was the tallest person in the group.

He smiled briefly. *So this is how Butler feels all the time.*

"We all have our reasons for wanting to go back," he began. "Holly and I have left friends and family behind who we would dearly love to see again. N°1 and Qwan, you need to get your people out of this dimension. The spell is unraveling, and soon nowhere on this island will be safe. If my calculations are correct, and I feel certain that they are, then not even silver can anchor you here for much longer. Now, you can go when the spell dictates, or *we* can decide when to make the jump."

Qwan did his sums in his head. "Not possible. It took seven warlocks and a volcano to move the island here. To get us back I would need seven magical beings. Warlocks, preferably. And of course, a live volcano, which we don't have."

"Does it have to be a volcano? Wouldn't any energy source do?"

"Theoretically," agreed Qwan. "So you're saying we could use the bomb?"

"It's possible."

"Highly unlikely, but possible. I still need seven magical beings."

"But the spell is already cast," argued Artemis. "The infrastructure is there. Couldn't you do it with fewer?"

Qwan wagged a finger at Artemis. "You are a smart Mud Boy. Yes, maybe I could do it with fewer. Of course, we would not know until we arrived."

"How many?"

"Five. Five at the absolute least."

Holly ground her teeth. "We have only three, and N°1's a novice. So we need to find two demons with magic on this island."

"Impossible," snapped Qwan. "Once an imp warps,

that's the end of any magic they might have. Only warlocks, like myself and N°1, do not warp. So we keep our magic."

Artemis brushed ash from his jacket.

"Our first priority is to get out of this crater and find some silver. I suggest we leave the bomb here. The temperature is not enough to ignite it, and if it does explode, the volcano will absorb some of the force. If we are going to find some other magical creature, we will undoubtedly have a better chance outside this crater. At any rate, the sulfur is giving me a headache."

Artemis did not wait for an agreement. He turned and made for the crater lip. After a moment, the others followed, struggling with each footfall through the crust of ash. It reminded Artemis of a giant sand dune he'd trudged up with his father once. Here, falling would have harsher consequences.

It was a difficult and treacherous hike. The ash concealed grooves in the rock and small crevasses that vented warm air from the volcano. Colorful fungi grew in clusters around these vents, and they glowed in the crater shadows like coral night-lights.

Nobody spoke much during the climb. N°1 muttered his way through large tracts of the dictionary, but the others realized that this was his way of keeping his chin up.

Artemis glanced upward occasionally. The sky was dawn-red, and glowed above him like a lake of blood.

306

That's a cheery metaphor, thought Artemis. Maybe it says something about my character that a lake of blood is the only image I can come up with.

N°1's build was best suited for the steep climb. He had a low center of gravity, and could rest on his stumpy tail if need be. His thick feet anchored him securely, and armored plates covering his body protected him from sparks or bruising in the event of a fall.

Qwan was clearly suffering. The old warlock had been a statue for the past ten thousand years and was still working the kinks out of his bones. Magic soothed the process somewhat, but even magic could not completely erase the pain. He winced each time his foot punctured the soot crust.

Finally the group reached the summit. If time had passed, it was impossible to tell how much. The sky still had the same red tinge, and all timepieces had virtually stopped.

Holly jogged ahead the last few steps, then raised her right hand, fingers closed in a fist.

"That means halt," Artemis told the others. "It's a military thing. Human soldiers use the exact same sign."

Holly poked her head above the rim for a moment, then returned to the group.

"What does it mean if there are a lot of demons on their way up the mountain?"

Qwan smiled. "It means our brother demons saw the flash of our arrival and are coming to greet us."

"And what does it mean if they are all armed with crossbows?"

"Hmm," mused Qwan. "That could be a touch more serious."

"How bad can they be?" asked Artemis. "We've faced trolls together."

"It's fine," said Holly, powering up her handgun. "They're not so big. We're going to be fine. Really."

Artemis frowned. Holly only bothered reassuring him when they were in deep trouble.

"That bad?" he said.

Holly whistled, shaking her head. "You have no idea."

CHAPTER 14: LEADER OF THE PACK

The Island of Hybras

While Artemis and company had been zooming around the time tunnel, Leon Abbot had been in council with the pride elders. Council was where all the big decisions got made, or more accurately, where Abbot made all the big decisions. The others thought they were participating, but Leon Abbot had a way of bringing them around to his way of thinking.

If only they knew, he thought, biting the inside of his cheek to prevent a smug grin spreading across his face. *They would eat me alive. But they can never know, because there is nobody left alive to tell them. That dolt N°1 was the last, and he's gone. What a pity.*

Abbot had something big planned for today. A big

departure for the pride, the dawn of a new era. The Leon Abbot era.

He looked down the table at his fellow demons sucking the bones from a bucket of recently live rabbits that he had laid on for the meeting. He despised the other council members. Every one. They were weak, stupid creatures, ruled by their baser appetites. What they needed was leadership. No arguments, no debates, just *his* word as law, and that was that.

Of course, under normal circumstances, the other demons might not share his vision of the future. In fact, if he suggested it, then they would most likely do to him what they were currently doing to the rabbits. But these were not normal circumstances. He had certain *advantages* when it came to negotiating with the council.

At the far end of the table, Hadley Shrivelington Basset, a recent addition to the council, stood and growled loudly. The signal that he wished to speak. In truth, Basset worried Abbot slightly. He was proving a little resistant to Abbot's regular powers of persuasion, and some of the others were beginning to listen to him. Basset would have to be handled soon.

Basset growled again, cupping both hands around his mouth to ensure that his words traveled to the head of the table.

"I would speak, Leon Abbot. I would have you listen."

▷ • ♟ ⊙ • ⊕ ▯ • ♒▷ ◉ • ♒♟ • ⊕ ▯

310

Abbot sighed wearily, waving at the demon to go ahead. The young ones certainly loved their formality.

"Things are happening that worry me, Abbot. Things are not as they should be with the pride."

There were murmurs of assent from around the table. Not to worry. The others would soon change their tune.

"We are known by human names. We worship a human book. I find this sickening. Are we to become human altogether?"

"I have explained this, Basset. Perhaps a million times. Are you so dull-witted that my words do not penetrate your skull?"

Basset growled low in his throat. These were fighting words. And pride leader or not, Abbot would soon find those words rammed down his throat.

"Let me try one more time," continued Abbot, plonking his boots on the table, a further insult to Basset. "We learn the human ways so we can better understand them, and so more easily defeat them. We read the book, we practice with the crossbow, we bear the names."

Basset would not be cowed. "I have *heard* these words a million times, and each time they seem ridiculous to me. We do not give each other rabbit names when we hunt rabbit. We do not live in foxholes to hunt the fox. We can learn from the book and the bow, but we are demon, not human. My family name was Gristle. Now that's a real demon name! Not this stupid Hadley Shrivelington Basset."

It was a good argument, and well presented. Maybe in different circumstances Abbot would have applauded and recruited the young demon as a lieutenant, but lieutenants grew up to be challengers, and that was one thing Abbot did not want.

Abbot stood and walked slowly down the length of the table, gazing into the eyes of each council member in turn. At first their eyes blazed with defiance, but as Abbot began to speak, this fire faded, to be replaced by a dull sheen of obedience.

"You are right, of course," said Abbot, running a talon along one curved horn. An arc of sparks followed the path of his nail. "Everything you say is exactly right. The names, that ridiculous book, the crossbow. Learning the language of English. It's all a joke."

Basset's lips curled back over pointed white teeth, and his tawny eyes narrowed. "You admit this, Abbot?" He addressed the council, "You hear him admit it?"

Before, the others had grunted their approval of the young buck's challenge, but now it was as if the fight had gone out of them. All they could do was stare at the table, as if the answers to life's questions were etched into the wood grain.

"The truth is, Basset," continued Abbot, drawing ever nearer. "That we're never going back home. This is our home now."

"But you said . . ."

"I know. I said that the spell would end, and we would be sucked back to where we came from. And who knows, it may even be true. But I have no idea what will actually happen. All I know is that for as long as we are here, I intend to be in charge."

Basset was stunned. "There will be no great battle? But we've been training for so long."

"Distraction," said Abbot, waving his fingers like a magician. "Smoke and spells. It gave the troops something to concentrate on."

"To *what* on?" asked Basset, puzzled.

"Concentrate, you moron. Think about. As long as there's a war to be planned, demons are happy. I provided the war, and I showed them how to win. So, naturally, I am a savior."

"You gave us the crossbow."

Abbot had to stop and laugh. This Basset really was a prize fool. He could almost pass for a gnome.

"The crossbow," he panted at last, when his mirth had petered away. "The crossbow! The Mud Men have weapons that shoot death. They have iron birds that fly, dropping exploding eggs. And there are millions of them. Millions! All they would have to do is drop one egg on our little island and we would disappear. And *this* time, there would be no coming back."

Basset did not know whether to attack or flee. All these revelations were hurting his brain, and all the other council members could do was sit there drooling. It was almost as if they were under a spell. . . .

"Come on," said Abbot mockingly. "You're getting there. Wring out that sponge of a brain."

"You have bewitched the council."

"Full marks!" crowed Abbot. "Give that demon a raw rabbit!"

"B . . . But that can't be," stammered Basset. "Demons are not magical creatures, except the warlocks. And warlocks do not warp."

Abbot spread his arms wide. "And I am so obviously a magnificently warped creature. Does your brain hurt? Is this all too much for you, Basset?"

Basset pulled a long sword from its scabbard. "My name is Gristle!" he roared, lunging at the pride leader.

Abbot batted the blade aside with his forearm, then pounced on his opponent. Abbot may have been a liar and a manipulator, but he was also a fearsome warrior. Basset may as well have been a dove attacking an eagle.

Abbot drove the smaller demon to the stone floor, then squatted on his chest, ignoring the blows Basset drove into his armored plates.

"Is that the best you can do, little one? I have had better tumbles with my dog."

He grabbed Basset's head between his hands and squeezed until the younger demon's eyes bulged.

"Now, I *could* kill you," said Abbot, the thought giving

him obvious pleasure, "but you are a popular buck among the imps, and they would pester me with questions. So I will let you live. After a fashion. Your free will shall belong to me."

Basset shouldn't have been able to speak, but he managed to moan one word. "Never."

Abbot squeezed harder.

"Never? Never, you say? But don't you know that *never* comes quickly here in Hybras."

Then Abbot did what no warped demon should be able to do: he summoned magic from inside himself and let it shine through his eyes.

"You are mine," he said to Basset, his voice irresistible, layered with magic.

The others were so conditioned to the *mesmer* that they succumbed to just a tinge of it in his voice, but for Basset's fresh young mind, Abbot was calling forth every spark of magic in his system. Magic that he had stolen. Magic that, by fairy law, was never to be used to *mesmerize* another fairy.

Basset's face turned red and his forehead plate cracked.

"You are mine!" repeated Abbot, staring straight into Basset's captive eyes. "You will never question me again."

To Basset's credit, he fought the enchantment for several seconds, until the magic's power actually burst a blood vessel in his eye. Then, as the blood spread across the orange sclera of his eye, Basset's resolve faded, to be replaced by docile dullness.

"I am yours," he intoned. "I will never question you again."

Abbot closed his eyes for a moment, drawing the magic back into himself. When he opened them again, he was all smiles.

"That's good. I am so glad to hear that, Basset. I mean, your other option was a quick and painful death, so you're better off as a mindless lapdog anyway."

He climbed to his feet and graciously helped Basset to his.

"You've had a fall," he explained, in a doctor-patient voice. "And I'm helping you to your feet."

Basset blinked dreamily. "I will never question you again."

"Oh, never mind all that now. Just sit down and do whatever I say."

"I am yours," said Basset.

Abbot slapped his cheek gently. "And the others said we wouldn't get along."

Abbot returned to his own chair at the head of the long table. The chair was high-backed and made from various animal parts. He settled into it, paddling the armrests with his palms.

"I love this chair," he said. "Actually, it's more of a throne than a chair, which brings me to our main

business here today." Abbot reached under a leather flap in the chair and pulled out a roughly fashioned bronze crown.

"I think it's about time the council declared me king for life," he said, fixing the crown on his head.

This new king-for-life idea would be a tough sell. A demon pride was always ruled by the fittest, and it was a very temporary position. Abbot had only survived as long as he had by *mesmerizing* anyone who dared challenge him.

Most of the council had been under Abbot's spell for so long that they accepted the suggestion as if it were a royal decree; but some of the younger ones shuddered with violent spasms, as their true beliefs wrestled with this new repugnant idea.

Their struggles didn't last long. Abbot's suggestion spread like a virus through their conscious and subconscious, subduing revolution wherever it was found.

Abbot adjusted his crown slightly. "Enough debate. All in favor, say *graaargh!*"

"*GRAAARGH!*" howled the demons, battering the table with gauntlets and swords.

"All hail King Leon," prompted Abbot.

"ALL HAIL KING LEON!" the council mimicked like trained parrots.

The adulation was interrupted by a soldier demon who burst through the lodge's flap.

"There's a . . . there was a big . . ."

Abbot whipped off the crown. The general population wasn't ready for that yet.

"There's a what?" he demanded. "A big what?"

The soldier paused, catching his breath. He realized suddenly that he'd better communicate the *bigness* of what had happened on the mountain, or else Abbot was liable to behead him for interrupting the meeting.

"There was a big flash." A big flash? That didn't sound *big* enough.

"Let me start again. A *huge* flash of light came from the volcano. Two of the hunting party were nearby. They say someone came through. A group. Four beings."

Abbot frowned. "Beings?"

"Two demons, maybe. But the other two, the hunter doesn't know what they are."

This was serious. Abbot knew it. These beings could be humans, or worse still, surviving warlocks. If it was a warlock, he would surely guess Abbot's secret. All it would take was one demon with some real power, and his hold on the pride would be gone. This situation had to be contained.

"Very well. The council will investigate. Nobody else goes up there."

The soldier's Adam's apple bobbed nervously, as he was about to bear bad news. "It's too late, Master Abbot. The entire pride is climbing the volcano."

Abbot was halfway to the door before the soldier finished his sentence.

"Follow me!" he shouted to the other demons. "And bring your weapons."

"*GRAAARGH!*" roared the spellbound council members.

Artemis was surprised at how calm he felt. You would think that a teenage human would be terrified at the sight of a pride of demons climbing toward him, but Artemis was more nervous than terrified, and more curious than nervous.

He glanced backward over his shoulder, into the crater they had just climbed out of.

"The pride comes before a fall," he said softly, then smiled at his own joke.

Holly overheard. "You certainly pick your moment to develop a sense of humor."

"Usually I would be planning, but this is out of my hands. Qwan is in charge now."

N°1 led them along the rim of the crater toward a low rocky ledge. There was a wooden rod jammed into the ground beside the ledge, and hooked over the rod were dozens of silver bangles. Most tarnished and soot-caked.

N°1 wiggled a bunch over the top of the rod.

"Dimension jumpers leave these here," he explained, passing them out. "Just in case they make it back. No one ever has, until now. Except Leon Abbot, of course."

Qwan slipped a bangle onto his wrist. "Dimension-jumping is suicide. Without silver, a demon will never be able to stay in one place for more than a few seconds. They will drift between times and dimensions until they are killed by exposure or starvation. Magic is the only reason we're here. I am amazed this Abbot person made it back. What is his demon name?"

N°1 squinted down the mountain pathway. "You can ask him yourself. That's him, the big one elbowing his way to the head of the group."

Holly squinted down at the pride leader. "The one with the curved horns and big sword?" she asked.

"Is he smiling?" N°1 asked.

"No."

"That's Abbot."

It was a strange reunion. There was no hugging, no champagne, and no teary-eyed reminiscing. Instead there were bared teeth, drawn swords, and threatening behavior. The latest batch of imps were especially eager to skewer the newcomers and prove their valor. Artemis was the number-one target in the group. Imagine, an actual live human here on Hybras. He didn't look so tough.

Artemis and company had stayed put on the ledge, waiting for the demons to come to them. They didn't have to wait long. The imps arrived, breathless from the climb and just dying to kill something. If it hadn't been for

Qwan, Artemis would have been ripped to shreds on the spot. In fairness, Holly had something to do with keeping Artemis alive, too. She tagged the first half dozen imps with a charge from her Neutrino strong enough to send them scurrying back to what they thought was a safe distance. After that, Qwan managed to hold their attention by conjuring a multicolored dancing monkey in the air.

Soon, every demon who was able to climb the mountain had done so, and they were all staring at the magical monkey.

Even Nº1 was entranced. "What is that?"

Qwan fluttered his fingers, causing the monkey to somersault.

"It's a simple magical construct. Instead of allowing the sparks to roam on instinct, I marshal them into a recognizable form. It takes time and effort, but in time you will have this micro control, too."

"No," said Nº1. "I mean what *is* that?"

Qwan sighed. "It's a monkey."

As their numbers grew, the demons became more and more agitated. The warriors crashed horns in a show of strength. They bashed each other's chest plates with their forearms and made a big show of sharpening their swords on stones.

"I miss Butler," said Artemis.

"Me too," said Holly, scanning the crowd for the greatest threat. It wasn't easy to decide. Every demon in the crowd seemed as though he were on the verge of hurling himself at the new arrivals. Holly had seen 3-D models of demons, of course, but she had never seen the real thing. The models were accurate enough, but they couldn't capture the bloodlust in the creatures' eyes, or the eerie whines that curled out of their noses as battle fever possessed them.

Abbot barged through to the front of the group, and Holly instantly trained her weapon on his chest.

"Qwan!" said Abbot, obviously amazed. "You're alive? I thought the warlocks were all dead."

"Except the one that helped you," said Nº1, before he could stop himself.

Abbot took a step back. "Well, yes. Except that one."

Qwan closed his fist and the monkey disappeared. "I know you," he said slowly, searching for the memories. "You were at Taillte. You were a dissenter."

Abbot drew himself up. "That's right. I am Abbot the dissenter. We never should have come here. We should have met the humans head-on. The warlocks betrayed us!" He leveled his sword at Qwan. "You betrayed us!"

The other demons growled and rattled their weapons.

Abbot took a moment to study the other members of the group.

"A human! That's a human. You have brought the enemy to our door. How long before the rest of them follow in their metal birds?"

"Metal birds?" said Artemis in Gnommish. "What metal birds? All we have are crossbows, remember?"

There followed a collective *ooh*, as the demons realized that this human spoke their language, albeit with an accent.

Abbot decided to change the subject. This boy was picking holes in his story. "And you brought an elf, too, warlock. Armed with a magical weapon. The elves betrayed us at Taillte!"

Qwan was getting bored by all this posturing. "I know, everybody betrayed you at Taillte. Why don't you give the order you're working up to? You want us dead. Give the order and see if our brother demons will attack the only being who can save them."

Abbot realized that he was on very dangerous ground. This poisonous little bunch had to be dealt with. Quickly and permanently.

"You want to die so much? So be it, you can die." He pointed his sword at the small group, and was on the verge of roaring *Kill them* or perhaps *Death to the traitors*, when Qwan snapped his fingers. He did this in a very showy way, setting off a magical mini explosion.

"I remember you now. Your name isn't Abbot. You're N'zall, the idiot who ruined the time spell. But you seem different. Those red markings."

Abbot flinched as if struck. A few of the older demons sniggered. Abbot's demon name wasn't brought up very much. Abbot was a little embarrassed by it, not surprising since N'zall meant *little horn* in the old demon cant.

"It *is* you, N'zall. It's all coming back to me now. You and that other moron, Bludwin, you were against the time spell. You wanted to fight it out with the humans."

"I still do," roared Abbot, overcompensating after the mention of his true name. "There's one right here. We can start with him."

Qwan was angry now, for the first time since he'd come back to life. "We had it all worked out. We had a circle of seven—in the volcano, the lava was rising, and everything was under control, then you and Bludwin hopped out from behind a rock and broke the circle."

Abbot's laugh was hollow. "This never happened. You have been away too long, warlock. You have gone mad."

Qwan's eyes burned with blue sparks, and magic rippled along the length of his arms. "I have been a statue for ten thousand years because of you."

"Nobody believes a word of this, warlock."

"I believe it," said Nº1. And there were some in the demon camp who believed it, too. It was in their eyes.

"You tried to murder the warlocks!" continued Qwan accusingly. "There was some commotion, and Bludwin went into the volcano. His energy tainted the spell. Then you dragged my apprentice, Qweffor, into the lava, too. Both of you went in. I saw it." Qwan frowned, trying to piece it all together. "But you didn't die. You didn't die because the spell had already started. The magic transported you away before the lava could melt your bones. But where did Qweffor go? Where did you go?"

N°1 knew the answer to that question. "He went into the future. He told our secrets to the humans in exchange for one of their storybooks and an ancient weapon from a museum."

Abbot pointed the sword at him. "I *was* going to let you live, impling."

N°1 felt a knot of rage in his stomach. "Like you *let me live* the last time. You told me to jump into the crater. You *mesmerized* me!"

Abbot was in a tough spot. He could order the council to attack, but that would leave many questions unanswered, and he couldn't *mesmerize* everybody. But if he let Qwan keep talking, every one of his secrets could be exposed. What he needed was some time to think. Unfortunately, time was something he did not have. He would have to use his wits and weapons to get out of this situation.

"I *mesmerized* you? Don't be ridiculous. Demons don't have magic. We abhor magic." Abbot shook his head in disbelief. "What am I even doing explaining myself to a runt like you. Shut your mouth, N°1, or I'll stitch it shut and throw you into the volcano."

Qwan did not appreciate his new apprentice being threatened.

"I have had enough of you, N'zall. You would threaten warlocks? N°1, as you call him, has more power inside him than you will ever have."

Abbot laughed. "For once you are right, old warlock. I have no power inside me. Not a single spark of magic. What I do have is the power of my fist, and the strength of the pride behind me."

Artemis was growing tired of this bickering. "We don't have time for this," he said, stepping out from behind Qwan. "The time spell is unraveling, and we need to make preparations for the journey home. For that journey, we need all the magic we can get. Including yours, N'zall or Abbot or whatever your name is."

"I don't argue with humans," growled Abbot. "But if I did, I might repeat that I don't have any magic."

"Oh, come on," scoffed Artemis. "I know the side effects of the *mesmer*. Including ragged pupils and bloodshot eyes. Some of your friends here have been *mesmerized* so much they barely have pupils anymore."

"And where did I get this magic?"

"You stole it in the time tunnel. I imagine you and Qweffor were literally melted together by the combination of lava and magic. When you emerged in Earth's recent past, you managed to hold on to some warlock magic."

This was a bit of a stretch for everyone present. Abbot realized that he wouldn't need the *mesmer* to convince anybody that the human's theory was ridiculous. He could destroy this human's argument before destroying the human.

Abbot made a great show of scoffing at Artemis. He did the whole big tribe leader bit, running his nails along the curves of his horns and barking out short bursts of laughter. Pretty soon, almost everyone else was laughing along.

"So, human," said Abbot, when the furor had died down. "I *stole* magic in the time tunnel. You must be losing your mind, Mud Boy. Maybe that's because I'm about to order my imps to skin your bones and suck the marrow from them. Even if that were possible, how would you know? How would a human know?" And Abbot grinned smugly, certain that no satisfactory answer could possibly be forthcoming.

Artemis Fowl grinned right back at him and pointed his index finger at the sky. Actually, it was his middle finger, due to the time tunnel switch. From the tip of this finger sprang a small blue spark that exploded like a tiny firework.

"I know magic can be stolen," said Artemis. "Because I stole some myself."

This piece of melodrama was greeted by a moment of stunned silence, then Qwan cackled loudly.

"I said you were smart, Mud Boy. I was wrong; you are

exceptional. Even in the time tunnel you were plotting. Stole a little magic, did you?"

Artemis shrugged, closing his fingers on the sparks. "It was floating around. I wondered what would happen if I embraced it."

Qwan squinted at him. "Now you know. You are changed. A magical creature like us. I hope you will use your gift wisely."

"Just what we need," moaned Holly. "Artemis Fowl with magical powers."

"I believe that if we count Mr. N'zall here, that makes five magical beings. Enough to reverse the time spell."

Abbot was sunk and he knew it. The other demons were looking at him curiously, wondering if he had been manipulating them magically. Even a few of the *mesmerized* council were struggling to shake off their mental chains. It was only a matter of minutes before his dreams of kingship floated forever out of his reach.

There was only one option left to him.

"Kill them all!" he roared, not quite as fiercely as he would have liked. "Imps, you have free rein."

The *mesmerized* council members lurched into action, not quite as graceful in battle as they would normally be. The imps were so delighted to be given a chance to kill something with only two legs that they barged forward with unconfined glee.

"Blood and guts!" howled one, and they all took up the

cry. It was not particularly eloquent, but it got the message across.

Holly was not particularly worried. Her Neutrino could fire as fast as she could aim, and with a wide-beam setting she could stun the entire line of demons before they could do any damage. In theory.

She elbowed Artemis aside, took a stand, and began firing. The beams erupted from the pistol in a spreading cone pattern, blasting the demons off their feet and keeping them down for at least ten minutes. Except for the ones that were getting back up immediately. Which seemed to be most of them. Even the imps were shaking off the blasts as if they were mere gusts of wind.

Holly frowned. This should not be happening. And she didn't dare raise the setting for fear of doing permanent damage. Something she would not risk under any circumstances.

"Qwan?" she said. "My beam's not having much effect. Any ideas?"

Holly knew that warlocks weren't much use in combat situations. It was against their credo to harm, and they would only do so in the most dire situations. By the time Qwan overcame his pacifist nature, it would be too late.

While Qwan scratched his chin, Holly kept firing. Each pulse brought down a bunch of demons, but they were back on their feet in seconds.

"If the council has been *mesmerized*, I can heal them,"

concluded Qwan. "But the brain is delicate; I need direct contact."

"No time for that," said Holly, loosing another burst. "Artemis, have you got anything?"

Artemis had his hand on his stomach. "I really need to use a bathroom. A second ago I was fine. But now . . ."

Holly really wished her wings were operational. If she could just get a bird's-eye view on the targets, it would be much easier.

"Bathroom, Artemis? Is this really the time?"

One demon made it past the laser bursts. Close enough to smell. Holly ducked under his swinging mace, kicking him in the chest. The air left his lungs in a whoof, and the demon went down gasping for breath.

"I need the bathroom, and your Neutrino is having barely any effect. Time is speeding up. We're in a surge." Artemis grabbed Holly's shoulder, causing a burst to sail off high and wide.

"I need to get to the bomb. It could explode at any moment."

Holly shrugged him off. "Safety tip, Artemis. Don't jiggle me when I'm firing. Qwan, can you buy us some time?"

"Time," said Qwan, smiling. "You know, it's ironic that we need time because . . ."

Holly ground her teeth. Why did she always have to end up with the intellectuals?

🌙 ◊ ෴ ⬠ ෴ ⚼ ჶ • ◔ ჶ • ⚼ • ⚞ ⚲ ⚮ ჶ • ⊛ ◊

N°1 had been equal parts terrified and thoughtful during the attack. Terrified for the obvious reasons: dismemberment, painful death, etc. But he was thoughtful also. He was a warlock. There must be something he could do. Before he left the island, he would have been stunned into inactivity by the suddenness and ferocity of this attack. Now it wasn't even the worst thing he'd faced. Those security Mud Men in the chateau. The big ones with the suits and fire sticks, guns. N°1 could see them in his head, clear as if they were here.

Instead of allowing the sparks to roam on instinct, I marshal them into a recognizable form.

N°1 concentrated on the human figures in his memory, wrapping them with magic, bringing them forth. He felt them solidifying as though the blood in his forehead were freezing. When the pressure became too much for his forehead, he expelled it into reality, conjuring up ghostly images of a dozen human mercenaries, blasting away with automatic weapons. It was a spectacular sight. Even Abbot reared back. The rest more than reared back, they turned and ran.

"Nice, Qwan. Good thinking," said Artemis.

Qwan was puzzled. "You can read my thoughts? Oh, you mean the soldiers. That was not me. N°1 is a very powerful little warlock. In ten years he could move this island on his own."

Abbot was left standing ten paces from the group with

his sword in his hand and a hailstorm of blue bullets cascading around him. In fairness to the pride leader, he stood his ground, facing certain death the demon way: with a sword in his hand and a snarl on his face.

Qwan shook his head. "Just look at that. It's that kind of idiocy that got us into trouble in the first place."

Abbot had some experience with magic, and he soon realized that these new humans and their missiles were mere illusions.

"Come back, you fools," he shouted after his soldiers. "They can't hurt you."

Artemis tapped Holly's shoulder. "Sorry to jiggle you again, but we need to get back to the bomb. All of us. And if possible, lure Abbot down there, too."

Holly put several bursts into Abbot's chest to buy them a couple of minutes. The pride leader flew backward, as though a giant had pounded his chest with a mallet.

"Okay. Let's go. Artemis, you go ahead, I'll hold them off from the rear."

They scrambled back into the crater, skidding on their heels through the ash crust. They made faster progress on the way down, but it was just as treacherous. It was hardest for Holly because she was moving backward, ready to take a potshot at anyone who poked so much as a hair over the crater rim.

It was a scene from a five-year-old's nightmare. Acrid smells that burned the eyes and throat, a surface that sucked at the feet, a red sky, and the sound of breath and heartbeats. Not to mention the constant fear that the demons were coming.

Things were about to get worse. The release of Qwan's displaced magical energy had accelerated the deterioration of the time spell, and it was on the point of collapsing entirely. Unfortunately, this would happen in reverse order, starting on Hybras. Artemis knew this, but he hadn't had a spare second to run any calculations. Soon, he guessed, it would happen soon. And who could tell when *soon* was during a time surge.

Artemis realized that it was more than a guess. He knew the collapse of the tunnel was imminent. He could feel it. He was in touch with magic now. He was part of it, and it was part of him.

Artemis pulled Qwan's arm around his shoulder, urging him forward.

"Quickly. We need to hurry."

The old warlock nodded. "You feel it? Chaos in the air. Look at N°1."

Artemis glanced behind. N°1 was on their heels, but his brow was furrowed with pain and he knuckled his forehead.

"He's sensitive," gasped Qwan. "Puberty."

Suddenly human puberty didn't seem so bad.

Holly was in trouble. Her years of training and experience hadn't prepared her for the moment when she would be retreating *into* a volcano, guarding a human and two members of a supposedly extinct species during a time surge.

The surge was playing havoc with her bodily functions, but it was also having an effect on her gunfire. She was laying down a covering fire on the ridge, but a cluster of blasts disappeared in midair.

Where do those shots go? Holly wondered briefly. Into the past?

Groups of ghost images fizzled into existence for a brief moment, giving the illusion that there were twice as many demons as there had been. Added to this, she was suddenly struck with hunger cramps, and she could swear her fingernails were growing.

Abbot's demons came fast, and not in a tight group as Holly had hoped. They had ranged themselves along the rim, and came over the top in a coordinated wave. It was a fearsome sight, dozens of warriors bounding over the lip, their markings glowing in the red light, teeth bared, horns quivering, and bloodcurdling battle cries echoing around the crater walls. This was not like fighting trolls. Trolls had some basic smarts, but these demons were organized and battle-ready. Already they knew to spread out and avoid the laser bursts.

Holly picked out the pride leader.

Hello there, Abbot, she thought. Whatever happens here, you're going home with a headache.

She loosed three bolts at him. Two disappeared, but one connected, sending Abbot tumbling into the dirt.

Holly did her best, widening the spread as much as possible, setting the trigger on automatic. If she'd had her full combat pack, then there wouldn't have been a problem. A few flash grenades at the right moment would have stunned the entire wave of demons, and a pulse assault rifle could have held them back for a few hundred years if necessary. As it was, she had one handgun, no backup, and a time surge gobbling half her rays. It seemed an impossible task to slow down Abbot and his goons long enough for Artemis to reach the bomb. And even if she did manage it, what then?

The demons kept coming, bent low and bobbing. They loosed bolts from their crossbows on the run, none of which were affected by the surge. Of course they wouldn't be. The rays from her Neutrino were calibrated to have a short life once they made contact with air; they would dissipate after five seconds unless specifically reset to hold together for longer.

Thankfully the bolts were falling short, but not as short as they had been a few moments earlier. Time was running out, in more ways than one.

A group of daredevil imps made it past Holly's arc of fire. Their method of travel was foolhardy and suicidal. Only idiot luck saved them from crushed skulls. Using a hide shield as a sled, three of them skidded down the crater's inner slope, being tossed hither and thither by rocks and changes in gradient.

One second they were fifty yards away, and the next, Holly could smell the sweat glistening on their brow plates. Holly swung her gun barrel toward them, but it was too late, she could never make it. And even if she did, the others would use the distraction to make ground.

The imps were leering at her. Lips pulled back over sharp pointed teeth. One was especially agitated and had some kind of slime flowing from his pores.

The imps seemed to hang suspended in the air for the longest time, and then *something* happened. The air pulsed, and reality momentarily split into colored pixels like a faulty computer screen. Holly felt sick to her stomach, and the imps winked out of existence, taking a six foot diameter tube of the crater with them.

Holly fell back from the hole, which collapsed in on itself.

N°1 fell to his knees and threw up.

"Magic," he gasped. "Breaking down. The lure of Earth is stronger than silver now. No one is safe."

Artemis and Qwan were in slightly better shape, but only slightly.

"I am older and have more control over my empathy," said Qwan. "That's why I didn't throw up." And having said that, he threw up.

Artemis didn't even give the old warlock time to

recover himself. There was no time. Time was surging and unraveling at once.

"Come on," he said. "Forward."

Holly backpedaled to her feet, pulling N°1 to his. Behind them on the slopes, the demons had frozen at the sight of the disappearing imps, but now were advancing again with renewed determination. No doubt they believed that Holly was responsible for the disappearance of their little brothers.

Temporal booms echoed around the island as chunks of Hybras spun into the time tunnel. Some would materialize on Earth and some in space. It was doubtful that any demons unlucky enough to be transported would survive. Not without concentrated magic to forge a compass for them.

Artemis dragged himself the last few steps to the bomb, dropping to his knees beside it. He wiped ash from the readout with his sleeve, then spent a while studying it, nodding along with the flickering of its digital timer.

The numbers of the timer were behaving erratically: jumping forward, slowing down, and even backing up slightly. But Artemis knew that there would be a pattern in here somewhere. Magic was simply another form of energy, and energy conformed to certain rules. It was simply a matter of watching the timer and counting. It took a while, longer than they could afford, but eventually

Artemis spotted the repeat. He ran the numbers quickly in his head.

"I see it," he shouted to Qwan, who was on his knees beside him. "It's mainly forward. An hour per second for a count of forty, followed by a deceleration to thirty minutes per second for a count of eighteen, then a slight jump backward in time, one minute per second back for a count of two. Then it repeats."

Qwan smiled weakly. "What was the first one again?"

Artemis stood, heaving the bomb from its cradle of ash and fungus.

"Never mind. You need to prepare to transport this place. I'll move the bomb to wherever you need it."

"Very well, smart Mud Boy. But we still have only four magical beings. We need N'zall."

Holly backed into the group, still firing. "I'll see what I can do."

Qwan nodded. "I have faith in you, Captain. Then again, I am a trusting person, and look where that got me."

"Where do you want this?"

Qwan looked around. "We need to form a circle around it, so somewhere flat. Look, that level spot. There."

Artemis began dragging the bomb toward the indicated spot. It wasn't so far. Then they could all stand around in a ring and watch it explode.

Everyone had their jobs to do now. The chances of their tasks coming to fruition were slightly less than the chances of a dwarf-goblin marriage ever taking place. And a goblin would rather eat his own feet than marry a dwarf.

Artemis had to position the bomb. Nº1 and Qwan were in charge of spell-casting, and Holly had the unenviable tasks of keeping them all alive and persuading Abbot to join their group. And all this while the island was disintegrating around them.

The volcano was literally being torn apart. Huge segments vanished into space like parts of a giant 3-D jigsaw. In minutes, there would be nothing left to transport.

Qwan took Nº1's hand in his own, leading him to the small level spot.

"Okay, young fellow. That thing you did up there with the soldiers, that was good. I was impressed. But this is the big time. I know you're in pain. That's just because you are now sensitive to the spell's breakdown. But you have to ignore that. We have an island to move."

Nº1 felt his tail vibrate nervously. "An island? An entire island?"

Qwan winked. "And everyone on it. No pressure."

"What do we do?"

"I need only one thing from you. Call up your magic, every drop. Let it pass through me and I'll do the rest."

That *sounded* easy enough. But calling up magic when there were arrows flying and chunks of the countryside disappearing was about as easy as going to the toilet on command with a dozen people watching. Who all hated you.

N°1 closed his eyes and thought magical thoughts.

Magic. Come on, magic.

He tried to open the same doors in his mind as he had when he had conjured up the human soldiers. To his surprise, he found the magic came easier now, as if it were ready to come out. The cage had been opened and the beast was free. N°1 felt the power surge through his arms, animating him like a puppet.

"Whoa there, big fellow," said Qwan. "No need to blow my head off. Put a leash on it until it's time to go." The old warlock shouted to Artemis, his thin voice almost whipped away by sonic booms, "How long?"

Artemis was dragging the bomb with some difficulty, digging his heels into the crust and heaving. He couldn't help thinking that Butler would have simply slung the bomb and its casing over one shoulder and hefted it onto the plateau.

"Count to three hundred. Maybe two ninety-nine. Providing the deterioration remains constant, which it should."

Qwan had stopped listening after the words *three hundred*. He gripped N°1's hands tightly.

"Five minutes and we're going home. Time to start the mantra." Qwan closed his eyes and bobbled his head from side to side, muttering in the ancient demon tongue.

Nº1 could feel the power of the words shaping the magic into rising circles of blue fire around them. He held on to his new mentor and joined in, repeating the mantra as if his life depended on it. Which, of course, it did.

Holly now had to draw Abbot into their little group and persuade him to join the magic circle. It seemed, judging by the way he was waving his fancy sword, highly unlikely that he would do this voluntarily.

The demon attack was mostly in disarray now, what with large tracts of their surroundings flashing off into another dimension, but Abbot and his council members were as dogged as ever, forging ahead with barely a pause when some of their number disappeared.

Holly held her fire, wondering what would be the best way to communicate with the pride leader. She was a trained negotiator, and suspected from her own observations and what Nº1 had told her, that Abbot had Acquired Situational Narcissism. He was completely in love with himself and his own importance in the community. Narcissists would often chose to die rather than accept what they saw as demotion. To Abbot, Holly would represent someone who was trying to remove him as pride leader, and therefore someone to be dealt with immediately.

Great, thought Holly. No matter what dimension you're in, there's a bigheaded male trying to take over the world.

The demons were advancing in a ragged line. Abbot was at the head, urging his *mesmerized* troops forward. The red sky was splitting into interwoven tendrils behind his head. The world, as Abbot knew it, was ending, but still he would not give up his position. Death for all before disgrace for him.

"Call off your warriors, Abbot," shouted Holly. "We can talk about this."

Abbot did not reply, as such. Not unless howling and stomping could count as a reply.

The demons were spreading out even more now, flanking her and avoiding being sucked off into another dimension all in one group. Abbot skidded ahead, digging his heels through the crust of ash, leaning his torso back to avoid tumbling. He was completely coated in ash now; even his ram's horns were gray. Gray maelstroms trailed behind him as each lurch forward threw up a thousand flakes.

There's nothing I can do, thought Holly. This guy wouldn't listen to his own mother. If he knew who his mother was.

There was no way out. She would have to up the charge and knock him senseless for a couple of hours. Qwan would have to put Abbot in the magic circle unconscious.

"Sorry," she said, and flicked up the power setting above the pistol's thumb-rest.

Holly aimed with practiced accuracy. The beam that pulsed from the Neutrino's barrel was a more dangerous red now, and should knock Abbot head over heels a couple of times.

I'll try not to enjoy that sight, thought Holly.

It was a sight she never got to enjoy, for at that precise moment, the time surge reversed for a count of two. The beam disappeared into the past, and Holly felt like throwing up as her atoms were scrambled once again by time quandary. She caught a glimpse of her ghostly past self a couple of feet to her right. Out of focus past versions of the demons scrambled behind them like speed trails. Then the past was gone for another minute.

Abbot was still coming. Dangerously close now. Holly reckoned she had time for another shot. And with any luck, the demon council would lose their singularity of purpose with their leader out of the picture.

She adjusted her aim, then the world shattered before her like a broken mirror. A curved section of the earth rose above her like a tidal wave, then dematerialized in a glittering flurry of sparks. Holly caught a glimpse of alternate dimensions through the gaps. There was sun and space and enormous multi-tentacled creatures.

The sheer amount of magic present in the air squeezed Holly's head like a vise. She vaguely noted as Artemis and the others succumbed to the magical overload.

But she could not succumb. Some of the demons may

have been sucked up into the time tunnel, but there could be more left. The air shimmered and settled. Rivulets of dust and rock spilled from midair. Huge chasms yawned all around, with nothing below but red space. There was more emptiness now than land.

Most of the demons were gone. Most, but not all. Abbot alone was left, grinning maniacally, his sword extended before him.

"Hello, elf," he said, and plunged the sword into Holly's chest.

Holly felt the steel slide through the delicate membrane of elfin skin, between the eighth and ninth ribs, and lodge a millimeter below her heart. It was cold as ice and more painful than words can describe. She fell backward, slipping off the slick blade, crashing through the crust of ash. Blood poured out of her like water from a ruptured vessel. Her own heart did gravity's work, emptying her veins with every beat.

"Magic," she gasped through the pain.

Abbot was jubilant. "Magic cannot help you, elf. I've been working on this sword for a long time, in case the warlocks ever showed up. There's enough enchantment in this steel to stop an entire magic circle." He shook the sword as he talked. Spittle sprayed from his mouth, and Holly's blood dripped from his blade, splattering lines on the ash.

Holly coughed, the action felt like it was splitting her in

two. Magic could not help her here. There was only one person who could.

"Artemis," she said, her voice weak and thin. "Artemis, help me."

Artemis Fowl glanced her way briefly, then returned his gaze to the bomb's timer, leaving Holly Short to die on the ground. Which she did.

CHAPTER 15: HOME AGAIN, HOME AGAIN

Artemis was hauling the bomb when the big shift came. The magical overspill hit him like a football tackle, driving him to his knees. For a moment his senses were completely overloaded and he was left gasping in a vacuum. Sight was first to return, distorted by tears and stars.

He checked the bomb's timer. Three minutes to go, providing that the pattern did not disintegrate. He glanced to his left, where Qwan and N°1 were returning to the business of conjuring, while over his right shoulder, Holly was holding whatever demons were left. All around, the world was vibrating itself out of this existence. The noise was hellacious and the smell coated the inside of his nostrils.

The bomb was heavy enough to make Artemis's

knuckles crack, and not for the first time, he wished Butler were at his side to take the strain. But he wasn't at his side, and wouldn't be again if Artemis did not get going. It was a simple plan: move the box to the plateau. Object A to point B. There was no sense thinking about it.

Then Holly got stabbed and the plan got a lot more complicated.

Artemis saw the blade going in out of the corner of his eye. And worse still, he heard the sound it made. A clean snick, like a key going into a lock.

This can't be real, he thought. We have been through so much together for Holly to be taken so quickly.

The sound the sword made coming out of Holly was hideous beyond imagination. Artemis knew that he would take that sound to his grave.

Abbot was gloating now. "Magic cannot help you, elf. I've been working on this sword for a long time."

Artemis sank to his haunches, fighting the urge to crawl to Holly's side. Magic could not help Holly, but perhaps a combination of magic and science could. He forced himself to ignore the spurts of deep red blood seeping from her wound. There was nothing in Holly Short's future but death.

Her current future. But the future could be changed.

N°1 and Qwan had not seen the assault. They were

deep in concentration, building the blue rings. Abbot was moving toward them now; the tip of his sword dripped blood on the ash like a leaky pen joining the dots to his next victims.

Holly spoke her last. "Artemis," she said. "Artemis, help me."

Artemis glanced at her. Once. Briefly. He shouldn't have. The sight of his friend dying almost threw off his count. And right now, the count was the most important thing.

Holly died without a friend to hold her hand. Artemis felt her go, another gift of the magic. He kept on counting, brushing away the tears on his cheeks.

Keep counting. That's all that matters.

Artemis rose and moved swiftly to his fallen friend. Abbot saw him go. He pointed the sword in Artemis's direction.

"You're next, Mud Boy. First the warlocks then you. Once you are gone, things will return to how they were."

Artemis ignored him, nodding along with the count in his head, making sure not to rush. The count must be accurate or all was lost.

Abbot elbowed his way between Qwan and N^o1. They were so focused that they barely realized he was there. With two strokes of his cursed sword, the job was done. N^o1 fell backward, blue magic trailing from his fingers.

Qwan did not fall, because the tip of Abbot's sword was keeping him upright.

Artemis did not look into Holly's eyes. He could not. Instead, he pried the handgun from her hand and pointed it away from him.

Be careful now. Timing is everything.

Abbot yanked his sword from Qwan's chest, and the small body slumped lifelessly to the ground. Three dead in less time than it would take to tie a shoelace.

Artemis ignored the last breaths, and the rhythmic crunching of ash that told him Abbot was coming. Not that the demon was trying to hide it.

"I'm back here, human. Why don't you see if you can turn around in time."

Artemis searched the volcano floor around Holly for footprints. There were many, but only two side by side, where Abbot had stood as he struck. All the while, he counted, remembering his own calculations.

An hour per second for a count of forty, followed by a deceleration to thirty minutes per second for a count of eighteen, then a slight jump backward in time, one minute per second back for a count of two. Then it repeats.

"Maybe I'll keep you." Abbot chuckled and prodded Artemis's back with his sword. "It'd be nice to have a pet human around. I could teach you tricks."

"I have a trick for you," said Artemis, and he fired a single blast from the gun.

The blast exited the barrel, and then was whipped one minute into the past, just as Artemis had calculated it would. It faded from the present and emerged just in time to strike the ghostly image of Abbot as he drew back his sword to thrust it into Holly.

The Abbot of one minute ago was lifted and tossed against the crater wall.

The present-time Abbot had barely time to say "What just happened?" before he winked out of existence, no longer flesh, merely unrealized possibility.

"You didn't kill my friends," replied Artemis, though he was talking to himself. "That never happened."

Artemis glanced down nervously. Holly was no longer there. *Thank God*.

Another quick glance told him that Qwan and Nº1 were back building their magic circle as if nothing had happened.

Of course not. Nothing did happen.

Artemis concentrated on the memory. Picturing Abbot spinning through the air. He wrapped the incident in magic to preserve it.

Remember, he told himself. What he had just done, now never had to be done, and so wasn't done. Except, of course, he *had* done it. Time quandaries such as these should be forgotten for the sake of sanity, but Artemis was loath to surrender any of his memories.

"Hey," said a familiar voice. "Don't you have a job to do, Artemis?"

It was Holly. She was hog-tying Abbot with his own bootlaces.

Artemis could only stare at her and smile. He still felt the pain of her death, but that would heal quickly now that she was alive again.

Holly caught him smiling. "Artemis, could you get that box onto the plateau? It's a simple plan."

Artemis smiled some more, then shook himself. "Yes. Of course. Put the box on the plateau."

Holly had been dead and now she was alive.

Artemis's hand tingled with the phantom memory of a gun it may or may not have held moments before.

There will be consequences for this, he thought. You can't alter time and be unaffected. But whatever the consequences are, I will bear them, because the alternative is too terrible.

He returned to his mission, dragging the bomb the final few feet to the plateau. He knelt, put his shoulder into the casing and slotted the bomb between Qwan and Nº1's legs. Nº1 didn't even notice that Artemis was there. The little apprentice warlock's eyes were solid blue now, flush with magic. The runes on his chest glowed, then began to move, swirling like snakes, slithering upward to his neck and swirling on his forehead like an enchanted Catherine wheel.

"Artemis! Give me a hand with this!"

It was Holly, struggling to roll Abbot's unconscious body across the bumpy crater. With each revolution, the demon's horns got snagged in the earth, plowing a small furrow.

Artemis plodded across to her, legs aching from the climb and descent. He grabbed one horn and heaved. Holly took the other.

"Did you shoot him?" Artemis asked.

Holly shrugged. "I don't know. Maybe. It got a bit hazy there for a minute. Must be the time spell."

"Must be," said Artemis, relieved that Holly didn't remember what had happened. Nobody should have to remember dying, though he would be interested to find out what exactly came next.

Time was running every which way, including out. One way or another, the island of Hybras was not going to be here much longer. Either the time spell would take it in pieces, or Qwan would get a grip of the bomb's energy and transport them back to Earth. Artemis and Holly dragged Abbot into the circle, dumping him at Qwan's feet.

"Sorry he's out," said Holly. "It was that or dead."

"Difficult choice with this one," said Qwan, grabbing one of Abbot's horns.

Artemis took the other, and between them they pulled Abbot into a kneeling position. There were now five in the circle.

"I had been hoping for five warlocks," grumbled Qwan. "One warlock, one apprentice, an elf, a human, and a snoring egomaniac were not exactly what I had in mind. This makes things a little more complicated."

"What can we do?" asked Artemis.

Qwan shuddered and a blue film passed across his eyes.

"D'Arvit!" he swore. "This young one is powerful. I can't hold him in much longer. Two more minutes of this and he's going to melt our brains inside our skulls. I saw that once. Fluid boiling right out of the ears. Horrible."

"Qwan! What can we do?"

"Sorry. I'm a little stressed here. Okay. Here's how it's supposed to work. I'm going to lift us off, with junior's help. When the device explodes, I'll convert the energy to magic. Captain Short, you're in charge of the where. Artemis, you're in charge of the when."

"Where?" said Holly.

"When?" said Artemis, simultaneously.

Qwan gripped Abbot's horn so tightly it creaked. "You know where this island goes, Holly, picture the spot. Artemis, let your time call to you. Allow it to reel you in. We cannot go back to our time. That would cause so many quandaries that the planet would probably just drop into a lower orbit and fry everything on it."

"I accept that," said Artemis. "But allow it to reel me in? I prefer some facts and figures. How about trajectories? Spatial addresses?"

Qwan was on his way into a trance. "No science. Just magic. Feel your way home, Artemis Fowl."

Artemis frowned, disgruntled. *Feeling his way* was not how he generally did things. People who *felt their way* without hard scientific facts generally wound up broke or dead. But what choice did he have?

It was easier for Holly. Magic had always been a part of her life. It had been her minor in college, and all LEP officers had to take regular in-service courses. In seconds her eyes were clouded with blue sparks and her inner magic had added a blue ring to the pulsing circles around them.

Visualize it, thought Artemis. See where you want to go, or rather, when you want to arrive.

He tried, but even though the magic was in him, it was not *of* him. The fairies were lost in the spell-casting, but Artemis Fowl could only gaze at the huge bomb at their feet and marvel that they were waiting for it to explode.

A bit late for doubts now, he told himself. After all, the whole "harness the bomb's power" notion was your idea.

It was true, he had conjured a few sparks earlier. But that was different; he had done it without thinking. The sparks had been a flourish to make his point. Here, his magic could be what kept everyone on this island alive.

Artemis studied each member of the circle in turn. Qwan and N°1 vibrated with unnatural speed. Their eyes were blue, and markings spun on their foreheads like mini-cyclones. Holly's magic vented through her fingers, coating her hand in an almost liquid blue light. Abbot, of course, was unconscious, but his horns glowed blue, and continuous streams of sparks shot from them, cascading over the group like the special effects at a rock concert. In fact, this entire episode would not look out of place in a music video.

Around them, the island was suffering its own trauma. The time tunnel's continued meltdown snatched up increasingly larger plots, whisking them off to other dimensions. The crackling hoops of power around them fused to form a magical hemisphere. It was not perfect, though; gaps flowed across its surface, threatening the integrity of the entire structure.

I'm the problem, thought Artemis. I am not contributing.

Artemis felt himself on the verge of panic. Whenever this feeling claimed him, he ordered his mind to shift gears and slip into a meditative mood. He did this now, feeling his heart slow and the impossible craziness around him slip away.

He concentrated on one thing: Holly's hand in his, clutching his fingers with life and energy. Holly's fingers twitched, sending magical tendrils along Artemis's arm. In his relaxed state, he was receptive, and her magic sparked his own, drawing it from his brain. He felt the magic ignite in his nerve endings, filling him up, elevating his consciousness to another place. It was a euphoric experience. Artemis realized there were sections of his brain opening up that hadn't been used by humans for millennia. He also realized that humans must have had their own magic once, but had forgotten how to use it.

Ready? asked Qwan, but not aloud. They were sharing consciousness now, as they had in the tunnel. But this was a clearer experience, like radio waves compared to digital.

Ready, replied the others, thought waves overlapping in a kind of mental harmony. But there was disharmony, too, and struggle.

It's not enough, thought Qwan. *I can't seal the hemisphere. I need more from Abbot.*

The others pushed as hard as they could, but none of them had any more magic to give. Abbot would kill them all in his sleep.

Hello? Who's there? said a new voice, which was something you don't expect in a closed magic circle, even if it is your first one.

Along with the voice came a series of memories. Great battles, betrayal, and a plunge into a fiery volcano.

Qweffor? said Qwan. *Is that you, boy?*

Qwan? Can it be you? Are you trapped here too?

Qweffor. The apprentice hauled into the volcano by Abbot back on Earth. Qwan instantly understood what must have happened.

356

No. We're in the magic circle once more. I need your power. Now!

Oh, gods, Master Qwan. It's been so long. You wouldn't believe what this demon eats.

Power, Qweffor! Now! We can talk at the other end.

Oh, okay. Sorry. Nice to hear a warlock's thoughts again. After so long, I thought——

Power!

Sorry. On the way.

Moments later, a strong pulse of power hummed through the circle. The magical hemisphere sealed, becoming a solid shield of light. Qwan redirected a small chunk of magic down to encircle the bomb itself. A high-pitched whistle emanated from the little golden sphere.

High C, thought Artemis absently.

Focus! admonished Qwan. *Take us to your time.*

Artemis focused on the important things he had left behind, and realized that they were all people. Mother, Father, Butler, Foaly, and Mulch. Possessions that he had believed important now meant nothing. Except maybe his collection of Impressionist art.

Leave out the art, Artemis, warned Holly, *or we'll end up in the twentieth century.*

Nineteenth, replied Artemis. *But I take your point.*

It may seem that all this bickering was a waste of valuable time, but it took place instantaneously. A million multisensory messages were exchanged along magical pathways, which made fiber-optic cables look about as efficient as two cans and a piece of string. Memories, opinions, and secrets were laid bare for all to see.

Interesting, noted Artemis. *If I could re-create this, I could revolutionize the communications business.*

You were a statue? said Qweffor. *Am I reading this right?*

At the circle's center, the bomb's timer was clicking toward zero. In a single second, the timer swept through the final hour on the clock. When the timer hit zero, a charge was sent to various detonators, including three dummies, to a block of plastic explosive the size of a small television set.

Here it comes, sent Qwan.

The bomb exploded, transforming the casing from a metal box into a million supersonic darts. The inner shield stopped the darts dead, but absorbed their kinetic energy, adding it to the outer shield.

I saw that, thought Artemis, impressed. *Very clever.*

And he had seen it somehow. Some kind of lateral vision that allowed everyone to view events at their own pace, and from whatever point of view they preferred. It also allowed his mind to fully concentrate on his home time, while also appreciating the spectacle. Artemis decided to move his third eye outside the circle. What-ever happened to this island was certain to be pretty spectacular.

The explosion released the power of an electrical storm

into a space the size of a four-man tent. Everything inside the space should have been vaporized, but the flame and shock waves were contained by the small golden sphere. They roiled about in there, punching through in several places. Wherever this happened, the errant force was attracted to the blue rings of power and stuck to them like flashes of cloud-to-ground lightning.

Artemis watched some of these flashes shoot straight through his body and out the other side. But he was not injured; on the contrary, he felt energized, stronger.

Qwan's spell is keeping me safe, he thought. It's simple physics—energy cannot be destroyed, so he's converting it to another form: magic.

It was a spectacular sight. The bomb's energy fueled the magic inside the circle until the rolling orange flames were tamed by blue ones. Gradually the bomb's power was consumed and transformed by sorcery. The rings glowed with a blinding blue light, and the figures inside the circle seemed to be composed from pure power. They shimmered insubstantially as the reverse time spell took hold of them.

Suddenly, the blue rings pulsed, injecting a shock wave of magic into the island itself. Transparency spread like water on the surface and below. Pulse followed pulse until the transparency spread beyond the crater. To the demons in their village, it must have seemed like the volcano was being eaten by the magic. The nothingness spread with each pulse, leaving only shimmering golden sparks where solid land was, moments before.

The dematerialization reached the shore, and beyond to the ten yards of ocean carried here with the island. Soon, there was nothing left but the circle of magic, floating blue in the red rippled space of Limbo.

Qwan reached out to them. *Concentrate now. Artemis and Holly, take us home.*

Artemis squeezed Holly's hand tightly. They were as close as they could ever be. Their minds were one.

Artemis turned and stared at his friend with the blue eyes. Holly was staring back, and she was smiling.

"I remember," she said aloud. "You saved me."

Artemis smiled back. "It never happened," he said.

And then their minds and bodies were split right down to the subatomic level and whisked across galaxies and millennia.

Space and time did not have any recognizable form. It was not like flying in a balloon over a timeline and saying "Look, there's the twenty-first century. Take us down there."

Everything was impressions and feelings. Artemis had to shut out the desires of the hundreds of demons around him and concentrate on his own internal compass. His mind would feel a longing for its own natural time, and he would just have to follow it.

The longing felt vaguely like a light warming his mind when he turned in its direction.

Good, thought Qwan. *Head toward the light.*

Is that a joke? Artemis asked.

No, replied Qwan. *I don't make jokes when there are hundreds of lives in the balance.*

Good policy, thought Artemis, and turned toward the light.

Holly was concentrating on where to land the island. She was finding this incredibly easy. She had always treasured her aboveground memories, and now could call them up with amazing clarity. She remembered a school tour to the site where Hybras had been. In her mind's eye, she could see the undulating beach, gold and shining in the summer sunlight. She could see the blue-gray glint on a dolphin's back as it breached the waves to greet its fairy visitors. She could see the silver-flecked blackness of the water in what humans called Saint George's Channel. The light of all these memories warmed her face.

Good, sent Qwan. *Move—*

I know. Move toward the light.

Artemis was trying to put this experience into words, for his diary. But he was finding it difficult, a novel experience for him.

I think I'll just concentrate on finding my own time, he thought.

Good idea, thought Qwan.

So you turned yourself into a statue? That was Qweffor again, dying to catch up.

Oh, for heaven's sake, grumbled Qwan. *See for yourself.* And he sent the relevant memories across to his old apprentice.

Everyone in the tunnel was treated to a cinematic rendering of the initial creation of the time tunnel, ten thousand years ago.

In their minds' eye, seven warlocks hovered above the very mouth of an active volcano, protected from the heat by a magical circle. This was an altogether more impressive affair than the improvised magic circle Artemis had previously witnessed. These warlocks were a confident crowd, swathed in elaborate robes. Their magical circle was actually a sphere of multicolored light. What's more, they did not need to get their boots dirty in the ash; they hovered twenty feet above the volcano mouth. Chanting in deep bass tones, they poured bolt after bolt of magic into the magma until it began bubbling and convulsing. As the warlocks concentrated on inducing the volcano, Abbot and his partner Bludwin crept out from behind a rocky outcrop farther up. And even though demon hides can endure great heat, both were sweating profusely.

With barely a pause to realize how moronic and shortsighted their plan was, the saboteurs leaped from an outcrop down toward the circle below. Bludwin, who was blessed with the twin gifts of idiocy and misfortune, missed every warlock in the circle and plunged flailing into the hissing lava. His body slightly raised the temperature of the surface lava, not significantly, but enough to taint the spell. Abbot connected with Qweffor, dragging him out of the circle to the lip of the volcano. Abbot's hide immediately began steaming, and poor Qweffor, still in a magical stupor, was as helpless as a newborn under his weight.

All of this happened at the worst possible time. The spell was loose in the volcano now, and the warlocks could no more stop it than a mouse could hold back the sea.

A magically enhanced pillar of solid lava spewed—red, orange, and magnificent—from the volcano, straight into the inverted cauldron of blue magic. Grimacing and in obvious distress, the warlocks converted the molten rock into pure power, pumping the energy back into the ground.

Abbot and Qweffor were caught simultaneously by the lava and the magical backwash. Qweffor, already in an insubstantial magical state, collapsed into a body-shaped cluster of stars, which were then absorbed into Abbot's body. Abbot twisted in agony, tearing at his own skin for a brief moment. Then he was smothered in a deluge of magic and disappeared.

The warlocks maintained the spell for as long as they could, until most of the island had been transported to another dimension. But the lava kept coming from deep beneath the earth, and with the circle broken, they could not contain its savage might. It swatted them aside like a bear would swat annoying insects.

The stricken warlocks spiraled through the air in a rough line, smoke trailing behind them from their flaming robes. Their island was gone, their magic was spent, and the ocean below was ready to crush their bones. There was only one chance for survival. Qwan called on his last sparks of magic and cast a gargoyle spell. The most basic of all warlock talents. In midair, the warlocks were petrified, and they fell in a tumbling line into the bubbling ocean far below. One died instantly when his head snapped off, two more lost arms and legs, and shock killed the rest. All except Qwan, who had known what was coming. They sank to the bottom of Saint George's Channel, where they would shelter generations of spider crabs for several thousand years.

For several thousand years, thought Qweffor. *Maybe being stuck inside Abbot wasn't so bad.*

Where is Abbot now? asked Artemis.

He's inside me, replied the apprentice. *Trying to get out.*

Good, thought Qwan. *I want a word with him.*

CHAPTER 16: POINT OF IMPACT

This time, the materialization was a painful process. Being separated from a thousand consciousnesses left Artemis with a deep sense of loss. For the first time in his life, he had completely belonged. He knew everyone, and they knew him. There would always be a bond between them all, though the specifics of others' memories were already fading.

Artemis felt like an oversize Band-Aid that had been ripped off an enormous limb and flung on the ground. He lay on the earth shivering. Sharing consciousness had felt so right, that now it was as if he had just lost the use of several senses, including balance.

He opened his eyes, squinting through the sunlight.

Sunlight! They were on Earth! Though where and when remained to be seen.

Artemis rolled onto his stomach, then struggled slowly to all fours. The others lay in the crater, disorientated like him, but alive, judging by the moans and groans. He himself felt fine, except for a darting pain in his left eye. His vision was sharp but slightly yellowed, as though he were wearing pale sunglasses. Holly, the soldier, was already up, coughing the ash from her lungs. When her airwaves were clear, she helped Artemis to his feet.

She winked at Artemis. "Blue sky. We did it."

Artemis nodded. "Perhaps." The wink drew his attention to her left eye. It seemed that they hadn't made it through the tunnel unaltered.

"Look at me, Holly. Do you notice anything different?"

"This doesn't have anything to do with puberty, does it?" said Holly, smiling. Then she noticed . . . "Your eyes. They've changed. One blue and one hazel."

Artemis smiled. "You too. We swapped in transit. Just the eye, as far as I can make out."

Holly thought about this for a moment, then ran her hands over her head and body.

"Everything's in place, thank goodness. Except now I have a human eye."

"It could have been a lot worse," said Artemis. "You could have been traveling with Mulch."

Holly winced. "Now that you mention it."

A solitary blue dot of magic sparkled inside Holly's new eyeball, reducing it in size slightly.

꙳ ꗻ ꘘ • ꙮ ꘓ ⊕ ⊕ ꙳ Ꙋ ☞ ➜ Ᏼ ꝏ ꙸ • ꙴ ꙅ

"That's better," she sighed. "I had a blinder of a headache. Your new eye must be too small; why don't you use your ill-gotten magic to fix it."

Artemis tried, closed his eyes and concentrated. But nothing happened.

"It seems as though the transplant did not take. I must have used all I had in the tunnel."

Holly punched his shoulder lightly. "Maybe you passed it on to me. I feel great. That time tunnel was like a magical mud bath. Maybe it's just as well that you lost your magic. The last thing the People need is a magical criminal mastermind running around aboveground."

"A pity," sighed Artemis. "The possibilities were endless."

"Here," said Holly, taking his head in her hands. "Let me fix you up."

Her fingertip glowed blue, and Artemis felt his new eye expand slightly in his socket. A single tear ran down his cheek, and the headache disappeared.

"A pity I was unable to do it myself. Being magical for even a short while was simply . . ."

"Magical?"

Artemis smiled. "Exactly. Thank you, Holly."

Holly smiled back. "It's the least I can do for someone who brought me back to life."

Qwan and N°1 were on their feet. The old warlock was trying not to look too smug, and N°1 was wiggling his tail experimentally.

"You never know what that tunnel will do to you," he explained. "I lost half a finger last time. It was my favorite finger, too."

"Rarely in my tunnels," said Qwan. "My tunnels are works of beauty. If the other warlocks were alive, they would give me a medal. Where is Qweffor, by the way?"

Qweffor was buried up to his waist in an ash mound, head down. Qwan and N°1 hauled him out by the boots. He lay spluttering and snorting on the ground.

"Do you need a handkerchief?" asked N°1. "All that ash and mucus coming out your nose is horrible."

Qweffor wiped his eyes with the back of his hand. "Shut up, Runt!"

N°1 took a step backward, which would prove not to be quite enough.

"Runt?" he squeaked. "You're not Qweffor, you're N'zall!"

"Abbot!" roared the demon, reaching up and grasping N°1 by the throat. "The name is Abbot."

Holly had her gun out and powered up before Abbot finished his sentence.

"Let him go, Abbot!" she shouted. "You can't escape. There's nowhere to escape to. Your world is gone."

The ex-pride leader was actually crying. "I know it's gone. This runt took it from me! Now I will take his life from him."

Holly sent a warning shot over Abbot's head. "The next one is between your eyes, demon."

Abbot hefted N°1, using him as a shield. "Shoot now, elf. Put us both out of our misery."

A change had come over N°1. Initially he had been sniveling—standard N°1 behavior—but now the tears were drying on his cheeks and his eyes were hard.

Every time things are going right for me, Abbot ruins it, he thought. I am so fed up with this stupid demon. I wish he was gone.

This was a big breakthrough for N°1. Usually when he found himself in a bad situation, N°1 wished himself away. This time he was wishing someone else would disappear. Enough was finally enough, so N°1 broke through a lifetime of conditioning and talked back to Abbot.

"I want to speak to Qweffor," he said in a trembling voice.

"Qweffor's gone!" shouted Abbot, spraying spittle onto N°1's neck. "All that is left is his magic. My magic!"

"I want to speak to Qweffor," repeated his hostage, with a little more volume.

For Abbot, this latest subordination was the wind that burst the dwarf's bum-flap. Even though he was bereft of land and lackeys, Abbot decided that he would not bear impudence from an imp. He tossed N°1 upward, spinning him in the air and gripping his shoulders as the imp descended. N°1 came down, face-to-face with Abbot, the demon's horns brushing his ears. Abbot's eyes were wide and crazy, and his teeth were slick with saliva.

· 🦀 🐾 ☽ · 🐚 🖱 ⬡ 🖴 · 🦀 🐾 ☽ ◊ · 🐾 🐚 ⴱ ·

"You're not long for life, little runt."

If Abbot had been paying closer attention to his captive, he might have noticed that Nº1's eyes were filmed with blue, and his markings glowed and shimmered. But, as usual, Abbot was only interested in his own plight.

Nº1 wriggled his hands upward, grabbing Abbot by the horns.

"How dare you!" said Abbot incredulously. Touching a demon's horns was tantamount to a challenge.

Nº1 stared into his captor's eyes. "I said, I want to talk to Qweffor."

Abbot heard him that time, because the voice wasn't Nº1's. It was a voice of pure magic, layered with undeniable power.

Abbot blinked. "I'll . . . eh . . . see if he's in."

It was too late for compliance; Nº1 wasn't about to rein in his power now. He sent a magical probe into Abbot's brain via the horns. Abbot's horns glowed bright blue and then began shedding large brittle flakes.

"Careful with the horns," said Abbot blearily, then his eyes rolled back in his head. "The ladies love the horns."

Nº1 rooted around in Abbot's head for a while until he found Qweffor sleeping in a dark corner, in a place scientists would call the limbic system.

The problem, realized Nº1, is that there is only room in every head for one consciousness. Abbot needs to go somewhere else.

And so, with this instinctive knowledge and absolutely no expertise, Nº1 fed Qweffor's consciousness until it expanded, occupying the entire brain. It was not a perfect fit, and poor Qweffor would suffer from twitches and sudden loss of bowel control at public functions, a syndrome which would become known as Abbot's Revenge. But at least he was in control of the body most of the time.

After several years and three hearings, fairy warlocks would rule to rehouse Abbot's consciousness in a lower life form. A guinea pig, to be precise. The guinea pig's own consciousness would soon be subjugated by Abbot's. Warlock interns would often amuse themselves by throwing tiny swords into the pig's pen, and cracking up while watching the little piggy try to pick them up.

Qweffor blinked Abbot's eyes.

"Thanks, Nº1," he said, placing the smaller warlock on the ground. "He's always been too strong for me, but now he's gone. I'm free." Qweffor studied his new arms. "And I have muscles."

Holly lowered her gun, resting a hand on her thigh. "That must be it. Surely our troubles are over?"

Artemis felt the earth tilt a fraction below them. He dropped to one knee, laying the flat of his hands on the ground.

"I hate to say this, Holly, but I think we're sinking."

* * *

The sinking thing turned out not to be as serious as it sounded. Of course, it *was* serious; after all, an island was sinking. But there was help at hand.

Holly realized this when her barely functional wrist computer was suddenly flooded with LEP chatter.

The sky is a projection, she thought. They're waiting for us.

Suddenly, where there had been nothing, hundreds of fairy vehicles appeared in the air above the island. Emergency services air ambulances flew in decreasing circles, searching for landing spots. Huge demolition platforms were guided down by tugpods, and an LEP shuttle dropped straight into the volcano.

The pod had the slick lines of a teardrop and a nonreflective surface that made it difficult to see, even with the shield powered down.

"They were expecting us," said Artemis, unsurprised. "I thought as much."

N°1 sneezed. "Thank goodness. I am so fed up with this volcano. It's going to take a month to get this crater stink out of my plates."

"No, no," said Qwan, linking arms with his new apprentice. "You can vent your pores magically. It's a very handy talent."

Holly waved to attract the shuttle, though there was no need. Even if her helmet hadn't had a nuclear tracker, the carrier's scanners would have already scanned, categorized, and checked the LEP database for a match for each one of them.

The shuttle spun and reversed down to them tail first. Its jets blasted, moving furrows in the ash.

"Wow," said Qwan. "Those ships are fabulous. The People have been busy."

"A lot has happened in ten thousand years," said Holly, holding up her palms to show the pilot she was not holding a weapon. Again, probably not necessary, but with Ark Sool in command of the LEP, nothing could be taken for granted.

Four grappler hooks shot from the corners of the shuttle, smashing through the crater crust into the rock below. Once they had a solid grip, they reeled the craft in for a landing. The rear door slid across, and Foaly came trotting down the ramp, dressed in a custom-tailored four-legged LEP jumpsuit. He skidded down the incline to Holly, digging his back hooves through the crust.

"Holly!" he said, hugging her tightly. "You made it back. I knew you would."

Holly hugged the centaur back. "And I knew you'd be here waiting."

Foaly reached an arm around Artemis's shoulders. "Well, when Artemis Fowl says he'll be back, you know it's going to take a lot more than space and time to stop him." Foaly shook hands with N°1 and Qwan. "I see you brought quite a few guests."

⊙ ◊ ß ⋓ • ✄ ⊛ § ß • ⊛ ▢ • 8 ⊙ ⊛ ✄

Holly smiled, her teeth white against a face of streaked ash. "Hundreds."

"Anyone we need to worry about?"

"No. A few have been *mesmerized*, but a couple of sessions in therapy should straighten that."

"Okay, I'll pass it on," said the centaur. "Now, we have to cut the reunion short and board immediately. We have thirty minutes to sink this island and pack up the entire facility."

Facility? thought Artemis. They've had time to set up a facility. Just how long have we been away?

They climbed the ramp and strapped into gel-padded bucket seats in the sparsely furnished rear. There were no comforts here, just seats and gun racks. A medic fairy scanned them all in turn, then shot a cocktail of inoculations and germ killers into their arms, just in case Hybras had brewed up any mutant diseases over the past ten thousand years. A true professional, the medic did not bat an eye examining Qwan and N^o1, even though he'd never met their like before.

Foaly sat beside Holly.

"I can't tell you how good it feels to see you, Holly. I requested this assignment. I'm on leave from Section Eight. This entire facility is my design. Biggest single project I ever worked on, designed for a thirty minute walkaway. I knew you'd make it back."

Holly thought about that statement for a moment. *She was an assignment?*

) ⊕ ⊕ ⅏ Ʊ ☎ • ℛ ♆ ⚘ ⃒ • ⚘ ♭ ⚵ • ⚘ • ◊

The shuttle reeled in the grippers and peeled away from the crater wall. In seconds they breached the mouth like a bullet from a gun. The vibration was enough to rattle teeth for the first few seconds, then the stabilization fins snicked out the side and calmed the ride down.

"I am glad to see the end of that volcano," said N°1, trying to appear casual, even though he was flying around in a metal teardrop. After all, this was not his first flight.

Foaly laid the heel of his hand on the porthole rim, peering downward.

"You really are seeing the last of it, as soon as we have everybody off the island. Those demolition rigs are going to turn the laser cutters on it. We're going to slice it up and then remote-deflate the buoys underneath. Let 'er down slow. That way, no tidal waves. The water displacement alone was enough to send a few big rollers in toward Dublin, but we boiled 'em up from space. Once the island is down, we can pack up the shield and go home."

"Oh," said N°1, who hadn't understood much of what had been said.

Artemis looked out the porthole at his elbow. Below on the island, demons were being guided into shuttles by rescue teams. Once the crafts took off, they switched on their shields and shimmered from view.

"You gave us quite a scare, Holly." The officer laughed. "Coming back twenty miles off target like that. We had to light a fire under our pilots to get over here and get the projection up. Luckily it's early in the morning, and the tide is low. We've got about half an hour before the first fishing boats get out here."

"I see," said Holly slowly. "Big-budget stuff. Sool must have been spitting fire."

Foaly snorted. "Sool? He can spit what he wants out of whatever end he wants. He got drummed out of the force a couple of years ago. Do you realize that traitor wanted to let the entire Eighth Family die off? The moron actually said as much in a memo."

Holly gripped the arms of her seat. "A couple of years ago? How long have we been gone?"

Foaly snapped his fingers. "Oh, uh, yeah. I wasn't supposed to just blurt it out. Sorry. I mean, it's not serious, like a thousand years or anything."

"How long, Foaly?" demanded Holly.

The centaur thought about it for a moment. "Okay. You've been gone for nearly three years."

Qwan reached over and slapped Artemis's shoulder. "Three years! Nice going, Mud Boy. You must have one hell of a brain to get us that close. I wasn't expecting to see this side of the century."

Artemis was stunned. Three years! His parents hadn't seen him for three years. What torture had he put them through? How could he ever make up for it?

Foaly was trying to fill the shocked silence with

information. "Mulch has kept the PI firm going. Well, more than that, actually, it's thriving. He signed up a new partner. You'll never guess who. Doodah Day. Another criminal turned do-gooder. Wait till he hears you're back. He's calls me every day. I have a pain in my tail trying to explain quantum physics to that dwarf."

Holly reached across and took Artemis's hand.

"There's only one way to look at this, Artemis. Think of all the lives you've saved. That's worth a few years, surely."

Artemis could only stare straight ahead. Dying in the transfer would have been a grade-one disaster, this was surely a grade-two. What could he say? How could he explain himself?

"I need to get home," he said, sounding for once like an actual fourteen-year-old. "Foaly, would you tell the pilot where I live?"

The centaur chuckled. "Like every law enforcement agent under the world doesn't know where Artemis Fowl lives. Anyway, no need to go that far. Someone is waiting for you at the shoreline. They've been there for quite a while."

Artemis placed his forehead against the porthole. He felt so tired suddenly, as though he had actually been awake for three years. How could he even begin to explain events to his parents? He knew how they must be feeling—exactly how he had felt when his father had gone missing. Perhaps he had already been declared dead, as his father had been. And even though his return would bring happiness, that pain would always be there under the surface.

Foaly was talking to the demons. "Who's this little guy?" he asked, tickling N°1 under the chin.

"That little guy is N°1," said Qwan. "He's the most powerful warlock on the planet. He could fry your brain by accident, say, if you were tickling him under the chin and he got irritated."

The centaur withdrew his finger sharpish. "I see. I like him. We're going to get along just fine. Why are you called N°1? Is that a nickname?"

N°1 felt the magic inside him, comfortable, like heated veins. "It was my imp name. But now I think I'll keep it."

Qwan was surprised. "What? You don't want a *Q W* name? That's traditional. We haven't had a Qwandri in a while. What about Qwerty?"

N°1 shook his head. "I am N°1. The name used to mark me out as different, now it makes me unique. I have no idea where we are, or where we're going, but I already feel more at home than I ever have."

Foaly rolled his eyes. "Excuse me while I get a tissue. Honestly, I thought you demons were warlike and stoic. This little guy sounds like one of those cheap romance novels."

"The little guy who could fry your brain," Qwan reminded him.

"One of those cheap romance novels that I happen to adore," said Foaly, backing away slowly.

N°1 smiled contentedly. He was alive, and he had helped to save the island. Finally he knew his place in the universe. Now that Abbot was taken care of, he could live his life the way he wanted to. And the first thing he would do, when things had settled down, would be to track down the demoness with the red markings very much like his own, and see if maybe she would share a meal with him. A cooked meal. It could be that they had a lot to talk about.

The shuttle slipped through the shield into the morning sky. The jagged rocks of the Irish coast jutted out from the waves, sun-speckled by the early light. It was going to be a fine day. There were trace clouds to the north, but nothing that could keep people inside for long.

There was a group of houses clustered around an inlet, and in the horseshoe harbor, fishermen were already on the sand, setting their nets.

"This is your stop, Artemis," said Foaly. "We'll drop you behind the quay wall. I'll give you a call in a few days, for debriefing." The centaur reached out a hand and laid it on Artemis's shoulder. "The People thank you for your efforts, but you know that everything you have learned is confidential. Not even your parents, Artemis. You'll have to think of something besides the truth to tell them."

"Of course," said Artemis.

"Good. I didn't have to say it, I know. Anyway, the man you want is in the little cottage with the window boxes. Say hello from me."

Artemis nodded numbly. "I will."

The pilot swung in low, tucking the shuttle out of sight behind a deserted, ramshackle, stone building. When he was certain that there was nobody in the sight lines, the pilot hit a green light over the rear door.

Holly helped Artemis out of his chair. "We never get to hang out," she said.

Artemis half chuckled. "I know. There's always a crisis."

"If it's not goblin gangs, it's time-traveling demons." Then Holly kissed him on the cheek. "That was probably dangerous. You being a pubescent volcano."

"I've got it under control, just about."

Holly pointed to her new blue eye. "We'll always be a part of each other now."

Artemis tapped the cheek below his fairy-brown eye. "I'll keep an eye out for you."

"Was that a joke? My goodness, you are changing."

Artemis was a little dazed. "Well, apparently I'm almost eighteen."

"God help us all. Artemis Fowl, eligible to vote."

Artemis chuckled. "I've been voting for years." He tapped his ring-phone. "Call you later."

"I have a feeling we'll have a lot to talk about."

They hugged briefly, but tightly, then Artemis walked down the ramp. He took three steps and looked back, but there was nothing but sea and sky.

Artemis Fowl made for strange early morning viewing in the village of Duncade: a lone teenager in a tattered suit, leaving a trail of ash behind him as he climbed through a stone stile and half stumbled along the quay front.

There was a small group ahead of him, leaning on a concrete bollard. One shaggily bearded fisherman was telling a wild story about a twenty-foot wave he had seen during the night, which had simply evaporated before it reached the shore. He told the story well, complete with big arm gestures and whooshing noises. The other men nodded to his face, while behind his back winked and made *drinky-drinky* motions with their hands.

Artemis ignored them, walking farther down the quay front to the cottage with the window boxes.

Window boxes? Who would have thought.

There was a keypad on the door. It looked out of place in such a rustic setting, but Artemis would have expected no less. He keyed in his own birthday, zero one zero nine, deactivating the lock and interior alarm.

It was dark inside, curtains drawn, lights off. Artemis stepped inside to a spartan living area with a functional kitchen, one chair, and a sturdy wooden table. There was no television, but rudimentary shelves had been erected to store hundreds of books on various subjects. As Artemis's eyes adjusted to the gloom, he could make out some of the titles. *Gormenghast, The Art of War,* and *Gone with the Wind* being among them.

"You are full of surprises, old friend," murmured Artemis, reaching out to touch the spine of *Moby Dick.*

As he traced the embossed title, a small red dot of light appeared on his fingertip.

"You know what that is?" said a low rumbling voice behind him. If thunder could speak, then this would be its voice.

Artemis nodded. This was no time for outbursts or sudden moves.

"Good. Then you know what happens if you do anything to upset me."

Another nod.

"Excellent, you're doing very well. Now lace your fingers behind your head and turn around."

Artemis did as he was told, and found himself facing a huge man with a full beard and long hair drawn back in a ponytail. Both were flecked with gray. The man's face was familiar, but different. There were more lines around the eyes, and a deep frown slash between them.

"Butler?" said Artemis. "Are you behind all that hair?"

Butler stepped back as though struck. His eyes widened

and he swallowed rapidly, suddenly parched.

"Artemis? Is it . . . You're the wrong age! I always thought . . ."

"The time tunnel, old friend," explained Artemis. "I saw you only yesterday."

Butler was not yet convinced; he moved quickly to the curtains, and in his haste pulled them, rail and all, away from the wall. The red light of sunrise flooded the small room. Butler turned to his young guest and took the boy's face in his hands. With massive thumbs he wiped the grime from around Artemis's eyes.

What he saw in those eyes almost buckled his knees.

"Artemis, it is you. I had begun to think . . . No, no. I knew you would come back." And then again with more belief. "I *knew* it. I always knew it."

The bodyguard wrapped Artemis in arms strong enough to break a bear's back. Artemis could have sworn he heard sobs, but when Butler released him, he was his usual stoic self.

"Sorry about the beard and the hair, Artemis. I was blending in with the natives. How was your . . . eh . . . trip?"

Artemis felt the sting of tears in his own eyes. "Um, eventful. If it hadn't been for Holly, we never would have made it."

Butler studied Artemis's face. "Something is different. My God, your eyes!"

"Oh, yes. I have one of Holly's now. It's complicated."

Butler nodded. "We can swap stories later. There are calls to be made."

"Calls?" said Artemis. "More than one?"

Butler plucked a cordless phone from its cradle. "There's your parents, of course, but I should call Minerva, too."

Artemis was surprised. Pleasantly so. "Minerva?"

"Yes. She's been here several times. Almost every school holiday, in fact. We've become good friends; she's the one who started me reading fiction."

"I see."

Butler pointed the phone at Artemis. "It's Artemis this, and Artemis that. She has really built you up to be something special. You're going to have to work hard not to disappoint her."

Artemis swallowed. He had been hoping for a break, not more challenges.

"Of course, she's grown up a bit, even if you haven't," continued Butler. "And quite the beauty. Sharp as a samurai sword, too. There's a young lady who could give you a run for your money at chess."

Then again, thought Artemis. Nothing like a challenge to keep the brain active. But that could come later.

"My parents?"

"You just missed them. They were here yesterday, for the weekend. They stay in the local guesthouse whenever

they can." Butler laid a hand on Artemis's shoulder. "These last few years. It's been terrible for them. I told them everything, Artemis. I had to."

"Did they believe you?"

Butler shrugged. "Some days they did. Mostly my fairy stories just added to their pain. They think I've been driven mad with guilt. And even though you're back, things will never be the same again. It would take a miracle to erase my stories, and their suffering."

Artemis nodded slowly. *A miracle.* He lifted his hand. On the palm was a slight graze from his climb over the quayside stile. Artemis concentrated and five blue sparks of magic leaped from his fingertips and zeroed in on the graze, wiping it out like a cloth wiping dirt. He had more magic left than he had pretended.

"Maybe we can arrange a miracle."

Butler was beyond further amazement. "That's a new trick," he said laconically.

"I picked up a little more than an eye in the time tunnel."

"I see," said Butler. "Just don't do it around the twins."

"Don't worry," said Artemis. "I won't." Then his brain computed what Butler had actually said.

"What twins?"

Butler punched in the Fowl Manor phone number, smiling. "Maybe time stood still for you, big brother, but it didn't for the rest of us."

Artemis stumbled to the room's only chair and sank into it.

Big brother? he thought, and then . . .

Twins!

EOIN COLFER

is the *New York Times* best-selling
author of the Artemis Fowl series,
The Supernaturalist, *The Wish List*, *Half
Moon Investigations*, and *Eoin Colfer's The
Legend of . . .* books. He lives in Ireland
with his wife and two children.

To learn more about Eoin Colfer,
visit his Web site at www.eoincolfer.com